Acknowledgements

Writing a novel is not a solitary journey. This story was made richer and more authentic when I sought wisdom and advice from the experiences of others. Any misinterpretation of facts would be my mistake, not theirs.

Thanks to Liz Valencia of the National Park Service for information on the volunteer program and other details of working on Isle Royale.

Gratitude also goes to Marshall Plumer, an Isle Royale District Ranger, who provided insight into the professional capabilities and structure of the law enforcement arm of the National Park Service.

The entire staff at Isle Royale National Park was knowledgable, friendly, and eager to provide information about the wolf packs that struggle to survive on the island and in balance with the moose. As a visitor, my thanks goes out to the rangers and volunteers who staff the park and to the conservation groups who maintain the trails.

Vic Foerster, arborist and author of *Naked in the Stream*, helped me understand the nature and habits of trees growing on Isle Royale and to get the names of flowers right and in the correct season.

Thanks, too, to Dr. David Ciambrone, retired coroner and author of *Poisons,* for his information about the effects of poisonous plants and to Scott Gamboe, medical examiner and author, for answering my dead-body questions.

I thank my Sierra Club friends for accompanying me to Isle Royale National Park and making the week-long hike safe and fun.

For giving me a taste of luxury, I thank Jack and Laura Lanigan for their hospitality and a wonderful day at sea on their yacht, "Extreme Machine" and Betsy and Harry Durbin, for a day in paradise aboard, "Fuelish."

Thanks and love go out to my friends and family for their encouragement and belief in me, especially my husband, my most ardent supporter.

Isle Royale National Park, Michigan.

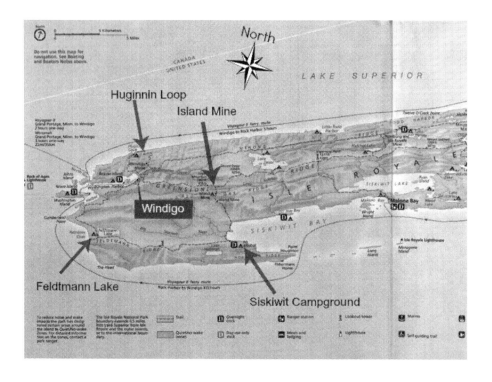

Those who dwell among the beauties
and mysteries of the earth
are never alone or weary of life.

- Rachel Carson

In wilderness I sense the miracle of life.
- Charles A Lindbergh,
Life, 22 December 1967

1

Lake Superior: 22 Nautical Miles

The yachtsman attracted me for a moment—before he spoke. Compliments fell from his mouth like trash slides through a garbage chute. He turned my stomach at that first meeting, and I liked him even less when I found the body. An accident, they called it, but I suspected otherwise.

That was on day three of our week-long backpacking trip. On day one Meagan and I gripped the railings of *Voyageur II* as the ferry churned through the choppy waters of Lake Superior. After three hours on the heaving deck, I was ready for dry land. Isle Royale lay like a dark oasis in the green waters, off to our left.

Suddenly, seafaring curses shot from the wheelhouse and a sleek yacht raced across our bow. A warning siren blared above our heads. *Voyageur II* heaved to starboard, throwing passengers in the open bow against the gunwales.

My land legs failed me. Lake Superior's icy fingers rushed aboard, pulling at our ankles, but retreated when the sixty-foot ferry righted itself. Mechanical noises growled from below decks. Powerful diesel engines pulled the boat away from jagged black rocks, but drove her directly into the trough of an eight-foot swell. A gray wave rose, curled and crashed over the railing. *Voyageur II*'s aluminum skin shook, but shrugged off the blow.

"Are you okay, Mom?" Meagan braced herself and helped me up from the deck.

My hip ached where I had fallen. "A bit shaken, but in one piece." I pushed wet hair from my eyes and fished a bandana from my fanny pack to dry my face.

Scouts, backpackers and other visitors to Isle Royale shook water from their clothing, regained their seats, and laughed in that thin, high-pitched tone common to those who have recently imagined their own demise. Scout leaders counted heads.

Meagan took her place again, like the Celtic Queen Maeve, in the prow of the boat leaning into the wind with her golden hair streaming behind her. Spray glistened in droplets on her cheeks. My daughter, the accountant. So accomplished, so independent. She had flown in from Atlanta, using her last vacation week for this trip. She had asked to come along. A contented sigh escaped me, though I wondered where the time had gone and why she seldom called. Surely, a week of backpacking would reconnect us.

Life is good, I thought, though I shivered in my wet nylon hiking clothes. To protect myself from the wind, I huddled below the gunwales but peered over the railing to keep my eyes on the steady horizon and my stomach in its place.

"Ironic," I murmured. "Lighthouses are built to prevent shipwrecks, and we nearly crashed into that one."

Meagan heard and turned, her eyebrows arched high in exaggerated fear. "Ten more feet and we'd be clinging to those rocks." She laughed and pointed out over the waves. "There goes the jerk in the yacht."

I leaned over the gunwale and shielded my eyes from the morning sun. The yacht gleamed white against the island's dark woods. Like a modern-day pirate ship on the run, the elegant vessel cruised into Washington Harbor churning up a trail of foam for us to follow.

* * *

My good friend Sarah accepted a position with the National Park Service as a volunteer for the summer. She had persuaded me to visit her on Isle Royale by hinting at a mystery and a rumored investigation. The island's isolation was enough to entice me, but the "strange vibes" she talked about clinched it. When Meagan agreed to join me in the wilderness, I packed my gear immediately.

Sarah stood alone on the dock waiting for *Voyageur II* to drop anchor in Windigo. Even from three hundred yards out, I saw the creases in her crisp new NPS volunteer uniform. She spotted the orange cap I waved and trotted to the end of the dock, her unruly dark curls springing from beneath her hat.

I'd met her last fall when she helped me survive a Grand Canyon trip. In March she had driven to Illinois to help me move out of my ex-husband's house, but since then we had exchanged only e-mails and quick phone calls. I missed her.

Sixty-two passengers funneled across the gangway and stood in a ragged line on the dock to unload backpacks and gear and pass each along to its owner. Meagan and I took our places.

"Amy!" Sarah grinned and stepped into line next to me, taking a bulky pack from my hands. She passed the pack along before greeting me with her trademark bear hug. "Hey! How was the ferry ride? When I came over, the lake was so choppy the trip from Minnesota seemed like six hours. Half the people were sick. Not good! You look great!" Sarah's words spilled out too fast for an answer, her energy and enthusiasm belying her retirement age. Her brown eyes sparkled as she surveyed me up and down.

"Your hair finally grew," she said. "You even have a stubby little ponytail going there."

I fingered my barely-there brunette hair, still wet with Lake Superior water.

Sarah's gaze came to rest on Meagan. "This is your daughter." She smiled into Meagan's face and gave her a hug. "You've got a great mom."

"I think so." My eldest maneuvered away from Sarah's embrace and stuck out her hand. "Nice to meet you. I'm Meagan." My daughter, with a runner's lithe body, had always seemed tall to me, but Sarah dwarfed her in height and solidity.

We passed backpacks of all shapes and designs along the line and chatted about Sarah's volunteer position, wolves on the island, the near-miss with the yacht. When the last of the packs was delivered, Sarah leaned down to ask, "What about Ranger Glen?"

Leave it to Sarah to barge right into that fragile area. I fended off the intrusion into my personal life as well as I could. "I e-mailed him last week to thank him for getting you into the volunteer program."

Sarah lowered her brows. "You know what I mean. Any romance blooming? Fireworks?"

My cheeks heated up, and I knew my fair Irish skin broadcasted my discomfort. "We're good friends," I said, "but I haven't seen him. He's still stationed at Grand Canyon."

"I know. I e-mailed him."

Before I could protest, a young male ranger, with a real badge hanging on his baggy shirt, corralled passengers at the end of the dock and herded us to the pavilion. Sarah joined him amid the picnic tables. The two uniforms got the milling crowd's attention as she and the ranger officially welcomed all of us to Isle Royale National Park and presented the obligatory orientation for new arrivals.

While we listened, Meagan and I found dry jackets in our packs and claimed seats in the sun. Sarah's humor kept the large group under control while she conveyed park rules and policies: low-impact camping; don't feed the wildlife; no pets; pack it in, pack it out. Her years as a teacher had prepared her well for public speaking.

The audience, eager to begin their adventure, responded cheerfully—except for my daughter. Meagan sat with her hands between her knees, her face pinched.

"What's wrong?" I whispered.

Meagan bolted from her seat and ran toward the latrine.

I started up to follow, then stopped. Forcing myself to stay with our gear, I watched her retreating figure as I listened to the park rules and regulations.

Minutes later, Sarah dismissed the campers and made a beeline for me. Her lighthearted demeanor had fallen away. Obviously, she had seen Meagan take off. "What's going on?" she asked.

"I guess Meagan had to make a pit stop." Over Sarah's shoulder I spotted my daughter emerging from the shower house. Relieved, I changed the subject. "You're a natural speaker, Sarah. Good job."

Sarah glanced at Meagan's approach and followed my lead. "Thanks." She grinned with pride. "I love this stuff."

Meagan's tan seemed to have faded, making the few freckles across her nose more pronounced. "Sorry," she murmured.

"Are you okay, honey?"

"I'm fine." Meagan didn't look me in the eye. "Freezing and wet, but I'll make it." Her tone meant the subject was closed. Further questions would be an invasion of her privacy.

"A little seasick?" Sarah asked.

Meagan looked out toward the boats bobbing in the harbor and sighed. "Maybe this camping thing isn't for me."

Sarah tried to help. "If you don't feel well, we can get you into the dorm for tonight. You can have my bunk, and I'll sleep in the shelter. I love waking up out there."

Meagan stared upward for a long few seconds, perhaps at the treetops or the few puffs of clouds in the cool blue sky. "No thanks," she said, giving Sarah a weak smile. She lowered her eyes to mine. "I'm sorry, Mom. I'm just..." She shook her head. "I need

5

to get dry clothes." Meagan shouldered her backpack and walked away.

Sarah's eyebrows went up, expecting an answer from me. I had none.

I shrugged, perplexed by my daughter's mood change. "I'd better go after her." I grabbed my backpack and cinched myself into the straps. "When can we talk about what's going on around here?"

"Soon, I hope," Sarah said. "There's too much secrecy, locked doors. A federal investigator is coming in a few days." She waved me away. "Right now, you have to figure out what's going on with Meagan."

Thankful she understood, I started down the path. "When are you off duty?" I called over my shoulder.

"Tomorrow. We'll talk then."

I ran as well as I could beneath the weight of my pack and caught up to my daughter, who dawdled at an intersection.

"Meagan?"

My daughter and I used to have an easy relationship, close and chatty. Just a few years ago—before my divorce, before her move to Atlanta with her husband. Longer than that, I realized. Before high school. *God! It's been sixteen years!* How did I let that happen? Was it too late to get her back?

Beating down guilt and sudden panic, I tried to calm my voice. "What's going on, honey?"

"Don't worry, Mom, I just need to get settled." She readjusted her hip belt. "Let's find this place."

I pointed her down the path along a thick row of flowering honeysuckle. Meagan didn't know where she was going, but she hurried along the gravel lane as if late for an appointment. Her long legs, strengthened by marathon training, gave her an advantage over me, but I had the map.

The path ran parallel to the harbor and past a line of moored boats. I wondered if the clean, white yacht hogging the one cement dock, relegating lesser boats to small piers, was the same boat that nearly ran *Voyageur II* aground on the lighthouse rocks. Meagan forged ahead without glancing at the boat. Only my haste and concern for my daughter prevented me from eavesdropping on the shrill female voice emanating from the impressive vessel.

The brisk walk must have warmed Meagan's body and cooled her impatience. She stopped at an array of posted signs pointing in various directions, turned and waited for me.

"I'm sorry, Mom. I don't know..."

"Is something wrong, Meagan?"

"Maybe I'm nervous. This trip is supposed to be a good thing for me and you, and it's not starting well."

Surrounded by wild roses, we stood in the dusty road. I felt awkward, like walking on eggshells. Between my business and a demanding spouse, I had almost lost my daughter. I wanted to do everything right.

"Our visit will be perfect," I assured her. "This beautiful island almost guarantees it."

Meagan smiled, but her eyes remained guarded. "Which way?"

"Washington Creek Campground," I read. "Turn left."

The trail led into the woods at the edge of Washington Harbor. A series of puncheons crossed the boggy areas and kept our boots out of the mud, but the narrow wooden walkways tested my balance. An unfamiliar wildflower caught my attention, and I almost walked off the edge. Bluebead lilies and bunchberry grew in abundance; others would have to wait to be identified.

I worried we were too late for a tent site and envisioned Meagan's disappointment if none were available. Plan B was to hike several miles to the next campground.

My motherly instincts, working overtime, caused me to bite my lip as we explored the quiet, wooded area. The puncheon branched off to numbered shelters. We walked past one after the other. All were occupied. Gear hung on pegs or had been dumped on the picnic tables.

Please let there be space for us—anything. I disliked being in charge of anyone else's vacation plans, expected to iron out all the wrinkles. This was worse. I wanted this week to be a memorable mother-daughter trip.

I glanced over my shoulder at Meagan. She had regained some of her color.

Why should I fret over my own daughter's reaction? She's a responsible adult. My stomach twisted as I tried to formulate a better Plan B.

Up ahead the puncheon ended in a mass of shrubbery. The end of the line. I crossed my fingers as we approached the last campsite. No gear. No movement. Empty.

"We're here!" My voiced sounded too bright, even to me.

Meagan stepped off the puncheon, nodded, and dropped her pack onto the picnic table.

"This is a great location," I said, hoping my daughter felt well enough to appreciate its beauty. "Maybe we'll see moose in the pond this evening."

Meagan eyed the rustic structure, which was nothing more than three wooden sides with a plank floor, a roof, and a door centered in the front wall of screen. "I don't know about this, Mom. Do we sleep on the bare floor?"

"You'll be comfortable enough on your sleeping mat."

"I'm too old for this." Meagan sighed and trudged up the wooden steps into the Spartan accommodations.

Perhaps primitive camping wasn't the best choice to rebuild a relationship with my daughter.

2

Welcome to Windigo

After a minute's rest, Meagan's energy returned. She pitched in to make the rough wooden shelter into our cozy, waterside cabin. We unrolled our sleeping bags, hung our packs on stubby pegs, and suspended our food bag from a center rafter to thwart hungry rodents. Satisfied with our work, we lounged at the picnic table, watching cormorants and hooded mergansers skim along the surface of the pond.

I hoped the lulling effects of the wilderness would loosen my daughter's tongue, and she'd share whatever troubled her. I knew there was something, but didn't want to probe. Didn't want to be rebuffed. Meagan and I chatted about the birds, the trees, and the weather. We tacitly agreed to shove important topics under the proverbial rug.

After a quiet afternoon hike on the Minong Trail and a dinner of dehydrated lasagna, we strolled up to the camp store and treated ourselves to ice cream cones. We scooted onto a log bench overlooking the harbor and swung our legs over the downhill slope.

"Is that calorie-free butter pecan?" Meagan teased.

I wiped a drip from my chin and groaned. "Let me have this little guilty pleasure. Besides, we burned hundreds of calories this afternoon, and we'll get plenty of exercise on this trip."

"I'm kidding, Mom," she said. "You always worry too much about your weight, and you look great."

"She's not dieting again, is she?" Sarah appeared behind us. "If you get any skinnier, you'll blow away."

I rolled my eyes, but greeted my friend warmly.

Meagan stood up and offered Sarah her seat, adding, "I'm afraid I didn't make a very good first impression, Sarah. I'm sorry I was rude."

Sarah waved away the apology and refused the seat. "Must have been jet lag or something. Hey, the visitors' center has great displays of Isle Royale flora and fauna. Geology and history, too, if that's what you like. Have you been inside?"

"Not yet," Meagan said, "but I do want to study the wolf information."

That was all she needed to say. Sarah played host with enthusiasm. "You'll love the exhibit. The visitors' center is officially closed, but I can get us in."

"You have keys?" I asked.

"Nah," Sarah said. "The volunteer coordinator was in her office when I left thirty minutes ago. She usually works late." Sarah leaned close to my ear. "Deborah is a few years younger than me and kind of cute. I want you to meet her."

An unexpectedly steep hill guarded the path to the visitor center's sturdy cedar deck. I trained my headlamp on the pavement ahead of my boots, but footsteps stomping down the plank stairs caught my attention. I meant to ask if the doors were locked, but the owner of the leather shoes veered to the side to avoid a collision with us and pulled the dark hood around his face to stave off a night breeze blowing off Lake Superior.

"Good evening," Sarah said, and Meagan and I echoed.

Humans are in the minority in wilderness settings and acknowledge each other when they meet. Relaxed camaraderie is common. The burly man in the hood apparently did not subscribe to that notion. To be fair, he may have grunted before he turned away.

The National Park Service had chosen the site of its visitors' center well. The building tucked itself into a hill among balsam firs, white cedar and paper birch overlooking the long view of Washington Harbor. I felt invited to lean on the railing to watch the moon rise, but the doors were unlocked, so we went in.

Faint light, emitted by exit signs, lit the center's display area and library. We were drawn to the brighter light that carpeted the floor outside an office door.

"Hello!" Sarah reached out to rap her knuckles against the door jamb, but instead gasped and stood stock-still.

I peeked in behind her. A woman in a tight-fitting Park Service uniform kneeled with her forearms on the desk, struggling to stand. Each grasp for a handhold sent more papers fluttering to the floor.

"Deborah!" Sarah yelled and rushed into the room. She grabbed the woman's elbow and helped her regain her balance. I took the other arm to guide the woman toward a chair.

Deborah sagged into the seat. Her long pale fingers held her forehead and then trailed through her thin coppery hair to the back of her head. Her hand came away smeared with red. She stared at the blood.

I feared Sarah might see the blood and keel over next to the injured woman, but Sarah steeled herself. I sent Meagan to find ice or a damp cloth and hovered over Sarah just in case her phobia kicked in late.

"What happened, Deborah?" Sarah said. "Did you fall?" In control of herself, she knelt before the woman, peered into her pallid face, and brushed back her short, red hair.

11

"You!" The woman struggled to focus on Sarah, as if just awakening. "You did it!"

Sarah sat back on her heels. "What are you talking about, Deborah? It's me, Sarah. Sarah Rochon."

"You hit me," Deborah snarled into Sarah's shocked face. "You saw the money in the file cabinet and you took it!" She used Sarah's shoulder to push herself to a standing position and staggered to an open file drawer. Papers flew. She emptied drawers below and to both sides of the first one before turning to confront Sarah.

"Where is it?" Spittle flew with her words.

"I think someone robbed her," I said. An image of the burly man stomping off the deck popped into my mind. I rushed to the window to catch a glimpse of him, but saw only the reflection of Deborah's office.

Poor Sarah, still on her knees like a supplicant, reached toward the frenzied woman. "Please. Tell me what you're talking about."

Deborah stopped. Confusion veiled her eyes before they lost their focus. Sweat beaded on her ashen skin, and she swayed against the file cabinet. Her legs buckled.

I rushed to catch her before her head hit the floor. Sarah jumped to my side to help ease the unconscious woman down. Deborah's breathing was weak, but her pulse was strong beneath her jaw bone.

"Is there a doctor on the island?" I asked. "She could have a concussion."

"The nearest doctor's in Thunder Bay. He'd have to come by sea plane." Worry etched itself on Sarah's face. "I don't know what to do."

"Take it easy." I laid my hand on her shoulder. "Why don't you run to the dorm or the store and find a ranger?"

Sarah dashed out and Meagan arrived with a towel soaked in cold water to apply to Deborah's forehead. I took pride and comfort in my daughter's sure, deliberate actions. She grabbed several jackets from the closet and covered the patient.

"She may be in shock," Meagan said. "What happened?"

"Deborah screamed at us, accusing Sarah of hitting her and stealing her money—then she fainted. She wasn't in her right mind." The woman's words disturbed me. Clearly, she believed what she'd said.

Meagan's forehead creased. "How well do you know Sarah?"

I bristled. "Don't even think that! Sarah saved my life in the Grand Canyon."

"Okay, okay." Meagan turned her attention to the unconscious woman. "But why would Deborah think Sarah would attack her?"

"I don't know." My eyebrows knitted together. What if Deborah persisted in her accusation? What if others believed her? Evidence. I needed evidence to prove Sarah innocent of the attack and theft. In a low voice, I said, "I'm going to look around, get to know this woman."

Meagan continued to monitor Deborah while I roamed the room. According to a plaque on the wall, the National Park Service designated Deborah Mitchell as Civilian Employee of the Year in 1998. Although now in disarray, her office had obviously been a clean, efficient workspace. Shelves, bins, and files were alphabetized and neatly labeled. Number two pencils sprouted from a cup marked "Pencils." Color-coordinated trays held neatly arranged pens, scissors, paper clips. Everything looked normal, but something was missing.

"What are you finding, Mom?" Meagan said from her position on the floor.

"Deborah seems to have an obsessive compulsive disorder." I looked across the surface of her desk. "But she has no stapler." I slipped my bandana from my pocket, wrapped it around my hand and yanked at the desk drawer. Locked. Each of the drawers was locked.

"It's under the desk," Meagan said, indicating the direction by tossing her mass of honey-gold hair over her shoulder.

I knelt and spotted a heavy-duty stapler lying on its side. With a #2 pencil, I reached under the desk to hook the device. "Just what I was looking for." I held the stapler by its edges and up to the fluorescent lights. Caught in the hinge mechanism were several short red hairs.

"This is how Deborah got her head injury." I held out the heavy item for Meagan to see. "I'm willing to bet there are traces of her blood, and the attacker's fingerprints, all over this."

In the supply closet I located a bin marked "Envelopes," chose a 9"x13" and sealed the stapler inside. Unless the attacker wore gloves, Sarah had nothing to worry about.

"Mom, Deborah looks better. I think she's coming to."

"Good, honey. Keep her calm." I hoped Deborah would join us only after I got a more thorough look around her domain. Her laptop's blank screen stared at me. Ever so slightly, the yellow pencil eraser grazed the touchpad. The screen came to life. A spreadsheet appeared with a list of twenty or so odd-sounding book or song titles: *Amazing Grace, The Dog House, All Mine, Spending Their Inheritance.* Each title corresponded with a four-digit number in the right-hand column. The pencil nudged the scroll key. The column heading read *Income.* I scrolled further up. A text box, perfectly centered both horizontally and vertically, read: *Wolf Pack—Profit and Loss Statement.* Before I could interpret the numbers or scroll down to the *Expense* section, several pairs of feet pounded across the outside deck. I lowered the screen with my elbow.

Sarah appeared first in the doorway. "How is she?"

"She's beginning to wake up," Meagan said.

I recognized one of the two rangers who knelt at Deborah's side as the thin young man who'd ushered us into the pavilion that morning and supervised Sarah's orientation for the new arrivals.

The female ranger seemed to have had first aid training and took control of the situation. She listened to the victim's breathing and checked her pulse, then called Deborah's name and patted her cheek.

Deborah's eyes fluttered open.

"Lie still, Deb," the first-aider said. "You've had a bad fall. We'll take care of you."

Color returned to the victim's cheeks. She wetted her lips. Her eyes roamed around as she tried to focus on those of us clustered around her. I held my breath. Her gaze lit upon Sarah, and she raised a thin finger and pointed. "She did it. She attacked me."

Sarah stepped back and shook her head. She sank into the desk chair, and I went to her side. The two rangers scowled at Sarah and me but continued to minister to their friend.

"Why would she say that?" Sarah muttered. "I thought... I thought she liked me. When I left her, she was friendly—though she practically shoved me out the door. I don't get it."

"Don't worry," I said. "I have proof someone else attacked her." Still perplexed, Sarah sat up straighter and rewarded me with a smile. Her complete faith in me weighed on my shoulders. *What if I'm wrong? What if he did wear gloves?*

* * *

"No. I don't want a doctor. Ouch."

Meagan and I stood off to the side while Deborah's friend examined the head wound. "But Deb, you may have a concussion."

"Do I need stitches?" Deborah snapped.

"The cut's not that bad, but..."

"Then I'll stay here, and we won't bother flying a doctor in." Deborah pushed herself up to a sitting position and her friends helped her to her feet. Sarah vacated the chair and motioned for Deborah to sit. Nose to nose, the tall, buxom woman gave Sarah a surly scowl but allowed the rangers to guide her into the chair.

I hoped no one had noticed Sarah's lip curl into a sneer.

15

"Do you feel like telling us what happened, Deb?" asked the fresh-faced, scrawny male ranger. A name tag introduced him as Ranger Zachary Weckman.

"All I remember is her being here." Her finger poked the air in Sarah's direction. "I worked late and was standing by the file cabinet. She hit me from behind."

"I didn't!" Sarah protested. "I finished assembling the handouts, said good-bye to you, and left. I didn't take anything from you, and I didn't hit you." Sarah corralled her vehemence, but indignation reddened her cheeks.

"Deborah, are you missing something?" The woman couldn't be much past forty, but Ranger Weckman coddled her as if she were a child or a senile octogenarian.

"No. I mean, yes," she responded and put her hand to her forehead. "I'm confused."

I wondered if she had also been as dramatic in her high school play. She stalled, seeming to roll each word around in her head before she spoke. "I keep a zippered canvas bag in the file cabinet—personal stuff. It's gone! You have to search her dorm." She jabbed her finger at Sarah again, but her agitation cost her. Color drained from her face.

"That's enough for tonight." Ranger Weckman stood and hitched up his pants, which threatened to fall from his hip bones.

"She needs to rest," said the first-aider, "and someone needs to be with her all night, checking her condition every two hours in case she does have a concussion."

Sarah stepped forward. "I'll stay with her. I'll check on…"

"Anybody but you," Ranger Weckman said. "Will you stay with her, Carolyn?"

The first-aider agreed, put her hand on Deborah's back, and led her out into the night.

I linked my arm through Sarah's and gestured to Meagan that we should go as well.

"I need to talk to you, Sarah." The remaining ranger pulled a chair up to the desk and sat with a notepad before him. A jerk of his head invited Meagan and me to leave. "I need to speak to Ms. Rochon alone." He seemed to be out of his element and covered his inexperience with unwarranted curtness.

We stepped out, but I stopped just beyond the door jamb.

Ranger Weckman didn't wait for Sarah to sit, just barged ahead. "What went on here tonight? What kind of argument did you have with Deb?"

"We had no argument." Sarah controlled her voice with effort. "Like I said, I finished the handouts and stepped into her office to say good-bye. I may have startled her. She jumped, and rushed me out the door."

"Did you hit her?"

"No! Of course not."

"Did you take her canvas bag?"

"No, I..."

"What was in the bag?"

Ranger Weckman continued to browbeat Sarah, cutting off her answers. I couldn't take the badgering any longer and stepped forward. "Listen, Ranger..."

He cut me off. "Who are you?"

I stood up straighter, arched my eyebrow, and pulled a smile across my lips. "Amy Warren. My daughter, Meagan, and I arrived on the island this morning."

He scribbled our names in his notebook. "Were you here when the attack occurred?"

"No, the three of us arrived together to find Deborah injured."

"Were you with Sarah all evening?"

"She had volunteer work to do here, so no." I stressed the word *volunteer*. His staccato questions ticked me off.

"So you can't vouch for Sarah's innocence in this attack."

"I certainly can vouch for her innocence!"

"I don't think so, Mrs. Warren." He slapped his notebook closed and walked toward the door. "Sarah, don't leave the island. The federal investigator will interview you in the next few days."

Sarah flinched like a puppy swatted across the nose with a newspaper. Her look of defeat broke my heart and unleashed my temper.

"Listen, Ranger Zachary Weckman," I read his name tag again with as much sarcasm as I could muster. "What kind of investigation is this?" I let my voice rise out of control. "Deborah couldn't see an attacker behind her. How dare you assign guilt when you have absolutely no facts!"

I caught sight of my wide-eyed daughter but didn't stop myself. "You haven't inventoried this room. Or secured the evidence. You believe the ramblings of a woman with a head injury. To top all that off, you won't listen to us about the man—the probable attacker—we saw on the deck. What kind of law officer are you?"

I was still holding the white envelope with the stapler inside.and slammed it on the desk. The stapler made an impressive crash. "Why haven't you asked about that?" Meagan and Sarah flanked me, holding my arms as if afraid I'd throw a fist at the young ranger.

"Take it easy, Amy," Sarah said. "I'm not worried about this."

Ranger Weckman, a bit pale, backed away. Suddenly he looked like a fifth-grader in the principal's office. "I am not a law officer," he mumbled. "I'm a naturalist, but today I'm the highest ranking ranger on the island."

He hung his head, and I wondered if my tongue-lashing had been too much. My muscles relaxed enough that Meagan freed my arm. I took a deep breath and raised my hand in peace. "I'm sorry to be so abrupt, Ranger Weckman, but I was afraid a janitorial crew would straighten up this mess, destroying evidence that will prove Sarah innocent."

As if used to being reprimanded, he nodded and accepted my apology with a shrug. "I just wanted to have a few answers before the park manager returns," the young ranger said, as if confessing that he'd forgotten his homework.

"I think we can help you find out who hit Deborah," I said. "While we waited for you to arrive, Meagan spotted this stapler under the desk." I held up the 9"x13" envelope. "I believe the attacker used the stapler to hit Deborah. Her hair is stuck in the mechanism, and no doubt his fingerprints are all over it."

The ranger cleared his throat and straightened his badge, then reached for the sealed envelope. "I assume you didn't leave your own fingerprints on the stapler?"

"Of course not." I resisted the urge to roll my eyes.

"Okay, Mrs. Warren." His official demeanor had returned, though muted. "I'll give this to the federal investigator, and we'll see what shows up."

Meagan smiled and nodded, building my ego. I looked at Sarah, expecting a proud grin. Instead her wide eyes stared from her slack and pale face. She grimaced and gave a slight shake of her head. I whirled around and thought to snatch the envelope from the ranger's hands, but he had roamed away, surveying the room.

I turned back to Sarah. "What?" I mouthed the word. Her shoulders went up and she made a squeezing motion with her right hand.

Good Lord! Sarah used the stapler. In my arrogance I had handed damning evidence over to those who already believed her capable of hitting a woman in the back of the head. "I'm so sorry, Sarah," I whispered.

"Hey, I'm innocent. Don't worry." She put her arm around my shoulders. "Should I tell him I used the stapler?"

19

Still kicking myself about handing over the attack weapon, I sighed. "That's your call. I've already done too much damage to your cause."

Ranger Weckman stood on the other side of the room deep in thought, surveying the scattered papers, and emptied file drawers. Sarah took a step in his direction, but I put a hand on her arm to stop her. "Not yet."

"Ranger Weckman," I said. He looked up, puzzled, as if he had forgotten we were in the room. I smiled. "I recall seeing surveillance cameras in the public area of the visitors' center. The recording will show the man who came in after Sarah left for the evening."

He looked at me skeptically but must have decided I was on his side. "Good idea, Mrs. Warren. There's a monitor behind the counter." He seemed thankful to have something to do and hurried out of the office into the darkened visitors' area. We filed out behind him. Sarah switched on the light to the large, open room.

The young ranger leaned on the counter's laminated surface and turned on the monitor. A view of the moose display blipped onto the screen; five seconds later, a scene from the darkened library section; five seconds after that, an image of the antique lighthouse lens. The camera then caught the four of us at the visitors' counter. The monitor cycled through the scenes again.

I sighed in disappointment. The cameras were trained only on the public areas; no offices, no outside entrances. Our only hope was that the intruder passed through the display area.

I waited for the ranger to realize the obvious.

He creased his brow and ran his fingers over and around the monitor. "How do we get a replay?"

"Most often," I said, "the DVRs are kept in a private location, maybe a storage room or office."

The three of them looked at me in surprise, and I shrugged. "I bought a camera and digital recording system for my business years ago after a robbery attempt."

"Maybe in the park manager's office," Sarah suggested.

"The manager is off-island for a few days. His door might be locked." Ranger Weckman led the way down a hall lit only at the far end by an exit sign. He flipped on a hallway light before opening the unlocked office door. The room was larger than Deborah's, but much less organized. A flat-screen monitor on the desk came to life when Weckman switched on the light. The same camera views we had seen up front cycled across the screen.

"The monitors all connect," Meagan pointed out.

That sparked an idea. Coaxial cable ran from the monitor, under the rug, and appeared again at the baseboard. A face plate guided the cable into the wall.

"What's on the other side of this wall?" I asked.

The four of us hurried into the hall as if on a scavenger hunt. The next door in the hallway was posted with a placard identifying it as a storage room. I was certain we had found the head-end of the surveillance system.

Sarah grabbed the doorknob, but the door did not yield.

"Shoot!" I said. "Do you have keys?"

Weckman's shoulders sagged and he shook his head. "Nope."

Perhaps the young ranger had imagined solving the case and impressing his supervisor. Maybe he didn't relish the idea of calling the park manager for permission—or dreaded involving a federal investigator.

"Who would have keys?" I asked.

"The manager and Deborah, of course," he said, "and the janitorial staff, but they're up at Rock Harbor tonight and tomorrow."

Sarah leaned her head against the door jamb. "I guess we wait until tomorrow to find out who sneaked in here."

At a loss for what more to do, we agreed to meet in the morning. Ranger Weckman turned off the light in Deborah's office. Meagan got the light in the hallway. I stood by the one in the display area and waited for the others to near the exit door before I flipped the switch. In the last second of illumination I spotted the large white envelope. Weckman had forgotten it. The attack weapon with Sarah's fingerprints lay on the counter next to the monitor. Then the room went black.

3

Day Two-Washington Campground

Wily old Ben Franklin drew a line on the surveyor's map in 1783 to create the United States' northern border. Somehow the Canadians got a nonexistent island to the north of the line and the U.S. got copper-rich Isle Royale. The state of Michigan claims the remote island, though Isle Royale is many miles closer to Minnesota and Ontario. I had studied maps and brochures before our trip and thought that perhaps the island's identity crisis keeps Isle Royale a secret and the least visited of our national parks.

Several hundred fortunate people shared the island that day, many of whom wouldn't venture far from the fancy lodge at Rock Harbor. Meagan and I survived her first night in the shelter and woke to a glorious morning. She said the view was worth the trouble. With a breakfast of oatmeal and hot tea, we sat on a bench at the edge of the pond hoping to spot moose grazing on grasses among the lily pads. I kept an eye on my watch.

"Almost eight o'clock," I said. "We should get going, if we're to meet Sarah and Ranger Weckman at the visitors' center on time."

Meagan stood and stretched, silhouetted against the sunlight reflected off the pond. My heart ached with love for my daughter. She linked her arm through mine, and we watched a blue heron stalking its breakfast. "I love this—in spite of what I said yesterday."

"I never doubted that." Bringing her to Isle Royale was a good move after all, a balm for our relationship.

"I'm excited to hike out to the next camp." Meagan unfolded a map from her pocket. "Which trail today?"

Her renewed enthusiasm for the island and backpacking thrilled me. "We have choices," I said, drawing my finger along a line on her map. "This trail to Feldtmann Lake or the Greenstone Ridge Trail."

"What's on the Greenstone?"

Finally, I got to impart bits of trivia I had discovered when planning the trip. "Ridges left by an ancient lava flow and the highest points on the island—and great scenery."

"Mmm. Feldtmann Lake. I want to try for bass." Meagan made a motion as if casting a line into the water.

"You mean fishing?" I sat back and stared at my daughter.

"Maybe pike." She laughed and reeled in an imaginary fish. "I'm good at fishing. Ed and I go several times a year."

What else didn't I know about my daughter? Her excitement for our hiking adventure reignited my own. "Okay, we're going fishing," I said. "Assuming the video recording clears Sarah, we can hike the trail to Feldtmann…"

"You mean we might stay here instead of backpacking the island?"

"I can't very well leave Sarah with an accusation hanging over her head," I said. A frown gathered on Meagan's brow, so I added, "I'm sure the security cameras will show the attacker, so we'll leave today as scheduled."

"Yes, of course. She's your friend and we should stay." Meagan's posture stiffened. She stuffed her bedding into a compression sack, and then methodically stowed her gear into compartments and pockets.

I hurried to pack and hefted my backpack onto the picnic table.

Meagan leaned on her pack. "What do you know about Sarah?" she asked from between tight lips.

"I know enough," I said. "Sarah's a retired teacher and travels the country as an independent consultant for school districts. And she'd do anything for me—for you, too."

"That's great, but…"

"But what?"

"Sarah looks like a hothead, and Deborah's obviously not the sweetest person on earth," Meagan said. "Isn't it possible she hit Deborah?"

Meagan scrunched up her face and waited for my answer.

Her logic was sound and she asked appropriate questions, but she didn't have the benefit of knowing Sarah for ten months. "She's not that sort of person," I said.

"Have you ever seen Sarah violent?"

She had me. I didn't want to admit that I once worried about Sarah's temper, but I couldn't lie to my daughter. "Technically, yes —when we fought the drug dealer in the Grand Canyon, but only to defend us."

Meagan cocked an eyebrow at me. "What if she suggested we go to the visitors' center together because she needed an alibi?"

Unhappy with the way the conversation was going, I sighed. "I suppose it's possible Sarah had a reason for us to go to the visitors' center, but…"

Meagan plunked her backpack on the table with more force than necessary. "Yes, and this is the person you want to spend time with on our vacation?"

My daughter had regressed into adolescence before my eyes. Obviously, something was wrong. The choice she gave me sat like a boulder on my chest. As much as I hated having friction with my daughter, I had to defend my friend. I glared across the picnic table. "Meagan! Sarah is honest and kind. She'd never attack an innocent person."

My tone brought Meagan up short. With some effort, she smiled and regained ten years of maturity. "Gad, Mom, I don't know what's wrong with me," she said. "I hope for your sake that you're right. Some parents are blind to the wrong their children do. Maybe you see Sarah in that way."

Odd choice of words, I thought. "I'm her friend, not her parent, and I'm certain my faith in her is well-founded." Relieved our confrontation was short-lived, I put my arm around my daughter's waist and tugged her to me. "You haven't been yourself, Meagan. What's bothering you?"

She flinched. Her skin twitched beneath my hand. After a moment's hesitation, she sagged into me. "Mom, I…"

"Hello, in the camp!" After rapping on the log siding, a middle-aged couple in safari outfits stepped from behind our shelter. "Mind if we watch for moose from your clearing?"

Our moment was lost.

* * *

Sarah waited on the deck of the visitors' center, her elbows propped on the railing. Her NPS shirt and short pants were ironed and creased. She waved to Meagan and me as we trudged up the dusty hill under the weight of our backpacks, ready for a day of hiking.

"Hey! Good morning!" Her voice rose above the mist hanging in the shrubbery, a little too loud for the early hour. She bounded down the steps to meet us and ushered us to the deck's seating area. I envied her energy.

"Good morning, Sarah. You look rested, like you don't have a worry in the world."

"I don't." She smiled. "Let's enjoy the gorgeous day. Coffee or tea, Meagan?"

A flicker of uncertainty passed across my daughter's face. "Coffee."

Given Meagan's silly suspicions, I was not surprised she was wary of Sarah's friendship. She accepted the steaming mug, but her eyes never rose above Sarah's chin. "Thanks."

"Great day for a hike," Sarah said. "Which trail did you decide on?"

"Feldtmann. Why don't you hike with us," I asked, "after we look at the CCTV recording?"

Meagan's jaw clenched.

Sarah glanced at Meagan and hesitated. "Nah." She shrugged. "You two need time to bond. Besides, they need me here, what with Deborah injured and *Voyageur* bringing in another sixty people this afternoon."

"How is Deborah this morning?" I asked.

"They wouldn't let me see her." Sarah's hurt showed. "She unlocked the visitors' center before I got here, so I guess she survived the night."

"Huh," I grunted, and hoped Sarah worried as little as she claimed.

"Uh, Sarah," my daughter said, standing up and motioning to the entrance doors. "We didn't get to see the exhibits last night. Will you show us the wolf display?"

Meagan's attempt to be civil pleased me, and Sarah brightened.

"Sure, come on in," Sarah said, jumping up. "You've got to see this antique lighthouse lens, too."

She led us to a hexagonal alcove where an eight-foot, multifaceted glass lens was displayed like a piece of artwork. The engineering impressed me.

"Hey, Mom, this is the lighthouse the ferry almost ran into."

I squinted at the placard rather than take out my reading glasses. "You're right. Rock of Ages lighthouse from 1910 to 1985."

Sarah stood back with her chin held high—proud, as if she had created the lens herself. I circled the unique bit of history again. "It's beautiful," I told her. She nodded and grinned.

Visitors straggled in and roamed through the displays and bookshelves. Meagan studied the wolf exhibit and I flipped through a wildflower field guide while we waited for Ranger Weckman to show up with the key to the storage room.

A familiar female voice caught my attention. When I heard her ask the clerk at the counter about an anchoring permit, I realized she was the angry woman we'd heard on the yacht moored at the dock yesterday.

"Valerie Kinzler, Ludington, Michigan," she told the volunteer who prepared her permit. In her white capris and sparkling jewelry, she looked more attractive than her voice indicated. I guessed her to be past fifty, but her forced tan may have added a few years and a layer of premature wrinkles. Her auburn hair probably came from a bottle, but the expensive cut framed her face well.

I ran my fingers through my own chopped-off, brunette mop and vowed to make a salon appointment one of these months. Curious about her yacht, I leaned on the counter as if waiting to ask the volunteer my own question.

Eavesdropping was forgotten when I realized the 9"x13" envelope containing the stapler was no longer on the counter. The stapler, covered with Sarah's fingerprints, was nowhere in sight. I scanned the array of office supplies and paperwork and moved the length of the workstation to check behind the monitor. *Maybe someone put the evidence away for safekeeping.*

I glanced toward Deborah's closed office, then beckoned Meagan away from the wolf display. She followed me to Deborah's door, which swung open easily. As I'd suspected, the obsessive-compulsive volunteer ranger had felt compelled to tidy her room. No hint of last night's chaos remained.

"What's up?" Sarah joined us in the doorway.

"Someone cleaned up the scene of the attack," Meagan said.

Sarah surveyed the room and whistled. "What does this do to the investigation?"

"Seems to me Deborah cares more about putting her paperwork in order than about finding out who stole her money," I said.

"Well, yeah," Sarah sniffed. "I'm her only suspect."

"So she says."

I wandered further into the room to get a look at the desk. A sparkling clean stapler sat innocently on the right-hand side. "You're in the clear, Sarah. The stapler looks like it's been polished to a high-gloss shine—no fingerprints."

Sarah raised both hands. "I'm not touching that thing."

"No, let's not," I said, but I was sorely tempted to get another look at the spreadsheet on Deborah's laptop. I lifted the screen with my bandana and started the computer, but the password request prevented me from going further.

"Pssst." Meagan hissed a warning from the doorway.

I moved away from the desk before Ranger Weckman entered the office. "What's going on in here?"

"That's what I want to know, Zak." I invaded his space, and he drew back. "What is this stapler doing here? I gave it to you for safekeeping. For you to protect the fingerprint evidence." I figured the best defense was a good offense. "And now we find the stapler polished clean, here on Deborah's desk. What did you do, Zak?"

He blanched and stared at the stapler, his mouth agape.

Behind him, Deborah marched into the room. "Why are these damn people in my office?" She skewered Sarah with her eyes. "You. Get out of here."

Sarah held her ground and returned the glare. Ranger Weckman stepped between them and regained his speech. "Deborah, someone cleaned your office…"

"*I* cleaned my office," Deborah snapped, ignoring Sarah. "How could you expect me to work in such a mess?"

Weckman sighed and rolled his eyes. "But, the evidence…"

"I don't need evidence." Her eyes narrowed to slits, and she turned to Sarah. "Give me my canvas bag and all is forgiven."

"Listen, Deborah…" Sarah jabbed her finger forward and advanced on the woman.

I linked my arm through Sarah's to stop her from making the accusation of attack into a real one. "Zak, did you bring the key to the storage room so we can view the surveillance video?"

"I have the key." Deborah took on a Queen Victoria persona and breezed past us into the hallway. We became her entourage and followed her to the storage room.

"Whoa. Where are you going?" Ranger Weckman stopped Sarah and me at the storage room door. "Please wait in the display area while we conduct our investigation."

"But viewing the recording was Amy's idea," Sarah protested.

"Even so, this is official business." He put his body between us and the door.

Deborah smirked and shooed us away with a wave of her hand.

I didn't like that Deborah seemed to be calling the shots for the official investigation and began to suspect that last night's stapler attack had been justified. "Let's go, Sarah."

The visitors' center provided many ways to kill time while we waited for the rangers to figure out how to operate the DVR in the storage room. Meagan wandered out to the deck to weigh her pack on the scale. Sarah busied herself by straightening the brochure rack. I flipped through mounting boards looking for wildflower specimens to memorize. I also kept an eye on Valerie, the woman from the yacht, who mulled over wild fruit descriptions.

She saw me watching her. "Do you know anything about these?" She eagerly held out a handful of red berries, her curt demeanor gone.

"That's thimbleberry," I said. "They're delicious and easily found inland."

"So, you can eat them?"

"Yes." I smiled at the woman. "They taste wonderful."

"Oh, good. I picked a bowl full." Valerie was as delighted as a child. "They'll be perfect for a fruit salad. I found blueberries, too."

"No." I frowned in a moment of confusion and ran through my memory for the details of berries on the island. "Blueberries ripen earlier. They're gone." I moved to the "B" section of the display to confirm my recollection.

"But I found a big patch of them."

My memory was a steel trap, though in the last decade, rust had hampered its operation. I couldn't name what worried me, but Valerie's naive smile urged me to protect her. She turned to leave.

"Wait." I grabbed her sleeve. "Was this what you found?" I released her shirt, but led her to a large display in the corner and tapped the picture with a skull and crossbones in the adjoining column. "Bluebead lily?"

"I found blueberries." She studied the picture and frowned.

"Blueberries usually ripen before these." My sharp tone made her listen. "Bluebead lilies are poisonous. Did you eat any?"

Color drained from her face. "I—I saved them for the fruit salad."

Embarrassed for her, I found a shellacked specimen card describing edible berries. "Raspberries are in season," I suggested with a smile. "I saw them along on the beach to the north."

Valerie studied the raspberry description for several seconds. "Thanks." She waved on her way out the door, and I wondered how she'd managed to pick juicy thimbleberries without staining her white capris.

The storage room door opened, and Sarah and I came to attention. Deborah sailed down the hallway and into her office, closing the door. Ranger Weckman beckoned to Sarah to enter the storage room.

"I'll be right back." She wiggled her eyebrows like Groucho Marx, but her playful swagger didn't fool me. Sarah's nerves were on edge.

I stationed myself against the wall outside the storage room's open door.

"Sarah, I thought you should see this, too," Weckman said. I heard taps on the keyboard. "Is that you walking toward Deborah's office?"

"Yes." Sarah's voice was more difficult to hear.

"There's no one else on the tape." More keystrokes.

"Oh." Sarah's dejection reached me ten feet away.

That couldn't be true. "Wait a minute." I stepped from behind the wall. "May I see the recording?"

"Mrs. Warren, I don't think you should see evidence." The young ranger's exasperation with me was clear. "The video shows that Sarah was the only one in the visitors' center last night."

"My daughter and I were both in here last night," I pointed out. "Weren't we on the recording?"

The poor guy looked shell-shocked.

I took a deep breath. "How familiar are you with that DVR?"

He rolled his eyes. "Deborah just showed me how to retrieve the images."

I bit my lip. "My daughter and I arrived in the visitors' center at 8:00 P.M. Can you fast forward to eight o'clock?"

He hit several key strokes. "I can't find you…"

"What does the time/date generator indicate?" I tried to hold my impatience in check.

"The what? Oh. 8:03 P.M., July 19," he read.

"What day is today?" I asked.

"The twenty-first," Sarah exclaimed.

Ranger Weckman put his hand to his forehead. "I'm just a naturalist." He groaned and stabbed furiously at the keyboard. "I can't find the archives."

"May I?" I didn't wait for an answer and pushed my way in to sit before the computer screen, moving the cursor over the menu. "Here's the archive and here's the video for the display room camera, July 20, 8:00 P.M." I tried to keep triumph out of my voice.

The jerky time-lapse recording showed Meagan, Sarah, and me walking through the display area. Deborah's door was off-camera; only a rectangle of light on the carpet showed our feet outside her office.

"Back up to seven-thirty," Sarah demanded. "That man in the sweatshirt had to walk through between 7:31 and 7:58."

I forgave her brusque excitement and pointed to the screen. "There you are leaving Deborah's door and exiting the visitors' center." We waited and watched five minutes of replay.

"Hmmm. Your mystery man is not on the video," Ranger Weckman said. He seemed disappointed, too. Sarah leaned against shelves of cleaning supplies, her shoulders slumped. I put my head in my hands to think.

"Time-lapse. You see only every fourth or fifth picture frame in time-lapse mode." I grabbed the mouse and ran the cursor around the screen until I found the correct menu. "There. Let's look at the same sequence in real time." I slowed the replay and clicked on 7:45 P.M. The three of us watched the darkened, empty display room for several minutes.

"What was that?" Sarah put her finger on the screen.

I scrolled through the video to 7:51. "There's a foot in the rectangle of light." The dark image was gone in a split second. I replayed the video and pressed pause. "That's a man's shoe."

Sarah lifted up her size-nine hiking boots. "They're not mine." Relief and giddiness were in her voice.

The ranger continued to study the recording and made notes, while Sarah and I turned into the hallway toward the exit signs to scope out the mystery man's route. Sarah hurried through a meeting room to locate the back door. She tested the crash bar and the unlocked door swung open.

"Oh!" A startled Meagan stood on the back deck with her hand on the door handle. She barged into the room and slammed the door shut.

4

Feldtmann Ridge

Meagan leaned her full weight against the door as if a grizzly waited to batter down the steel to gain entry. Sweat glistened on her pale face. Her breathing came in quick bursts.

"Meagan, what's wrong?" I reached for her in an instant panic. She let me hug her, though she was loath to remove her weight from the door.

"I'm okay." She held up a trembling hand.

I held my daughter at arm's length and studied her troubled face. "What is it then?"

"Just some creep...behind the building. Ugh." She exhaled and shook her head. "I was exploring back there and he cornered me under the deck—tried to lure me aboard his boat!"

"Are you hurt?" Sarah demanded. "Did he grab you? Touch you?"

Meagan lowered her chin and shuddered. "No. No. He ran his finger down my forearm." She demonstrated the move, the invasion of her personal space. "He was so...eeyew. Cigarette breath. I jabbed my elbow in his ribs and ran." She sought out my eyes as if for approval and tried to grin.

"Good," I said, though no sound made it past my lips.

"What's he look like?" With a scowl, Sarah yanked open the door and hurried out and around the deck.

I gripped Meagan's wrist and rushed to follow Sarah. We jogged along the deck, stopping at vantage points with views of the woods behind the building, the path, harbor, bath house and dock pavilion.

"Do you see him?"Sarah leaned over the railing like a panther perched on a cliff, ready to pounce.

"No, I don't," Meagan said. "He wore sunglasses, hair pulled back, big."

Few people were in sight, and none fit Meagan's description.

"What did he wear? Jacket, boots, shirt?" I asked and watched my daughter struggle with her memory.

"Blue jeans. I think a green shirt with buttons. I have no idea what kind of...they were shoes, boat shoes."

"Just like the burly guy last night," I said. "If it's the same man, he has brass coming back here after attacking Deborah. What if... We'd better check on her."

The three of us filed into the visitors' center and made a beeline for Deborah's office. The door was ajar. Sarah pushed it open.

Deborah looked up from her computer screen, startled. "What the hell do you want?"

Sarah shrugged and slammed the door. "She's fine."

Out in the bay two boats steamed out of the harbor: Valerie's sleek white yacht and a cabin cruiser with a blue stripe from bow to stern. I felt sure Deborah's attacker was on that boat. How could he have dared to return in daylight to the scene of the crime?

* * *

"Don't worry. I can handle her." Sarah jerked her thumb back at the visitors' center where Deborah stood on the deck glaring down on us. "You two need to stick to your itinerary. Do your mother-daughter bonding. I'm going to nose around here to see what old Deb is up to."

We had convinced Ranger Weckman that the real attacker had been caught on the surveillance video and Sarah should be allowed to perform her volunteer duties in spite of Deborah's surliness. Sarah would keep a lookout for the burly mystery man and the cabin cruiser with the blue stripe. I would be a mom to my daughter and try to heal her jangled nerves.

Sarah walked with us along the Greenstone Trail past the airdock where a float plane had just moored. We chatted with the pilot, who had flown in from Houghton, MI with two passengers, hikers with full backpacks.

"Maybe Deborah should fly out with him to visit a doctor," I said, and watched the pilot follow his passengers up the hill. "She wasn't smart to refuse treatment."

"I was wrong about Deborah." Sarah shook her head. "At first I liked her, but she's odd—or crazy. She can't bear to be away from her office."

"Like a trusted employee who won't take a vacation because his replacement will find he's been cooking the books." My daughter's offhand remark hit home.

"Meagan's right, Sarah. Snoop around a little for anything about Wolf Pack." I told them about the Wolf Pack spreadsheet and recited the titles I could recall from the file on Deborah's laptop. "I'd like to know what those song titles mean."

"Maybe the report refers to the three wolf packs here on the island," Meagan suggested.

"Could be, but the file didn't read like a scientific report." I sighed. I tended to see conspiracies and intrigue where there were none, so I set my suspicions aside.

We walked easily along the well-marked trail with lovely views of the harbor and Beaver Island. Meagan outpaced Sarah and I, so we lagged behind catching up on our lives.

"Meagan's rough on you," she observed. "What's up with that?"

"She's upset over my divorce, like John's rejecting her too, especially since we found out he's remarrying and she's pregnant."

"Who's pregnant?"

"Kim." I tried to keep bitterness out of my voice. "John's secretary."

"Ouch."

"Yeah. Meagan doesn't know who to blame and thinks her life must mirror mine, so she's afraid an unhappy marriage is in her future, too."

"She better fix her attitude, or that will be a self-fulfilling prophecy."

My eyes darted to Sarah, and she cringed. "Oops, my big mouth…"

"No, you're right. Something has soured my daughter. She needs me now." I quickened my pace to keep Meagan in sight. "Thanks for understanding, Sarah."

She shrugged. "Hey, this is great scenery." She stopped and made a sweep of her arm. "When things settle down, I'll come back this way with my watercolors."

"You should," I said. "It will calm you and you can stop biting your nails."

"Ach!" My talented friend rolled her eyes and shoved her hands in her pockets. "This is where I turn around," she said. A rustic sign announced the juncture of the Greenstone and Feldtmann trails. "*Voyageur* docks at ten-thirty, so I'd better get back. Take care of yourself." She laid her hand on my shoulder and headed back down the trail.

"See you in three days," I called.

"Stay out of trouble." Sarah waved over her shoulder. "Meagan, take care of your mom."

My daughter came to my side, and we stood in the shade of aspen, birch and balsam fir watching her march away.

"I was wrong about Sarah," Meagan said. "She's a good person."

"Thank you. That makes me happy." I put my hand through the crook of my daughter's arm. "Now let's get moving. We have eight miles to go."

The Feldtmann Trail tested Meagan and me by rising steadily to a ridge overlooking Grace Harbor. Our thirty-pound backpacks made the slight change in elevation seem significant. We were both in good shape, but a half hour passed before our trail-legs kicked into gear. At the top of the ridge we sat on a downed aspen for a water break and exclaimed over the leaf-filtered view of the valley and Lake Superior in the distance. I forgot about Deborah, the creepy man from the boat, and the misunderstandings with Meagan. In time she would tell me what bothered her. At that moment, I was content to simply be with my daughter. Everything else paled in importance.

The next hour brought us down from the ridge into lush woodlands with a damp floor carpeted in a wondrous display of wildflowers. Flower identification occupied my thoughts: marsh marigold, wood-nymph, joe-pye weed, and the bluebead lily Valerie had confused with blueberry.

Meagan sniffed loudly. "What's that smell?" She wrinkled her nose.

"Whew. Smells like a zoo." I put my nose in the air and walked slowly. The odor dissipated, so I retraced my steps to where the smell was most concentrated. My excitement grew, and I half expected to spy a little animal crouched in the shrubbery. Nothing appeared. "I don't know what it was."

"I'll bet wolves are nearby," Meagan said.

I opened my eyes wide, realizing she was right. We hadn't seen a human since Sarah left, and I suddenly felt alone and vulnerable.

Meagan surveyed the area and continued, "The display at the visitors' center says the West Pack hunts throughout this end of the island. They spray urine to mark their territory."

The foreign odor raised a primal alarm. Adrenaline pricked my skin. Suddenly on alert, I feared for my daughter's life. "We need to keep moving." I prodded her from behind, pushing against her backpack.

She laughed and sidestepped my efforts. "Don't worry, Mom. Wolves only eat moose, maybe a hare or beaver, but nothing else. They're afraid of humans, and we'd be lucky to see one."

As exhilarating as a wolf sighting would be, I didn't want to be a statistic for researchers who study the feeding habits of *Canis lupus*. "We'd be much easier to hunt down than a moose for some hungry wolf willing to sample new meat. Let's get out of here."

* * *

Later that afternoon Meagan and I walked along a beaten path camouflaged by honeysuckle and dogbane, both intent on reclaiming the area for their own species. The further we hiked from Windigo, the fewer people we passed. After the hubbub last night and this morning and the threat of wolves in deep woods, the open sunlight of Feldtmann Ridge was a relief. The trail snaked across dry, rocky fields and then tunneled through thickets of choke cherry, aspen, and hazelnut. My mind traveled back in history to a time when island visitors were not greeted by the same lush views. Lumberjacks once had their way with the island in the logging frenzy of the last century. Old pictures at the visitors' center had shown proud, roughly dressed men with the tools of their trade, peavies and pike poles, at the ready, posed in a work camp. Behind them were endless acres of stumps to the exclusion of every living thing. In 1936 a fire finished off the landscape. I marveled at nature's powers of rebirth.

"Are these thimbleberries?" Meagan's call from ahead brought me into the present. She waded into shrubbery to the side of the path, and I quickened my pace to join her in the thicket.

"Yep. Juicy and ripe." My mouth moistened as I plucked a swollen red berry. "When they're ripe these caps pull right off." I fitted a berry cap on my thumb like a thimble as a visual aid for its name and then settled the thimbleberry on my tongue, feeling the texture of an apricot's skin. Sweet, tart juice startled my salivary glands. "Mmmm."

Meagan watched me skeptically. "You sure they're not poisonous?"

I pointed out the plant's size, location, and leaf structure. "I'm sure. Nothing else on the island looks or tastes like this."

My daughter touched her tongue to a fat berry. Her eyes grew large. "Oh, my God." She quickly plucked another. We treated ourselves to a handful of fruit, savoring every one.

"How about thimbleberry cobbler tonight?"

Meagan's eyes lit up. "Yummy! You brought a recipe?"

"Nope. We'll create our own."

I tied my bandana into a little pouch, and we gathered berries until the improvised sack bulged. When we had our fill of berries and the hot sun in the open fields, we headed toward the forested area along the shore. Progress was slow because we veered frequently from the trail to grab just one more of the thumb-sized berries.

After an hour's walk, the ground became softer, damp. Puncheons bridged the bogs and put us slightly above grasses and reeds that tugged at our ankles. In the mid-afternoon Meagan and I took advantage of the boardwalks, dropped our backpacks, and sat to rest in a clearing where sunlight dried the wooden planks.

We chatted amiably, woman to woman, but stuck to safe topics. She enjoyed her responsibilities as CFO for the company in Atlanta. Her husband's golf game had improved along with his salary level.

I told her about my new condo and my friend, Glen, but avoided mention of her father. She stiffened whenever I got close to that subject.

I felt unsure of myself, timid. We used to talk nonstop. Back then I'd fill her imagination with stories, and she loved to learn everything I had to teach. Where had that ease gone?

"Are you enjoying yourself, Meagan?"

"Sure, Mom. These woods give me peace." Her eye flinched ever so slightly.

A thousand questions came to mind. I bolstered my courage and tried to probe. "You've been distant, honey. Is something wrong? Do you need..."

Meagan gasped. "Look!" She pointed behind me.

A moose calf stood motionless thirty yards away, watching us. His doleful eyes peered through thick foliage and stared from an impossibly long face with wide nostrils twitching in the air, buzzing with flies. Meagan and I stood for a better look. My impulse was to grab my camera, but we had been warned. A one-thousand pound mama moose packs more powerful fury than a mother bear. She was out there somewhere.

"Shhh. Don't move."

Meagan slowly reached for her camera and advanced ten feet with the calf framed in the digital screen.

"No, Meagan," I hissed. "Stay back!"

"I'm okay."

She zoomed in, and her shutter whirred. "Got a good one." Satisfied with her nature photo, she backed up and slipped the camera into her pocket.

For several minutes we held our positions, silent and still, in the pastoral scene surrounded by tall grasses and dense shrubbery. Bees visited star flowers and gentian, a warbler sang from a white pine, and one of God's ugliest creatures munched on birch saplings. The calf became curious. His ears quivered and his lip curled toward us. He took one step, and then another.

"No. Go away, moose." Perspiration dampened my armpits. "Meagan, walk slowly backwards." I retreated, but the inquisitive three-hundred-pound calf matched me step for step.

Suddenly, a roaring snort filled the air, thundering feet broke branches, and trees crashed to the ground. Mama moose had a full head of steam and charged from the deep woods straight for us.

Meagan screamed somewhere behind me.

"Run!" I screeched, but there was no time. I threw myself on the ground and squirmed under the puncheon. Meagan shinnied up a tree, climbing like a monkey on steroids. I tucked my arms and legs in just in time to avoid being trampled by six-inch hooves stomping the ground in rage. The moose kicked the walkway and raised her leg to hammer on the wooden planks. I gritted my teeth and prayed that the forest service bought the strongest possible wood to build the puncheon. I was terrified that a hoof would splinter the fragile cage and crush my skull. I squeezed my eyes shut while the moose snorted and dug a rut in the moist earth next to my head.

The bashing went on for an eternity, but then all went quiet. I risked opening one eye and peeked sideways. The hooves were still there, but the beast had found the succulent aspen trees irresistible. She chewed docilely. I tried not to breathe. Through the cracks between the planks I could see my daughter clinging to a branch, fifteen feet in the air.

"Get out!" Meagan yelled. "Go away, you big ugly animal!" With a vise grip on the tree, she threw leaves and small branches at the behemoth, but mama moose would not move while good food was at hand and her calf was safe.

I had no idea where her baby had gone and did not want to spook the moose again, so I shrank myself and waited. Occasionally, the huge snout came to ground level and snuffled around. She pawed the dirt nervously, but didn't budge. Through the slats I got a close-up view of her hairy snout, the disgusting dewlap hanging from her chin, and mangy patches of black fur on her neck. She hung her head, and I squinted to examine her coat more closely. That wasn't black fur; she was infested with ticks feeding on her blood. I almost lost my breakfast.

"Mom! Mom, are you okay?"

Meagan sounded frantic, but I couldn't answer her or even wave for fear of a moose reprisal. My daughter clung to the tree, sobbing. I prayed she wouldn't do anything brave.

Adrenaline drained away and the puncheon felt like a crypt. A rank, wild smell permeated the air. My skin crawled. I imagined ticks jumping from their current host to sample fresh human blood and promised myself a thorough body check.

The dull-witted creature munched on grass further and further away, out of my vision. I waited. Minutes later I heard Meagan jump from the tree and run down the puncheon. I poked my hand out of my safe haven to signal my survival, and she threw herself to her knees at my side.

"Are you hurt? Did she kick you?" Tears streaked Meagan's face.

"She missed. I'm okay. Now haul me out of here."

Getting into the cramped space was much easier than getting out, but Meagan yanked on my arm to free me. Then she gave me a hug, turned me around to brush dirt and mud from my clothes, and hugged me again.

"Really, Meagan, I'm fine. You don't have to fuss."

"I'm sorry, Mom. I was stupid to take pictures and felt so guilty in the tree while that monster tried to stomp on you."

"She was only trying to protect her baby. I'd probably do the same if someone threatened you." I smiled at my flushed and worried daughter.

"Well, I should hope so." She grinned like the eight-year-old I used to know.

Our quiet laughter relieved the pent-up tension.

"Now, let's get out of moose territory," I said, scanning the thick shrubbery.

Mother and baby browsed a hundred feet away, but they paid no mind to us. I pulled my bandana from the mud where the moose's hooves had ground it into the earth, and scraped off the pureed thimbleberries and dripping juice. The image of a human hand minced into pulp ingrained itself in my mind.

5

Feldtmann Lake

A blue oasis fringed with wilderness lay before us—Feldtmann Lake. We had the place to ourselves and claimed a patch of beachfront property for our campsite. I postponed the pleasure of dipping my sore feet into the clear, shallow water and instead set up camp. I pitched our tent away from an overhead dead tree limb that threatened to become a "widow maker" in a stiff wind, choosing instead a safer spot with a lesser view. Meagan threw a rope over a thick, healthy branch high in a sugar maple to hang our food bag to thwart mischievous mammals.

After the chores, I sat in the shade with my toes dug into the red sand and watched a beaver paddle across the smooth water, a widening vee streaming behind him. Meagan walked around the inlet to fish and soon caught a thrashing northern pike. She gently unhooked and released the fish. Minutes later she landed another, bigger northern. I wandered over to get a closer look.

"Hey! You're quite a fisherman," I called.

Meagan held up the line and grinned as if posing for a picture. "Thirty inches. We'll eat good tonight." Giddy, she slogged out of the knee-high water and pulled a heavy cord through the pike's gills. "Fishing near Atlanta was never like this."

I fought down my aversion to killing a living creature and thought of our ancestors hunting for food. I didn't want to touch the pike, but contributed to the hunt by carrying her fishing gear. We followed our own footprints along the arc of the beach back to camp where Meagan threw the cord over a branch to hang the writhing fish until its life drained away.

I stood back, a bit squeamish, while she expertly filleted the fish and tossed the head and entrails into deep water. "For the turtles."

Once the fish looked store-bought, I helped her wash the delicate fillets and lay them on paper towels on a flat rock. After we sanitized our hands, Meagan rummaged in her pack. "I told you I'd make use of this skillet."

We had examined the collapsible skillet at the outfitters in Duluth, but my pack had already exceeded my self-imposed weight limit. Meagan insisted on the purchase and promised me I wouldn't be sorry. She wasn't joking. The smell of sizzling fish was well worth the extra weight. The fish extended over the edge of the pan, but she fried the fillets to a golden brown. Her skills amazed me.

We stuffed ourselves and offered the last large piece to a passing fisherman who had come up empty. He strolled down the beach to brag to his friend that he had caught, cleaned, and fried the fish he was eating. Meagan and I laughed to ourselves and kept his secret.

I spotted a pair of hikers coming through the clearing; a big man following a woman half his size. "We have more company."

Meagan squinted into the bright sunlight. "That's the woman from the yacht."

"I think you're right."

Valerie could have posed for an outfitter's catalog in her neat, formfitting nylon pants, cotton shirt, and safari hat. She carried next to nothing. The beast of burden behind her carried the biggest backpack I'd ever seen, with a folding chair, lantern and miscellaneous gear tied on the outside, swinging back and forth.

"What kind of self-respecting woman does that to her husband?" Meagan shook her head. The duo passed our camp and dropped their packs in the grassy site a hundred yards from ours. We shifted our position on the log to watch the newcomers. Valerie found a shade tree, set up the folding chair and fanned herself while holding her water bottle to her forehead. She talked and fanned and talked and pointed. The husband lumbered around the pile of gear, but didn't join Valerie's running commentary. Even from a distance I could see he was perplexed. He examined each item of camping gear and removed price tags and packaging.

Spying on others got uncomfortable after a while, so we turned away, though we were not above sneaking a peek on occasion. For alternative entertainment I watched several grebes paddle across the water twenty feet from shore.

"That poor man. She must be a real shrew." Meagan clucked her tongue and busied herself with cleaning her folding knife.

"She seemed pleasant when I met her at the visitors' center, but not real bright." I adjusted my sitting pad on the ground so I could lean against the fallen log next to my daughter and attempted to create a personal conversation. "Where did you learn to fillet fish like that? From Ed?"

She heaved a happy sigh. "No, I taught him. Grandpa taught me."

"Grandpa? My dad?" My mind raced through our history to find a time when that was possible.

"He took James and me up to Lake Delavan once when you and Dad went to some convention for the week."

"Wow. I don't remember that."

Meagan shrugged as if to say, *What else is new?*

I ignored her attitude. "He tried to teach me, too, when I was six or seven, but I didn't care for fishing." I remembered rocking in the waves and sleeping on the warm wooden planks. "But I loved being in the rowboat with him."

48

"Me, too. I miss him." She ducked her head to my level and smiled.

At least that old rowboat was a memory we shared. I closed my eyes and breathed in the remembered smell of Dad's rich cigar smoke.

A high-pitched ruckus shook me from my memories. Meagan pointed her knife in Valerie's direction and sniggered. "They're trying to put up the tent, and she's ragging him something fierce."

Like gaping at a car wreck, I watched Valerie pick up a corner of the tent, try to fit a pole into a grommet, and then throw the pole on the ground. The man tried to calm her, smoothing the air between them with his bear-sized hands. She picked up the pole again and pointed to his end of the tent. Determined to jam it into the corner pocket, Valerie bent the pole to her will. I heard the snap three hundred feet away. She looked at the fiberglass pieces in her hands, threw them at her husband, and stomped off in the direction of the latrine.

"We should help them." I got myself off the ground with a groan. "Sarah told me how to fix a broken tent pole with duct tape."

Meagan shook her head. "You go, if you want to. I think we should stay out of their business."

"Be back in ten minutes."

I stopped five yards from where the man stood, scratching his head. "Hello," I called.

Distracted and unfocused, he pushed his wire-rimmed glasses to the bridge of his nose. "Oh, hi." He studied the poles laid out on the ground and stroked his smooth cheek. "Ah." He quickly assembled the poles in the correct order and stood the tent up with his hand holding the broken ends together.

I held up the duct tape.

A shy grin lit his face. "Excellent, but I need a stick or something for a brace."

49

"How about the extra tent stake?"

"You've done this before." He wound the tape around the pole ends and the brace, and then stood back to admire his handiwork.

"Is Valerie okay?"

He looked surprised that I would know her name, and we both glanced in the direction she had taken. The care and concern in his eyes said more than a thousand Valentines.

"She just needs time to calm herself." He dropped his hands against his thighs in a helpless gesture. "She's had a bad day. Forgot to pack her medication."

I held out my hand. "I'm Amy Warren. I met Valerie yesterday at the wildflower display at the visitors' center."

"Patrick Kinzler." His huge paw could have broken the bones in my hand. His gentleness surprised me. "Yes, Valerie loves flowers and photographs them everywhere we go."

He shuffled around and looked anywhere but in my eyes, the sort of man who didn't know he presented an imposing figure—the sort whose low self-esteem prevented him from seeing a tall, strong man in the mirror. I pigeonholed him as a brilliant computer geek or internet guru.

"My daughter and I are camped at the shore there." I nodded to our campsite where Meagan stood on the sand. "If you need help with anything, just shout."

He glanced with a bit of panic at his pile of gear. "Valerie will want dinner when she gets back. Will you show me how to work the stove?"

I hooked up the fuel canister, got water boiling, and explained how to prepare their dehydrated meals. He plunged into the project with confidence, determined to have a hot meal ready for his wife. I headed for my own campsite and hoped Valerie knew she had a gem.

* * *

Campfires were not allowed at Feldtmann. Without smoke to deter them, mosquitoes swarmed when dusk arrived. Meagan and I retreated to our tent before the sun set. Meagan had a novel. I had my journal and wildflower guide, but neither of us picked up our distractions. Instead, we tried to communicate. We talked mostly about her childhood, her current job, and her angst as a teenager.

Meagan laughed. "It's taken me ten years, but I think I'm finally over the worry of not fitting in and what the other girls are wearing."

"You certainly outgrew all that," I agreed. "I'm very proud of you, and I hope that we'll be close again, like we were back then." I envisioned more frequent visits—sharing secrets and intimate aspects of our lives.

Meagan laughed lightly. "Oh, Mom. We were never close."

"Never close?" My breath stuck in my throat, and I bit back the hurt.

She caught my reaction. "I mean, you're a great mom, but I always felt that James and I were on your to-do list." She took care with the words and a moist haze muted her brilliant blue eyes.

I grasped for happy memories. "Don't you remember when you'd curl up on the couch with me, and I'd stroke your hair while you told me about the girls at school?"

"Sure, I remember that."

"And when Tommy Schmidt broke up with you to date that Amanda girl?"

"I remember I came to you to talk and practically had to make an appointment. You were always running around for Dad or worried about Grandpa's business. You never had time for us. I forced you to listen to me."

"No, I loved listening to your stories and problems. Remember when I drove you to all those soccer games and tae kwon do lessons? I thought we could talk about anything." My heart ached.

51

Of course, two people can remember the same incident in vastly different ways, but my own daughter…

"I made you listen."

Her heavy assertion beat me down. I couldn't argue with her memories. "I'm sorry, Meagan. I always meant to be close to you, to be a good mom." I wanted to run away from the conversation, but I rooted myself. "I'm trying, Meagan. I'm here now and want to listen." The break in my voice threatened to surface. "Our regular phone calls and e-mails are good." I gave her a wary glance. "Aren't they?"

Meagan nodded with a wan smile. "I hate to say this, but it's better since your divorce, you seem more interested in me. Before that…" She shook her head. Her words crushed me into silence.

"So when you invited me on this crazy vacation," she said. "I dropped everything and here we are." Meagan shrugged off her melancholy, but the mood hung on me.

"And your brother must feel this way, too," I moaned. "I'll call him the minute we get home."

"That would be good, Mom. James needs you."

She rocked herself against me, and I linked my arm through hers. My eyes filled with tears—maybe for the years I'd missed, maybe in thanks for the promised years ahead. Small talk lost its importance.

"Mom?" Meagan shifted away from me. "I want to tell you about…"

Suddenly, we were startled by a commotion outside the tent.

"Mrs. Warren! Help!" A booming voice rocked the night and silenced the cicadas and tree frogs.

I shot to a kneeling position. "What? Who's there?"

"Please, you've got to help me find Valerie."

I grabbed my headlamp, which had been suspended from a loop at the ceiling, hung the strap around my neck, and crawled out of the tent to find Patrick Kinzler pacing the shore. His fluorescent lantern illuminated the entire area. Clouds of moths followed his progress.

"Patrick, what's happened?"

"Valerie never came back. I can't find her, and I'm worried sick." Panic garbled his speech.

I caught up with the big man and laid a hand on his arm to halt his pacing. A cold sweat layered his skin. "She'll be all right, Patrick."

Tears glistened on his cheeks in the manufactured light.

"Come sit and calm yourself. Tell me what's going on."

Patrick poured out his heart. Meagan and I flanked him and held him with conversation to prevent him from dashing headlong into the night, searching in a panic for his wife.

"Where have you looked, Patrick?" I kept my voice patient and bright.

"She walked toward the latrine, so I searched around there, and around the campground. I didn't go too far. Valerie would be angry if I wasn't here when she got back."

"You mentioned that she forgot her prescription," I said. "May I ask what the medicine is for?"

"The pills calm her down. Without them she gets depressed and angry and doesn't think straight." He hung his head and his body shuddered. "She hates to take them."

"She was angry when she left. What does she do to calm herself down?"

"I don't know." He put his face in his hands. "She bakes, or cuddles up with the dog, or goes for a swim."

Meagan and I exchanged a look of foreboding and glanced behind us at the black lake.

"Meagan, run down to that other campsite and ask those two fishermen to walk north along the shore." On full alert, she bobbed her head. "Make sure they have whistles. Three blasts and we'll come."

"Okay, Mom." She laced up her boots and switched on her flashlight.

"Then come back here in case Valerie returns to camp. Whistle for us if she does. Patrick and I will walk along the lake to the south."

Meagan ran off. Patrick still wrung his hands, but his shoulders squared up, ready for action and eager for any plan. He grabbed the fluorescent lantern and we set off along the sand—past where Meagan caught the northern pike, past a trail of moose tracks, and on until the shore turned sharply to the east. Patrick yelled Valerie's name over and over, his voice raw with desperation. We halted where the rocky beach and dense tree cover made swimming in the area unlikely.

"Let's retrace our steps and cast the light further over the water." The image of her pale body floating in the black water refused to go away. "She may have swum too far out to hear us."

That little bit of hope allowed Patrick to swing his light high and shout his wife's name again.

"Shh, Patrick, listen." I grabbed his wrist. A shrill blast of sound carried over the water, followed by another. I held my breath during the pause. Three more quick blasts. "They found something."

"Valerie!" Patrick dropped the lantern and ran.

I retrieved the light and jogged along the wet sand, no match for his rabbit speed. I rounded the end of the lake, ran past our campsite, and continued toward several lights dipping and bobbing in the dark distance. I slowed to a walk, breathing heavily. My heart sank to see Patrick's shadow hunched over, kneeling in the sand near a downed tree.

I reached the small group of searchers, pulled Meagan to the side and whispered, "What did they find?"

"Clothes. Pants, shirt and hat."

I brought the lantern to where Patrick sat back on his heels with the clothes gathered in his arms. "Patrick, are these Valerie's clothes?"

"Yes, yes."

"May I look at them in the light?"

He nodded and held them out toward me, though he wouldn't let go. The clothes looked whole and clean. I looked at the tags. Size four. The safari hat looked like hers, too. I sighed.

"So, she went swimming," I said. "Let's keep looking. Has anyone been further down the beach?"

"This is as far as we got," the young fisherman said.

Patrick jerked his head up and stared with a wild new hope in his eyes. He jumped to his feet and bolted off to the north. The rest of us followed, searching, fanned out across the beach and into the thick brush beyond. Patrick ran and shouted her name into the night.

Feldtmann Lake drew me to its edge. I shone my lights over the water, hoping to see the surface unbroken and still. The lake gently lapped at my boots, undisturbed. One of the searchers took in a sharp breath of air, and I looked up in time to see Patrick's lantern take a left turn and dart into the underbrush three hundred yards ahead. When his light became stationary, we quickened our steps.

Moments later, Patrick walked out of the night into our beams of light with Valerie cradled like a child against his chest. I ran the last two yards to his side and shone my headlamp over her body. She was purple with cold. Patrick sobbed and shook.

So did Valerie. She feebly clutched her husband's shirt.

"We have to warm her." I shouted a little too loud. "Who has a lighter? Gather firewood."

Meagan wrapped her jacket around the shivering woman and helped me strip off her wet underwear. Patrick's jacket gave Valerie another layer, but left her feet exposed, so I swaddled her freezing

55

feet in my fleece sweater. The big man rocked his wife in his lap while the others piled driftwood and coaxed a flame to life.

"I... I dove in," she whispered. "Too cold to breathe."

"Shh, Val. I've got you."

"Clothes were gone. I walked and..."

"You're okay, baby. Shh."

To give them their private moment, I busied myself with the illegal fire. I supposed that the rangers would make an exception to the rule, especially if we cleaned up the charred mess in the morning.

Meagan knelt at my side. "I ran back to get tea." She put a metal mug onto the hot coals and waited for the water to heat. Why hadn't I thought of that? I patted my daughter's knee.

After five or six minutes, Meagan wrapped the mug in a bandana and offered the tea to Valerie. Patrick took the mug and coaxed his wife to sip the hot liquid. She breathed in the rising steam and soon stopped shivering.

A half hour later Patrick picked up his wife and carried her to their campsite. The fishermen had already wandered to their tents after wishing Valerie well and receiving thanks from Patrick. Meagan and I stayed with the fire, enjoying its heat and watching the coals burn down.

"You really took charge, Mom."

"What do you mean, honey?"

"I mean, we saved that woman because everyone listened to you. You were wonderful." She laid her head on my shoulder.

The shock of her compliment silenced me. I needed to tell her how proud I was of her quick, thoughtful actions during the evening's emergency, but I was afraid my voice would crack with emotion. Instead, I kissed her forehead and stroked her golden hair while we watched the fire gutter out.

6

Day 3 - Siskiwit Bay

We slept later than usual the next morning. Most of the fog had burned off the lake by the time I stuck my head out of the tent. I started breakfast, and Meagan joined me before the pot of water boiled. She tousled her unruly hair, yawned, and stretched. My mind jumped back two decades to pink footed-pajamas—the pair with the bunnies and the trapdoor—and the smell of baby shampoo.

Meagan returned from the latrine and reached for the hand sanitizer. "They're gone."

I peered over the edge of my steaming mug of hot chocolate. "What's gone?"

"Patrick and Valerie's site is empty." She pointed her thumb toward the clearing. "They left our jackets hanging in the tree at the entrance to our site."

"That's really strange that they left so early." I took my fleece from her and slipped my arms into the sleeves. "I wonder if Valerie got sick."

"He would've called for you." She smiled and stirred a packet of cocoa into her mug. "They probably wanted to get back to that fancy yacht and cuddle in comfort."

"I hope so." We had seen the last of the couple, I was certain, but Valerie's odd behavior and the bizarre control she had over her husband continued to bother me.

A mosquito landed on the back of my hand, but I swatted her before she could draw blood. "You really helped those people last night, Meagan." I raised my voice, wanting her to hear me. "I'm very proud of you."

"Thanks, Mom. We worked well together."

Our eyes locked. We nodded in unison and grinned.

I knew then that I'd made the right decision to hike with Meagan rather than stay at Windigo to support Sarah. Still, I cringed to think of my friend being hounded by Deborah and treated like a criminal by the federal investigator. I hugged my daughter.

* * *

The loop around the western end of Isle Royale was a total of thirty miles. The longest leg, ten miles from Feldtmann to Siskiwit, lay ahead of us. Meagan and I walked at a leisurely pace up and down in elevation, sometimes through leafy forest, sometimes on the thin soil of the exposed ridge. The fire tower at the halfway point was our destination for lunch. While Meagan's strong legs took her up the one hundred steps to the top of the tower, I inflated my sleeping pad and lay in the shade.

"Come on up, Mom." Meagan waved from the top floor of the tower. "I can see Lake Superior. What a view!"

I waved and took her picture, content to stay below to re-energize with food and rest.

"There's a group of kids headed this way," she called from the heavens.

Dang. I wondered if they were headed to Siskiwit and if there'd be room in the shelters or campground for us. I rolled up my pad and collected my lunch debris.

Meagan descended quickly. The metal stairway shook and clanged beneath her feet. "We'd better go." She jumped down the last few steps and gathered her gear.

Before we could leave, I spotted a skinny little guy racing up the trail, competing with a much older, taller, blond boy. Red in the face, the little rascal tagged the leg of the tower and whooped in triumph. The older boy gave him a friendly shove in the shoulder. The two scouts argued and joked until they realized we were there. Self-conscious, or maybe reminded of their manners, they straightened up and shuffled their feet in the dust.

"Where are you headed?" I asked the fidgeting boys.

"We're camping at Siskiwit tonight," said the older scout, glancing at the remainder of the troop coming up the hill and antsy to be the first to climb the tower.

"We'll see you in camp, then." I motioned toward the metal stairway and released them from their obligation to be polite. He and the skinny rascal jumped and jostled to run up the steps before the others arrived.

Meagan and I gave up our lunch spot to the eight scouts before the two leaders crested the hill. We nonchalantly set out at a good pace, not wanting to trigger a competition with the scout troop to get to Siskiwit to claim a shelter.

"We'll have to move fast," Meagan said, once we were out of earshot.

"With so many of them, we may not even get a campsite." I didn't have a Plan B and certainly didn't want to continue hiking to the next campsites at Island Mine. "They'll probably play on the tower for a while. We'll be okay."

Racing ahead of the scouts turned out to be fun. We breezed along the twisting trail through fields of grasses and wildflowers as deep as our waists. The hours went quickly. Our noses caught the scent of water before we saw the lake. A half mile later, we topped a rise and were suddenly presented with a panoramic view of Lake

Superior. At the bottom of the hill lay a wide arc of beach bisected by a long cement pier. Meagan gave me a high-five.

"But we have company." I gestured toward a ribbon of trail snaking down a long slope off to our left where a lone hiker with a royal blue pack made progress toward our coveted shelter.

"I'll go." Meagan took off at a steady jog before I could stop her—or urge her to hurry. I lagged behind.

Much to our surprise, the backpacker hiked past the two shelters and into the woods at the far side of Siskiwit. We had the place to ourselves. We sat on the wooden steps to Shelter #1 and laughed, tired and relieved.

Someone had dragged a picnic table into the shelter, so we dumped our gear there and set up housekeeping before we wandered down to the beach to explore our home for the next two nights. I had thoughts of cooling off in the lake and stuck my foot in.

"Whoa! I change my mind." My foot, tinted blue, reminded me of Valerie's limp and pale body after her foolish plunge into the lake last night. She had been lucky. I sat on the pebbled shoreline and returned my socks and boots to my feet.

"You won't catch me in forty-two degree water." Meagan laughed. "I'll collect firewood."

A blazing campfire and a bubbly berry cobbler sounded like a great idea. I had spotted a patch of thimbleberries in the fields during our rush to the shore and backtracked to pick a pot full. I waded into the thicket and got into the routine of plucking the fruit, but stayed on alert, looking over my shoulder, in case another moose tried to trample this collection of berries—and me along with them.

* * *

Thirty minutes later I returned to the beach with a batch of thimbleberries and another of raspberries. Meagan had a good blaze going in the community fire-ring. She tended the fire, adding fuel, while I located her skillet and prepared our dinner.

The first crab-cake was a success, and I flipped the patty onto Meagan's plate.

She bit into the steaming treat tentatively. "That's really good, Mom."

I ignored the urge to scold her for talking with her mouth full and nodded in agreement. "Sarah's recipe. She gave me a sample on our first night in the Grand Canyon."

Meagan stopped chewing and turned toward the beach view without comment.

"She's a great outdoor cook. I wonder how Deborah is treating her." I sighed, anxious about Sarah's predicament.

Meagan's silence disconcerted me. I fidgeted with my food, pushing peas around my plastic plate. "Try these peas," I said, trying to make conversation. We had gathered the peas from bushes scattered along the beach and boiled them in a bit of water. I handed her the cooking pot.

Meagan also seemed to prefer to focus on the food and scooped a spoonful. "They turned out great, Mom. Fresh makes a big difference." Her face relaxed into a slight smile.

We ate quietly, looking out over the water, until Meagan straightened up.

"Well, here come the scouts." She pointed her spork at the top of the hill where the troop made their way through the deep grasses. All eight boys seemed to notice the lake at the same time. With a sudden shot of energy, they ran the last quarter mile and exploded onto the beach. They shrugged their heavy packs off their shoulders, dropped them, and struggled to yank the boots from their feet. I watched and envied their youth. Meagan wore a big grin.

The adult leaders arrived, but went directly to the second shelter. They let the boys burn off their exuberance, but eventually came to the beach to corral them.

"I apologize if the boys disturbed you," the man nearest to us said.

The linebacker-sized leader had pink cheeks and friendly jowls. He probably had been a scout himself and knew that hiking, gorging on thimbleberries, and the crazy run to the beach into the freezing water was stuff these kids would remember for the rest of their lives. I hoped so, anyway. The other man looked less comfortable in the out-of-doors, but amiable enough.

"Your boys don't bother us a bit. We enjoy watching them." I indicated the log on the opposite side of the fire ring for them to sit.

The two men settled themselves with a groan just as the skinny rascal we'd met at the tower ran up to them. "Can we jump off the pier?" He couldn't contain his excitement.

"After chores," the jowly man said.

"Oh, please, Mr. Domkowski, please."

"The sooner the chores are done, the sooner you can swim."

The young boy ran off to gather the others. They grabbed their packs and ran up the hill to their shelter.

The thinner leader nudged Mr. Domkowski. "I'd better follow to oversee the chaos." He grinned at us and shook his head with obvious affection for the energetic boys up at the shelter. "Do you mind if we share the campfire after you've had your dinner?"

"We'll keep the fire going for you." Meagan cracked another branch over her knee and threw the ends onto the flames.

"I'm making a raspberry-thimbleberry cobbler here." I showed off the pot of berries. "There will be enough for each boy to have a dollop."

"They'd love cobbler." Mr. Domkowski smacked his lips. "A dollop will hold them while they cook their dinner."

Screams came from up the hill. Scouts streamed out of Shelter #2, slamming the screen door. Younger boys jumped and shouted, while older scouts laughed and tried to calm them. The tall blond boy, armed with a broom, re-entered the shelter.

"A spider." Mr. Domkowski rolled his eyes and grinned. Both men pushed themselves off the log, said good-bye, and lumbered up the hill.

Meagan watched the leaders go. "They must be wonderful dads."

I nodded while I covered the skillet with tinfoil. "Spending time together is good for both father and son." I laughed. "And that spider reminds me of a story Sarah told about a tarantula." I stretched my fingers out like spider legs. "She said the hairy thing crawled…" I stopped in mid-sentence when I noticed Meagan's gloomy expression. "What?"

She shook her head. "Nothing."

"Tell me."

"It's just that you're always talking about Sarah this, and Sarah that."

I didn't try to hide my irritation. "Meagan, Sarah's my friend, and she's on my mind because I'm worried about this accusation against her."

My daughter hung her head. "You're right, Mom. I'm being a baby." She brought her eyes level with mine. "But I wanted this trip to be about you and me. I didn't want to share our time with Sarah, but I apologize. I understand that you're worried."

I patted Meagan's knee. "It's okay. We have lots of time, and I think we're doing fine. Are you enjoying yourself?"

Meagan nodded, a small smile brightening her face. "I am. I forgot how much I love camping." Her smile slid away. She shrugged and got up to add kindling to the fire, poking and prodding the wood, not looking at me.

Baffled, I watched pine sap ooze from a smoking log. Why was communication with my own daughter so difficult? I was afraid to say the wrong thing, to touch the wrong subject. Our reconnection was more nebulous than the smoke billowing skyward.

After several minutes, Meagan gave up her fire-stoking job and sat on the log to stare at the flames leaping from the dry wood. I picked up her stout stick and rearranged several logs, looking for glowing coals for the cobbler.

"Mom, I have to tell you something."

I stopped poking at the fire and sat back on my heels. Something in her voice warned me to prepare for a shock. My mind flew ahead, picturing her losing her job, or worse, her husband.

"Tell me anything." I brushed the grit from my pant legs and joined her on the log.

Meagan inspected her fingernails for dirt and wiped her hands on her shorts. She cleared her throat. "I was hospitalized a few months ago."

My breath caught in the back of my throat, and I sat up straight. I sent a quick prayer upwards. Please not cancer. Please not cancer.

"I had a miscarriage," she said.

My relief mixed with grief. "Oh, honey, I'm so sorry." I put my arm around her shoulders, but that wasn't what she wanted. She needed to talk.

"My second miscarriage."

"Second?" I was shocked and hurt. How could a daughter not tell her mother such a thing—twice! How could a mother not know? "Meagan, I'm... Why didn't you tell me?"

She shrugged. "The first one was...well, I felt bad. I was three weeks along and Ed told me to stop running, but I wanted to stay in shape. I had a little spotting and then nothing—as if I never had been pregnant."

"I wish you had told me."

"It's such a personal thing, and you had so much going on with Dad springing the divorce on you, and selling the house. You didn't need my bad news."

I silently berated myself for being so self-centered when my daughter needed me. She continued, as if compelled to spill out her side of the story. "The second pregnancy followed quickly and thrilled Ed. I was so careful. I stopped running and rested, but maybe the second pregnancy was too soon after the first. I ended up sitting on the toilet with blood pouring out of me. I was so weak I couldn't call Ed for help, but heard him laughing on the phone with my best friend."

I watched a war play out on her face between her logic and a sense of betrayal.

"He didn't know, or he would have helped you," I said.

"I know." She sighed. "When I struggled up from the toilet and flushed, the amount of blood shocked me." She put her head in her hands and filled her fists with thick hair. "And I saw a—a kidney bean shape swirling around in the red water."

Meagan untangled her fingers from her hair and stared at them, showing me a half inch. I winced at what was to come.

She whispered, "A second too late I realized that the little bean was my baby." Her eyes pleaded for release from her pain. "I flushed my baby," Meagan sobbed.

I choked back tears and pulled her into my arms. "No, sweetheart, don't think that."

"I could have grabbed her," Meagan insisted. "I should have held her. But like a zombie, I stared and—watched her disappear."

My precious daughter sat in misery, and I waited for her to empty her soul of useless guilt. She spoke from behind her trembling hands. "Now I dream of her golden curls and blue baby eyes, smiling from the bloody water, swirling away from me."

Meagan laid her head in my lap, and I ran my fingers through her thick, golden waves, pretending to be the mother I obviously wasn't. I must have overestimated my daughter's strength and independence. Maybe my view of her through her teenage years had been wishful thinking, hoping that she'd thrive without me. I had spent too many hours at the office and stressed out about things that now seemed so unimportant. I vowed to take away Meagan's pain, to do the mom thing. I prayed I wasn't too late and searched the vast lake, the sky, and the dark woods for wisdom. None came.

The fire needed tending, but I sat still, careful not to disturb my daughter. I mourned the years I'd wasted, and I mourned the granddaughter I might have had—a golden-haired toddler, like Meagan had been, a cherub.

The scouts burst upon the scene, running pell-mell down the hill. They buried each other in pebbly sand and did cannonballs off the long pier, shrieking as they came to the surface of the frigid water. They were in a blissful world. We were not.

My leg grew numb and I shifted my position. Meagan sat up and dabbed her eyes with the sleeve of her shirt. "Thanks, Mom. I needed to tell someone." She hung her head. "I'm so afraid I can never have babies."

"What does the doctor say?"

"He says I'm healthy and strong, and we can try again in a few months."

"Well, there you are. That's wonderful." I tucked a stray strand of hair behind her ear. "By this time next year you'll welcome a little Eddie into the world."

"No, that's too soon."

Her abruptness surprised me. "If the doctor says it's okay, then…"

"I can't." She sat up straight and took charge of her body and emotions. "I have several half marathons to run this summer and the Atlanta Marathon in November."

"Meagan, twenty-six miles is tough on your body, if you're trying to get…"

"And I'm scheduled for the Disney run in January." She frowned as if envisioning her calendar. "Maybe we'll try in April."

"Meagan, are you sure you want to get pregnant?" I asked softly, carefully. "Sounds to me like you're procrastinating."

Her face turned pale. "Of course I want to." She stopped and stared at her hands in her lap. "I'm afraid, Mom. What if I lose another baby?"

I took a long breath and peered into my daughter's troubled face. "Did I ever tell you that I had a miscarriage when your brother was fourteen months old?"

Her mouth opened. She shook her head and put a comforting hand on my knee.

"But six months later I was rewarded with a healthy pregnancy —and then, you."

"You never mentioned a miscarriage," she scolded.

"Too personal, I guess." I smiled and hugged my daughter. "I should have shared that with you once you grew up. Neither of us should go through grief alone."

Her pain didn't leave her. "I don't want to disappoint my husband again," she said. "He really wants to be a father. I think he blames me for running and losing our…the babies. He's different now, remote. What if he leaves me, like Dad left you?"

A few moments elapsed before I recovered from the blow. "No comparison." I breathed in cool, calming air. "Don't you think Ed is grieving, too? Give him time. He loves you, and the two of you will figure out what to do—together."

She smiled weakly. "I'd die without him."

7

Message From Windigo

Fire lured the scouts closer. Shivering, they crept in shyly, draped in sleeping bags, raincoats and extra clothes, but barefoot with purple feet and lips. Meagan and I roused ourselves to welcome our guests to the community fire ring.

"Come get warm, boys." I put on a pleasant face and waved them into the sitting area. "We'll need more wood."

They became a flurry of activity. The tallest boy, Conor, stirred up the flames and added sticks from the pile, placing them just so. "Who's on fire duty? Collect more fuel."

The younger boys respected Conor's authority and hopped into action. The skinny rascal scurried down the beach for driftwood. The others gathered downed branches from under nearby trees or from amongst the raspberry bushes and beach pea dotting the shoreline.

Conor poked the logs, and I chatted with him about their troop. "The boys certainly listen to you."

"I'm the patrol leader today." He spoke without looking at me. Several boys returned with twigs and branches and threw them on the flames. Conor frowned and rearranged the wood, jealously guarding his fire-building responsibility.

Unwilling to trespass on the terrain he'd staked out, I said, "I'll need hot coals to bake our cobbler. Will you dig out a few for me?"

He took to the project in earnest and selected the best of the glowing embers, but our conversation stalled. After Meagan's news, my heart wasn't into coaxing a teenager to talk. I went through the motions of baking a golden brown cobbler over Conor's coals.

Meagan and I sampled a small portion of the dessert before we let the scouts dig in. The boys pronounced the cobbler "Awesome!" They scraped the last of it from the skillet, licked their fingers, and then scoured the pan with sand before returning it to us sparkling clean.

Wyatt, the skinny rascal, sat on the end of the log warming himself. His thin face, which hadn't yet grown into his adult teeth, was spattered with freckles. With infectious enthusiasm, he fought for my attention by maintaining a steady stream of disjointed stories: a frog jumped into the laundry basket, his brother's arm broke while they wrestled, he got lost in a cornfield. His mother could have named him *Trouble*.

The boys roasted sausages over the campfire and vied for the honor of being the fire-master. Meagan observed the youngest boys with a softness in her eyes. We watched the scouts' antics, coaxed them to forage for wild beach peas and raspberries, and leaned comfortably against a log trying to replace sadness with life. The presence of youth worked on us like a tonic.

A change in wind directions caught my attention. I watched in fascination as a gray wall advanced across the open water, cutting the day in half. Lightning streaked within the heavy clouds. "There's a storm coming."

Meagan and the scout leaders jumped up. The boys couldn't be bothered, until a sudden wind whipped sand into their faces and kicked up whitecaps in the bay. Heavy droplets pelted us, making the boys hoot and holler. Everyone grabbed for gear and made a mad dash for the shelters, laughing all the way.

Refreshed, brought back to life, and relatively dry in our shelter, Meagan and I watched the storm roll over Isle Royale. Sheets of rain slashed across aspen and birch, flattened wild flowers and filled mud holes at our doorstep. The bay roiled and churned. Staccato drumming on the roof eliminated discussion, so my daughter and I linked arms and found peace in nature's fury.

From our perch on top of the bluff, we surveyed the cleansing of the earth. Trees bent and branches flew. A bright yellow movement caught my eye. A backpacker under a heavy load trudged into the driving rain, making slow progress along the trail leading to camp.

"Hey! Hello! Come out of the storm." I yelled, and Meagan joined me, but the wind stole our voices. She put her fingers to her mouth and whistled shrilly—a talent inherited from her father. No response. Meagan grabbed her raincoat from a peg and darted out the screen door. When she intercepted the hiker, his head jerked up as if surprised to see he was in Siskiwit campgrounds. She tugged his arm and led the drenched backpacker to our shelter. They burst through the door and stamped their boots on the wooden planks, spraying water droplets over me and all our gear. Our cozy shelter suddenly seemed too small.

"Thanks." He threw back his hood, and I was met with the startling gray eyes of a young man. Those thick, black lashes belonged on a girl—a model. A mane of dark, wet hair curled on his forehead. His five-o'clock shadow, so sexy to the younger crowd, masked his pale skin. My daughter thought nothing of him and pushed our gear to the far side of the shelter to make room for our guest. He hung his rain jacket on a nail and smiled down on us like a scalawag, flashing his perfect teeth and a deep dimple.

I stared, remembered to smile, and wished he were thirty years older.

"Amy?"

Startled that he knew my name, I stepped back.

"Sarah sent me."

I hate being the butt of a practical joke and suspected Sarah of putting this guy up to a prank, so I gave him a withering look.

He had a magnificent laugh. "I'm sorry. I should have introduced myself. Taylor Lorenz." His delicate hands embraced mine and then Meagan's. "I'm a visiting biologist researching the Isle Royale wolf packs." He fished a folded paper from his pack. "Sarah said I'd find you and your daughter here and asked me to give you this note. She's my best student. I've given several orientations about the wolves, and she's attended every one."

Though curious to read what Sarah had written, I tucked the note into my pocket and cleared a place at the picnic table for Taylor.

He stepped over the bench to sit. "Sarah and I have gotten to know each other well in the past few weeks. I'm very much on her side with this Deborah fiasco."

I was relieved that Sarah had allies among the island's hierarchy. "How's Sarah doing? Has anything new happened in the past two days?"

"As far as I know, there's no real news." Taylor paused, his head tilted slightly. "Deborah has been sniping at Sarah behind her back, trying to turn the other volunteers against her. The ostracism hurts Sarah more than she lets on, I think."

Taylor didn't have much more to say about Deborah's harassment of Sarah, so I worried alone, letting my daughter keep the conversation going with our guest. Meagan was most interested in his wolf research. While Taylor spoke with near reverence of the misunderstood wolves, I fired up the stove and made three mugs of hot chocolate to ward off the chill of the damp air.

"We thought we caught a scent of wolf this morning on the Feldtmann Trail," Meagan said. She rested her chin on her hands with her elbows propped on the table.

"Really? That would be West Pack." His eyes lit with interest. "We believe they just had a pup. They're down to five and need to rebuild the size of their pack. I'm on my way to the interior, trying to follow their hunting routes."

I didn't know whether to be afraid of marauding wolves or not. "Does the pack hunt here at Siskiwit? Are we in danger from them?"

Taylor must have heard the questions before. "Humans are not their prey, but don't get yourself in between a hungry pack and a sick or helpless moose they're stalking."

The moose reference launched Meagan and me into our story of the mama moose attack. Taylor listened, concern creasing his flawless features. "You were lucky. People have been killed by enraged moose."

"So I've heard." I shivered from more than the chill in the air. "The moose's rage certainly gave me a new appreciation for motherly love." I opened my eyes wide in an exaggerated expression.

"And me, too," Meagan said with a smile.

I didn't think she referred to the moose and her ugly calf. The scare was worth having my daughter realize her love for me. Nothing could have made me happier.

The drumming on the roof ended, replaced by the occasional splat of water from the leaves sloughing off the weight of the rain. The scouts' voices drifted to us as they escaped from the confinement of their shelter. The decibels increased, tinged with excitement.

"What are they saying?" I asked.

"Sounds like 'rainbow,'" Meagan said.

We all rose to our feet. I grabbed my camera and rushed outside. The boys were scattered about the hillside, pointing to the east. A magnificent rainbow rose from Lake Superior and arched across the water to end behind the treeline. Wanting to see a complete rainbow, I jogged down to the end of the pier. Meagan and Taylor followed. The boys soon joined us.

"Roy G. Biv," Meagan said.

Taylor laughed. "Roy G. Biv."

The Roy thing thoroughly confused me. "What are you saying?"

"Red, orange, yellow, green, blue, indigo, violet. The colors are always in that order." Meagan grinned at Taylor as if they shared some secret code. I heard the scouts chanting the colors, too. Either I hadn't paid attention in science class, or the acronym became standard only for the younger generations.

I snapped a dozen pictures and pondered my lack of knowledge for a moment. A second rainbow formed above the first. The complete double rainbow kept the Siskiwit crowd entertained for fifteen minutes.

The arches eventually faded away, leaving the sky plain and ordinary, and me a little melancholy. I hoped the rainbows were visible from the Windigo pier and that Sarah was cheered by them. I retrieved her note and read:

> The federal investigator arrives in three days and will
> get this mess straightened out. Deborah stays out of
> my way. She's been out hiking much of the time.
> Keep your eyes open for her. Hope you're bonding.
> —Sarah

Meagan joined me at the picnic table. "What'd she say?"

I returned the note to my shirt pocket. "Just saying *Hi*. She figures the investigators will be on the island in three days to clear her of Deborah's charges."

"And they'll find who really attacked Deborah." Meagan patted my knee. I appreciated her support and belief in Sarah's innocence.

"Taylor's not staying." She nodded toward the gaggle of boys gathered around the biologist at the fire ring, no doubt listening to wolf tales. "He's hiking through to Island Mine."

Eventually, Taylor gathered his gear, and the scouts scampered off. We walked with him a quarter mile to the top of the hill and the junction with the trail to Island Mine.

"Thanks for giving me shelter and hot chocolate." His beautiful smile could melt the right girl's heart.

"Thanks for delivering Sarah's note." I squinted up at him with the low-hanging sun in my eyes.

"No problem." He shrugged, then frowned. "It's the least I could do. By the way, Deborah's giving Sarah more grief than she admits. I had only two semesters of psychology, but to me Sarah seems depressed."

My heart sank. I questioned Taylor, but he couldn't give me any further details. We waved good-bye to him and turned back toward Siskiwit. I walked mechanically, not noticing the freshly washed flowers and clear blue sky.

"Mom, are you worrying about Sarah?"

"I guess I am."

"How about tomorrow we'll hike back to Windigo?" She picked a white campion and handed the flower to me. "We'll do what we can to help when the investigator arrives."

Meagan's new attitude took a weight off my shoulders, and my pride in my daughter grew immeasurably. Worry for Sarah grew as well. Taylor had said that the habitually cheerful, fearless Sarah was depressed. What was going on back at Windigo?

8

Day Four - Remington

My baby lay on the worn planks of the shelter. Inches from the weathered gray wood, her smooth round cheek flattened itself against her bedding, forming her mouth into pink cupid lips, slightly open, breathing deeply.

Meagan is a beautiful girl, I thought, but corrected myself. At twenty-eight, she was a woman—still, she'd always be my baby. Dawn's soft, gray light crept across her face, revealing her flawless skin. She certainly did not inherit her tan from me. John contributed his genes for her golden skin and honey blond hair, though I claimed her hair's wave and thickness as my gifts—or curse, depending upon the day.

John gave me two beautiful children. I could not harbor complete resentment against him, but my mind still reeled from the quick chain of events: his proclamation of independence, the divorce, the sale of the house, his pending marriage. All in the last nine months. Well, if one can create a baby in nine months, why not a whole new life for myself? I was trying.

To forestall any further thoughts of my ex-husband, I roused myself from my drowsiness and prepared to greet another perfect day in God's country. My clothes had been stashed in the bottom of my sleeping bag to warm them with my body heat during the night. I ventured into the damp air only after I donned nylon hiking pants, woolen socks, a shirt, and a fleece jacket.

Meagan continued to sleep, so I rolled off my sleeping pad and tiptoed out the screen door with my shoes and fanny pack in hand. I brought my cooking supplies down to the beach in hopes of catching the sunrise while my tea brewed. When it was ready, I cozied the hot mug in my gloved hands against my chest. I stood on the long pier, waiting for the purple dawn to surrender to the rising sun.

Far out over Lake Superior an arc of orange peeked over the horizon. A golden spear drove through the thin fog and into Siskiwit Bay, seeming to point directly at me. I shielded my eyes as additional rays lanced through the fog in all directions—the original compass rose glittering in a sea of spangles. Behind me the moon slipped toward the treeline, dragging the gray night down with it. Perfectly balanced, the day began.

Meagan loved glorious sunrises, but she craved her sleep even more. I cradled my lukewarm tea and fretted about her lost pregnancies and the effect they'd had on her relationship with her husband. If she was worried, so was I. My own surprise divorce taught me not to take marriage for granted.

In full daylight I could see our wooden shelter three hundred feet back from the beach, up the hill, tucked in amongst the balsam fir and paper birch. As much as I love tent camping, I coveted the luxury of a clean, spacious shelter. Staying dry is the biggest benefit. Summer storms, like yesterday's, march in from Lake Superior without warning, engulfing Isle Royale in deluges and pounding the sandy shores with massive waves.

I saw no movement inside the shelter, so I left my cooking supplies on the picnic table on the beach. My destination was the far shore of the inlet where I hoped to spot moose grazing along the edge of the water—from a safe distance, of course. For my birthday in April, Sarah sent me a pair of digital binoculars designed for long-distance photography. They hung from my neck, and I intended to stalk whatever wildlife I could find.

Overnight, a seiche had rolled ashore. The retreating water and yesterday's storm had smoothed the sand and cleared the shoreline of footsteps. Driftwood littered the beach. Anticipating a campfire that evening, I collected a pile of firewood to pick up on my return to our campsite.

On the west side of the inlet a line of tracks, unmistakably moose, led from the thick foliage at the treeline, across thirty feet of beach and into the water. I stopped immediately to listen and look. Though seeing a bull moose with a full set of antlers would thrill me, yesterday's scare was fresh in my mind. To my relief, the cloven prints pointed toward the bay. Either he swam out to deeper water or clomped through the shallows to the opposite shore. I fumbled with the binoculars, brought them to my eyes, and scanned the inlet and the far side repeatedly. Nothing.

Disappointed, I sat on a log. Thoreau or someone once wrote that if you sit in silence long enough, nature will come to you. So I waited. I enjoyed the gulls wheeling over the water and the sun burning off the last of the fog, but the elusive moose did not make an appearance. I brushed off the seat of my pants and continued along the shore.

Scattered driftwood, solid and dry, drew me along the beach. Former campers had not ventured this far to collect firewood. I felt compelled to take advantage of the bounty and gathered a pile too big to carry, but the work satisfied me. I wandered the sand, picking up sticks and throwing them back to the pile. A white object, at odds with the beige sand and gray water, caught my eye. Always eager to explore nature's cycle of life and death, I approached it, expecting to see the white belly of a fish or a gull felled from the sky.

My heart sank as I recognized the form of a little dog. I rushed to his side, kneeling in the shallow water. The lapping waves rocked him and moved his legs as if he'd jump up and run from me in an instant. But his neck hung limp at an odd angle and his eyes

77

were open, unseeing. Long white hair floated about him like a halo. Poor little guy. My throat tightened up and tears blinded me. How did such a pretty lap dog get to the wild shore of Isle Royale?

I lifted the dog out of the water. His small chest in my hand still held warmth. My pulse quickened—or did his heart beat against my thumb? I laid him on the shore, put my fingers in his armpit and held my breath. Yes. Another beat. Was it possible to give CPR to a dog? If I didn't do something quick, he'd die. Grasping him by his back feet, I held him upside down. Water ran from his mouth. I swung him gently. More water. Now what? I positioned him on my arm as if treating an infant and massaged his back. With a gurgle of water, a wheeze escaped his lungs. I laid him on the sand and held my ear to his muzzle. A tiny breath!

"Come on, buddy. Breathe."

A light came into his eyes. He whimpered.

"Yes!"

I wrapped the little dog in my jacket and held him to my chest. He needed warmth. He didn't struggle against me, but his legs twitched and his chest spasmed with a cough. He spit up more water and gave an exhausted sigh.

Every time I jostled him, he jerked as if in pain. His ribs are bruised, I thought, so I rocked gently and sang a lullaby as I had for my babies. "Too-ra Loo-ra Loo-ral…" We sat on that lonely beach for some time, me staring out over Lake Superior, and him fighting to live.

What stupid person brought him to an island famous for its wolves? To find out, I searched beneath his silky hair for his tags. I unbuckled his collar to ease the dog's breathing. An engraved silver heart identified him as 'Remington' and gave a phone number with a Michigan area code. The glittering rhinestone collar meant that someone missed him dearly.

Remington looked like a show dog: a fancy breed, clipped nails and well-groomed hair, though now the silky strands were tangled with debris. He hadn't been on the beach for long. I stroked the wet hair back from his face.

"You shouldn't have run away, Remington. There are wolves out here." The thought made me scan the area for territorial wolves that may have gotten the scent of another canine on their island. My spine stiffened. Taylor had said that a wolf pack will kill a lone wolf from another pack. Remington didn't have a chance in the woods. I held the dog closer and got to my feet.

Only then did I notice tiny paw prints in the sand at the edge of the water. The prints led out of the lake for about a yard, staggered along the shore, and ended where Remington had collapsed in the water. Did he swim ashore? I walked along the water's edge for one hundred feet in both directions, searching for additional footprints. No human prints, no little paw prints. I was certain the pup had come out of the lake.

Remington slept in my arms, breathing rhythmically with the occasional ragged cough. Careful not to jostle his painful ribs, I hurried along the beach, retracing my steps, surprised at the distance I had covered earlier. The heavy sand dragged at my feet and the little dog's weight increased with each step. Intent on listening for water in his lungs, my progress became slow and irregular, but in the general direction of the Siskiwit pier.

Suddenly, a familiar odor assaulted me. I lifted my nose to the breeze and flared my nostrils. Wolf! My eyes darted to the treeline forty feet from the water's edge. The bushes rustled, reeds parted. Maybe the wind played tricks on me.

I started to run.

With the awkward bundle in my arms and the wet sand dragging at my feet, the Siskiwit pier seemed miles away. Outrunning a wolf pack was a foolish hope, but I prayed for that miracle and barged ahead.

From a distance Meagan spotted me and waved. As if nothing was wrong, she carried a mug and walked toward the beach, picking her way along the rocky path lined with hawkweed and yarrow. She stopped. Realizing I wasn't jogging for my health, she ran to meet me on the sand.

"What's going on, Mom? What do you have there?"

My lungs bursting, I could only motion for her to come closer. I laid my twelve-pound burden on the sand next to one of the large logs around the campfire. "We need to build a fire," I gasped.

Meagan knelt at my side. "A dog! What happened? Is he hurt?"

"Wolves might be after us."

We both scanned the arc of the beach. No menacing wolf pack stalked us, not even one.

Meagan frowned. "They might come after a dog, but Taylor said they wouldn't attack humans." She gently stroked the dog under his chin, cooing and clucking. "What's he doing here?"

"I found him collapsed on the beach on the other side of the inlet. His name is Remington."

"Can I hold him?" She reached for the little dog without waiting for my answer.

"Careful, his ribs seem tender. Keep him warm while I build the fire." I helped her tuck the dog into her jacket, and a little pink tongue licked my finger. With a sigh the pooch closed his eyes again and settled beneath Meagan's breast.

With a last scan of the beach for phantom wolves, I stirred up the coals from last night's fire and added tinder. Embers began to glow. Soon flames flared upward and warmed us. Meagan knelt with Remington in the radiant heat.

"He's so adorable." Meagan cocked her head to the side and her ponytail fell over her shoulder. "You surprise me, Mom. You've never been a dog lover."

"I'm not. They're too much trouble."

Meagan shook her head. "Nice try, Mom. I remember you and Smokey."

Fifteen years ago, our Sheltie had walked into the woods to die alone. I promised myself back then that I'd never go through the heartache again. I sighed. "If I do ever get a dog, a cute one like Remington wouldn't be bad."

Meagan gave me a knowing smile. "How do you suppose he got here?"

"My guess is he fell overboard from some boat. The incoming seiche must have brought him into the bay, and he swam for shore. That's a long swim for those little legs."

Meagan opened her jacket to study Remington. "He looks like someone's prized pet. Havanese, I think."

"Take a look at his collar." I pulled the heavy bauble from my pocket.

"Wow. Silver tags." She let the sun shine on the collar. "I think these are diamonds."

"You're kidding." I couldn't tell rhinestones from cubic zirconia. "That pup leads a pampered life. When we get back to Windigo, we'll call that number and give his owners the good news."

* * *

For the remainder of the morning, Meagan and I took turns nursing our patient. The exhausted Havanese coughed up the last of the lake water and breathed more deeply. Once the scouts were up and about, we secreted the dog in our shelter. The boys' excitement would be too much for him. Remington stopped shivering, so we cocooned him in my sleeping bag and let him sleep. He awoke later with brighter eyes, but when I offered him food, he let his chin fall on his paws and fell asleep again.

"Once Remington is stronger, maybe tomorrow, we'll carry him to Windigo." I watched the little guy snooze peacefully and reminded myself not to get attached.

"Maybe I should stay here with him, while you go," Meagan suggested. "The park service issued a pet ban because visiting dogs might infect the wolf population with parvovirus."

I looked at my daughter in wonder. "Do you remember everything you read?"

"I try." She laughed. "If you want to get to Windigo to check on Sarah and call the Michigan number, I can stay here until the owners come to get him. I wouldn't want the park service to take custody."

"Surely, they'd try to find the owners or put him on a boat for the mainland."

"I don't know." Meagan shook her head and scratched behind the pooch's ear. He gazed up at her with total trust. "But right now, I plan to go for a run. On the way back I'll gather raspberries and beach peas to add to our lunch." She gave the dog a gentle pat and strolled down the hill.

Remington crawled into a spot of sunlight, settled in on the warm wooden planks and slept soundly. His fur dried, making him a white puff ball. His quality breeding and long pedigree were evident beneath his tangled hair. I took his picture to show the rangers, cautioned myself against a growing fondness. Even so, I enjoyed having the little guy near me as I recorded the day's events in my journal.

Before long my backside ached. I eased away from the dozing dog, stretched, and searched for a chore to keep myself busy. Our sleeping bags were damp from the morning dew, so I stepped out of the shelter to suspend a line between two trees to air the bags.

I reached for an aspen branch above my head, attempting to attach the rope with a clove-hitch knot. The bushes rustled behind me, and I had the feeling of being watched. Expecting a confrontation with a wolf, I whirled around, ready to defend Remington and myself with my bare hands.

"Sorry I startled you."

The polished male voice did nothing to stop the adrenaline charging through my bloodstream, but I came out of attack mode. At the edge of the campsite was an expensive shirt filled with broad shoulders and tucked into belted khaki slacks. Longish blond hair tickled the collar. The man was rugged, suave, and the type of guy my mother should have warned me about. The twenty-first-century Viking stared at me, stealing my ability to speak.

"A beautiful woman in the wilderness. What a pleasant surprise." The silky words came through even white teeth, which contrasted with his sun-burnished skin. He was as smooth as a soap opera villain.

Trying to gain control, I retrieved the rope from the ground, straightened up, and surveyed the handsome Norseman. He was too glib, too practiced. The guy had *salesman* written all over him, but—dang!—I wanted whatever he was selling.

I steeled myself against his wide smile and cornflower eyes, but he stared so blatantly, as if I were—a goddess. He advanced toward me. My fingers instinctively formed an X, a talisman to ward off his effect, to keep his sexiness at bay. I held the hex sign up between us.

He laughed, but stopped.

My body said, 'Panic! Run!' I forced myself to be civil to the man who had snuck up on me like a thief. I dropped my hands and laughed too, to cover the hex sign silliness—and my apprehension. "After so many years in business, I can spot a salesman a mile away, but I'm sorry to be so rude." I glanced around looking for a rock or stout stick just in case.

"Relax. I'm not selling anything." He held out his empty palms and stretched his lips in a smile. "Brad Olson. I'm captain of that yacht and just wanted to see if these shelters were occupied." He nodded toward a white boat, very similar to Valerie's, tied at the dock. "Another storm is forecast for tonight."

In profile he was the iconic ship's captain, wind in his face, hair ruffling. I could smell salt water. Whether the scent came from him, the approaching storm, or my imagination, I didn't know. "The shelters are full. I'm sorry." I still marveled at the power of my hex sign. The control felt good; control over the choice of who could sweet-talk me, who could beguile me.

He gazed into my eyes, regarding me with his head slightly tilted, waiting. He clearly knew the effect he had on women, expected my arousal.

That ticked me off. The man exuded sexiness but wore it like a Halloween costume. I stared back and did not flinch. "I have this shelter, and a scout troop has the other, though they're out on a hike."

"There are only two?"

He moved forward, pickpocket close, making me aware of his muscles and smoky, masculine scent. My hex sign failed. A quick image of a warlord in a romance novel swept into my mind. Fear tainted the attraction. I stepped back with my fist pressed to his chest to pin him in place. I surveyed my surroundings for an escape and spotted Meagan down the beach at the water's edge.

"My daughter and I will be here for two nights."

His gaze shifted from me to my lovely daughter bent over the beach plants, collecting peas. The sheep's clothing slipped off the wolf as he assessed my Meagan. "If that's your daughter, what does that do to you?"

I wished to hide her from his leer; wished that her golden hair didn't curl over her shoulder, that the sun didn't cast a warm glow on her runner's legs. "It makes me old enough to know better. You need to go now." I inched toward the shelter door. "There's room for you at the campground."

"I'm not staying at a filthy campground." All signs of his sexy veneer disappeared, replaced by a menacing sneer. "Boaters have precedence at these shelters. You'll have to vacate." He shifted his weight from one Italian leather shoe to the other and folded his thick arms across his chest.

I clenched my teeth to hide my fear in the face of his hostility.

A low growl came from within our shelter.

"I'll be damned. You have a dog—an illegal dog." Brad sniggered. "The park service will confiscate your mutt and impose a hefty fine." He stared through the screen trying to see Remington.

I took advantage of his distraction and dashed into the shelter. A blur of white fur flew past my ankles before I could slam the door. The dog barked and snarled. He attacked Brad's pant leg, jumping away from the man's kicks. Afraid for the dog's life, I rushed out, scooped him up and retreated into the shelter while Brad collected himself.

"I'll wring that mutt's neck," he bellowed. He mounted the steps and jerked open the door.

Remington squirmed from my arms and bared his teeth with more confidence than a pit bull. Brad lunged for him, but the scrappy dog ducked beneath his grab and scampered down the steps. Brad slammed the screen door in triumph.

"Get out!" I shouted. Scared and angry, I shook my clenched fist at him.

Brad's raucous laugh clattered off the bare wooden walls. "You gonna hit me with those bony little knuckles?"

Feeling foolish, I let my paltry weapons fall to my sides.

He stepped forward. His eyes, slits of blue, appraised me. "That's better." His handsome face contorted into a smile, close and intimate. "You want to be nice to me." That low, breathy voice had surely lured women into danger before.

"Go back to your boat!" There was no power behind my demand. I inched away. "I want nothing to do with you."

"If you treat me right, I can keep your buddy back at Windigo out of prison."

Startled out of my weakness, I lifted my chin and straightened my backbone. "What are you talking about?" The little dog throwing himself against the screen gave me courage.

"I spotted you two together," he sneered. "She attacked that woman and you covered it up."

"Liar. She's completely innocent." My stare, determined and steady, locked onto his cold blue eyes.

"No," he said. The emphatic word hung in the air, fouled by the stink of stale cigarettes. "They searched her dorm—and found Deborah's money bag." Smug and imperious, he looked down from his full height.

Doubt held my tongue.

His argument made and won, he fingered a button on my shirt. "You should be friendly to me."

My fist flew from behind my back, and the heel of my hand caught him in the jaw. My screaming fury stunned him. He stumbled against the screen door and down the step. Remington attacked, tearing at Brad's Italian loafer. The man hopped to his other foot and kicked at the dog, but the fluffy ball of agility skipped aside. The boatman's leg swung at empty space. His expensive shoes slipped in the slick mud, and he went down in a rut of rainwater.

Mud streaked his khaki trousers. Favoring his left elbow, he struggled up from the puddle and lurched toward me. Shrieking in panic, I slammed the flimsy door and fumbled with the hook lock, praying to put even the slimmest of barriers between me and the enraged womanizer. Remington attacked his bare ankle while Brad cursed and howled.

To my dismay, Meagan appeared at the side of the shelter, panting heavily. My lovely daughter towered over Brad in his crouched position. She leveled her jackknife at his nose and hissed, "Back off, buddy." She prodded the belligerent man toward the edge of the campsite.

I flung open the door and jumped to Meagan's side, doubling our power over Brad. His angry glare shifted to Meagan's fierce face, to her four-inch blade, to the snarling dog and back, considering his options.

"This isn't over!" Brad thundered and threw a scowl at us like a weapon. He kicked at Remington, missed widely, and stomped toward the beach path.

Meagan brandished her knife. "You're a pathetic bully!" she yelled after him.

Remington's lionhearted bark followed the man's retreating figure until a coughing fit shook the little dog's body. He fell on his side in the wet weeds, wheezing. Meagan scooped up the exhausted dog and crooned. "You scared him good. Such a brave puppy." She nuzzled her face in his silky fur.

The sound of breaking branches and thundering feet came from our right. Fearing another stampeding moose, I grabbed Meagan's arm and yanked her toward the shelter wall. The thick foliage shook and rattled.

The burly scout leader crashed into our clearing. "You ladies okay?" Sweat poured from Mr. Domkowski's flushed face. "What's all the screaming about?"

I was so startled that I merely put my hands up in a signal to stop.

Eight boys thrashed through the bushes from various directions and mobbed around their leader. Some had sticks in their hands. All were ready for battle. Skinny little Wyatt, red in the face, started down the hill toward the yacht.

"No, stop," I cried. "We're fine."

"Wyatt, come back!" Mr. Domkowski demanded.

"There he goes! We can get him!" Wyatt insisted. The other boys echoed him, twitching and flexing, ready for the hunt. Testosterone levels ran high.

"Please, boys, no more fighting," I pleaded. "He's just a bully who backed down when my daughter threatened him with her knife."

To distract them, Meagan held up her weapon with a flourish. The boys stared at the jackknife as if it were a saber, until their gazes fell upon the fluffy little animal in her arms.

"Where'd he come from?" Wyatt asked, his exuberance getting the better of his manners.

"Can I hold him?"

"What's his name?"

They gathered around. Eight pairs of hands reached to pet the dog. He backed into the crook of Meagan's arm.

"Remington found us. He's a hero," Meagan crooned and stroked his head. "He attacked that bad guy and ran him out of camp." She snuggled the dog close, safe from his adoring fans. "You scouts are heroes, too. Thanks for coming to our rescue."

"Yes, thank you, boys," I added. "You were so brave."

A few of the young men blushed, and all of them puffed up their chests.

"Poor Remington's exhausted. Let me get him inside." Meagan extricated herself from the group and mounted the steps to the shelter. "That man won't come back knowing you're here. We'll sleep better tonight."

"Yeah, if he comes back, we'll get him," Wyatt declared.

Many of the boys repeated his assertion. The teenagers set about devising perimeter protection in case Brad did sneak back in the night. They had plans for snares in the trees, silverware on string, and tin cups with pebbles. Their youthful energy and enthusiasm was infectious.

While they invented our protection and Meagan tucked Remington into his bed, I filled the two adult leaders in on the details of yachtsman's visit. They frowned in the direction of the lake just as the white yacht pulled from its mooring, throwing a wake against the iron pier. A woman stood alone in the stern of the boat, her hand raised to shade her eyes. She stared through the distance.

"I guess you won't need us for protection after all," Mr. Domkowski said. The shoulders of that goodhearted man finally relaxed. "But we'll be here if you do."

Meagan joined me to thank the scouts again and watched the leaders march down the hill, shepherding their energetic charges toward their shelter, collecting firewood along the way. She slid her arm around my waist.

"You know, Mom, that man looked familiar."

Her protective hug brought tears to my eyes. "Which one?"

"The one who almost got my knife stuck up his nose." My peace-loving daughter sounded like she wished she had opened up his nasal passages.

"Brad?"

"Whatever his name was, I think he's the one who freaked me out on the visitor center's deck. This time he was better dressed, no sunglasses, and his hair hung loose." She blew air from her cheeks in disgust. "But he's the same size, body shape. Walks the same. I'm pretty sure."

"Meagan, you could be right." A moment of "Duh!" hit me. "He said Sarah was going to prison. How could he know anything about the incident with Deborah?"

"When was that?"

"Right before I clocked him for trying to cozy up to me—and before you and Remington jumped to my rescue." I cradled my bruised hand.

My daughter winced. "Eww. That smarmy guy came on to you?"

I nodded and didn't admit to my initial involuntary attraction. "Brad wore leather shoes rather than hiking boots, just like the burly guy back at Windigo."

"So you're saying a guy from that fancy yacht stole Deborah's money?" Meagan looked askance at me.

"I don't know. We know he's a bully. What I can't figure out is, why would Deborah accuse Sarah instead of him?" I shrugged. "Maybe he has something over our pal Deb. I think we had our man and let him go."

"If I hadn't been here, he would have hurt you." Meagan's outrage heightened her color. "I won't forget him next time."

My daughter continued to surprise me. "Thank you for being here." I smiled at her and glanced at the flimsy lock on the screen door. Nerve endings prickled at the nape of my neck. Even with perimeter protection and Remington on guard, I'd sleep with my ears on alert.

9

Day Five - Lost and Found

Hiking solo was a new experience. I was wary on the eleven-mile shortcut to Windigo, expecting Brad, or wolves of another sort, to jump out of the bushes; or an angry moose to charge through the wet grasses and reeds that tangled with my boot laces. After last night's thunderstorm, the sun hid for much of the morning. A gothic, grey mist clung to the earth and did nothing to quell my apprehensions.

Meagan and I agreed that I would hike out early to Windigo to report Brad's aggressive behavior and the presence of the dog on the island. Meagan promised to keep an eye out for the yacht and stay under the watchful eye of the scout leaders until I returned in the evening.

After two hours and several miles of hiking in shadow, solar power brightened the day and calmed my nerves. Solitude settled upon me like a silken shawl, an extraordinary luxury. Birds sang, rodents rustled, a fly buzzed in a spiderweb. These small things might have escaped my notice if I weren't alone—if I had worried about falling behind my partners or tried to hold a conversation. The scenery tempted me to blend in, to sit quietly and view the wildlife in its natural state, but I was on a mission.

Footsore and thirsty, I plodded into Windigo not long after Voyageur II disgorged another band of newcomers. Some loitered on the dock, but most obeyed the rules and sat in the pavilion, listening to the orientation program. I slipped into a seat in the shade at the back of the crowd and listened to Sarah and Ranger Weckmen tag-teaming each other, giving information and answering questions about what the visitors could expect on the island. Sarah's already ebullient manner brightened when she caught sight of me.

After the program, she threaded her way through the visitors. "Hey, you're back early."

I stood to receive her bear hug.

"Where's Meagan? Is she doing okay now? You've got no backpack. What's going on?"

I waited for her to take a breath. "Done?"

She rolled her eyes and nodded.

"I left my backpack at Siskiwit with Meagan, so I could travel fast to get here and back there tonight. We—"

"Why? What's wrong?"

"Nothing big. Some jerk harassed us yesterday, but he sailed off."

Sarah bristled. "What did he look like? Can you identify him?"

"I know his name."

While trudging up the hill to the visitor center's deck where we had a clear view of the harbor, I filled Sarah in on the skirmish with Brad. I scanned the several boats bobbing at the dock, but none were as big as Brad's sleek, white yacht.

Anger creased Sarah's forehead until I got to the part where my daughter came to my rescue. "So, Meagan's a warrior—just like her mama was in the Grand Canyon. Atta girl!" She beamed with pride, but grew serious again. "Let me get this straight," Sarah said. "You think this Brad is the same guy who bopped Deborah, and we're no longer looking for the cabin cruiser that raced out of here."

"That's my theory."

Sarah propped her elbows on the railing, thinking. "I know I didn't see the cruiser with a blue stripe, but I don't recall if a big yacht's been here in the last two days."

My growling stomach interrupted her thoughts.

"You haven't eaten lunch?" Sarah frowned at the shake of my head and pulled a granola bar from her pocket. "Here, eat. Emergency food. I don't want you to bite my head off in a hunger-induced bad temper."

I protested my innocence, but took the bar. While I munched, I watched Sarah from the corner of my eye to assess her stress level. Her ragged fingernails looked inflamed. "You've been biting your nails."

"I'm a nervous wreck." She hid her hands in her pockets. "I've been snooping around Deborah's office, trying to get into that computer file. Zak would kill me if he knew."

"Zak?"

"Ranger Weckmen."

"Ah," I said. "Find anything?"

"No, but I know old Deb's guilty of something. She's too obsessive. I placed her stuff exactly as she had it, but I'm sure she'll notice a thing an inch out of place and have a fit." Sarah tore at the cuticle of her index finger.

"Okay, stop the snooping," I said. "She wouldn't leave incriminating evidence laying around in any case."

"Thanks. You go for this mystery stuff, I don't. Besides, I'd rather stay out of trouble. I enjoy giving the orientations to the new arrivals and don't want to lose this job."

It was as important to me to save Sarah's volunteer position as it was to catch Deborah in her game, whatever that was. "By the way, I got your message the day before yesterday."

Sarah leaned forward, earnest and eager. "And you came all this way to thank me for sending such a cute messenger to deliver my note." She raised her eyebrows in an exaggerated expression and wanted details of my reaction to the attractive Taylor.

I clucked my tongue. Her meddling irked me. "Sarah, I don't need you fixing me up with every man we meet. Besides, Taylor's barely out of college." My irritability grew. My relationship with Glen was enough for me. How could Sarah insinuate that I'd rob the cradle?

Sarah grinned. "Take it easy. Don't explode on me. I'm teasing." She motioned for me to eat more of the granola bar. "Taylor's a great guy and happily married. He happened to be going through Siskiwit, so I asked him to check on you."

My indignation petered out. I felt idiotic and needed real food. "Well, Taylor was worried about you. He thought you were depressed and got me worried, too."

Sarah sobered. "I'm fine. The federal investigator arrives in two days on other business, but according to Zak, Deborah doesn't want an investigation any more than I do. She's not cooperating with him."

"What about the bag they found?"

"Somebody found a bag?" Sarah's confusion could not have been faked.

"The money bag Deborah accused you of stealing." Saying the words gave me pain, but I forced myself to continue. "That captain guy, Brad, said they searched your dorm and found the canvas bag."

"That's news to me." Sarah deflated like a party balloon snagged by a tree. She leaned against the railing, her chin upon her chest. "I'm doing everything I can to be accepted here."

"Don't worry about Brad. The man's a gifted liar." I linked my arm through hers.

"Looks like you have Ranger Zak on your side now."

"Yeah, Zachary and I get along..." She stood up straight. Optimism and spunk returned color to her cheeks. "Who searched my dorm? Deborah? Zak would have told me."

I shrugged my shoulders. "Brad didn't say...just *they*."

"Let's find Zak." She jerked her head toward the visitors' center. "I'm tired of pussyfooting around. I'm going to get some answers."

Her forcefulness brought me to my feet, and she ushered me toward the visitors' entrance. I hesitated with my hand on the door handle and glanced inside.

"Don't worry. I won't hurt her." Sarah sniffed. "Deborah's out somewhere monitoring volunteer groups doing trail maintenance. She's hiding from me."

"Or maybe from the federal investigator."

"You may have a point." She yanked open the door.

Zak wasn't in his office either, so Sarah stewed in her adrenaline, pacing around the table in the volunteers' break room. I finally coaxed her into a chair by pleading starvation and persuading her to share her bag lunch. Clean hands, a cool drink, and a peanut butter sandwich revived me.

"Here's another reason I came to Windigo." I fished through my fanny pack for my camera and scrolled through the pictures until I found one of Remington.

Sarah patted her pockets and came up with her reading glasses. "That's a dog."

"Yeah. Meagan guesses he's a Havanese. I found him floating in the bay yesterday morning."

"Wow." Sarah studied the picture and forwarded to the other views. "Sounds impossible that he survived." She nodded her approval of my good deed. "But what's he doing here? Dogs aren't allowed on the island. Protects the wolves from some virus canines carry."

"Meagan warned me about the virus. That's why I came here alone. I plan to call the phone number on his tags, but what do I do with him in the meantime?"

"Mmm. With the park manager still off-island, that will be Zak's call, too." Sarah chuckled. "He'll be glad to see us."

"Yeah, I'll bet."

Sarah led me from the break room and toward Zak's office where the lights were now on. At that moment, the entrance door banged open. A woman dressed in a white outfit, glimmering with jewelry, stormed into the display area. Valerie. She ran to the counter.

"I want to report a missing dog." Red in the face, she waved her arms. Her bangles clinked like wind chimes.

The startled volunteer on duty chewed on a pen. "A dog? Dog's aren't allowed…"

"I know, I know," Valerie screeched, brushing aside legalities. "But he ran off the night before last, and I can't find him!"

Sarah and I approached the woman to rescue the stammering clerk.

"Valerie?"

Her eyes registered only the slightest hint of recognition. Sidestepping me as if I was inconsequential, she poked her finger at Sarah's uniformed chest. "You need to send out all these rangers to look for my dog!" She then remembered her manners. "Please."

I felt sorry enough for the frantic woman to forgive her high-minded arrogance. "Valerie, look at this picture." I pushed myself in front of her. "Is this your dog?"

She grabbed my camera and stared, struggling to focus. Sarah handed her bifocals to Valerie.

"Yes, yes. That's my Remington." Suddenly, she liked me. "Where is Remmy? Give him to me."

With a nod to the relieved volunteer clerk who hung on every word, Sarah escorted Valerie into Deborah's office and sat her down.

"Where's my dog?" Valerie scanned every corner of the room.

I pulled up a chair in front of the woman and tried to catch her attention. "Valerie, were you on your yacht at Siskiwit yesterday?"

"Siskiwit? Yes, why? We were looking for Remington. Patrick and I couldn't stay there and got a room at Rock Harbor during the storm." She fidgeted on the edge of her seat. "Where's my dog?"

"Do you know a man named Brad Olson?"

Valerie screwed up her face. "No. What's this got to do with Remington?" She stood up, angry.

Sarah laid a gentle hand on the agitated woman's shoulder. "Remington's safe. Please answer Amy's questions."

Valerie gave a quick nod and plopped herself on the chair in a huff.

I kept my voice patient and neutral. "A man by that name said he was the captain of a boat just like yours."

Valerie rolled her eyes and shook her head in disgust. "Erik Jansson pilots our yacht. Now tell me where my dog is, or I'll charge you with kidnapping."

I blew air from my cheeks and sat back in my seat, too exasperated to argue with the woman.

Sarah stood, hands on her hips, and loomed over Valerie. "You should be thanking Amy. Your dog would have drowned without her. She gave him CPR, for cripes sake!"

Valerie gasped, lost color from her face, and pleaded with her eyes for more information.

I ignored Valerie's rudeness and continued the story. "I found Remington floating in the water. Apparently, two nights ago he swam to shore from out in the lake somewhere. My daughter is caring for him at the shelter in Siskiwit."

Valerie stood up so fast her chair fell over. "I'll kill that man! He's always hated Remington."

She rushed through the door before we could stop her—not that we would have gotten any more information out of her in the state she was in. From the windows I watched her dash down the stairs and run toward the dock.

"That went well." Sarah flopped in Deborah's chair and swiveled around towards the desk. "Now what?"

"My guess is Valerie and Patrick will sail for Siskiwit to retrieve Remington. I wish I could let Meagan know they're coming."

"Patrick?"

"I didn't tell you the best part."

Sarah listened with interest to the details of Patrick's search for Valerie at Feldtmann Lake. "She doesn't show gratitude well."

"I wonder if she'll blame Patrick for Remington almost drowning." I shrugged and began to feel the effects of my eleven-mile hike. "Right now, I don't care. I have no clue what her husband sees in her."

"Money?"

"I doubt it, but who knows?" I scowled out the window and watched Valerie's big yacht maneuver through Washington Harbor, headed for open water.

10

Inside Job

Ranger Zachary Weckman poked his head in the door of Deborah's office. "What's all the commotion in here?" He smiled at Sarah as if they were old friends.

"Hey, Zak." Sarah swiveled the chair to face him. "You remember Amy Warren."

I regretted berating this pleasant young man at our last meeting and apologized again.

"Don't worry about it," Zak said. "You reminded me of my mother giving me heck for breaking curfew."

The young can be so heartless. "Thanks. I'm sure your mother is a lovely woman."

"He's kidding," Sarah said. "Maybe he owed us a barb or two for giving him a hard time the other night."

Zak grinned like a bad boy caught with his finger full of frosting. "Forget about it. I figured out that I believe Sarah's version of events much more than Deborah's. My job is to keep peace around here and keep an eye out for who really attacked our beloved Volunteer Coordinator. I'll be glad to turn the whole mess over to the investigator—who doesn't much care about the case." Zak looked around quickly. "I'd better keep my mouth shut."

Sarah jumped out of the chair. "Which reminds me—we came here to find out who searched my dorm." She looked pointedly at Zak.

"Not me. We don't have that authorization yet." Zak shook his head and raised his hands in mock surrender. "Unless you give me permission." He arched his eyebrows to make it a question.

"I don't care." Sarah's voice rose in frustration. "It's just very fishy that some guy Amy met at Siskiwit told her my dorm had been searched and that Deborah's canvas bag was found there."

The young ranger frowned. "That's bogus."

"Maybe Deborah searched without authorization," I suggested. "But why would she tell Brad and not you, Zak?"

Neither Zak nor Sarah had the answer.

"This is crazy." She headed for the door. "I'm going to tear apart the dorm myself."

"Let me know if you find the bag," Zak called after her.

I followed Sarah from the office, past the volunteer desk and the eavesdropper whose chair was still spinning after her quick return to it. I leaned over her desk to read her name tag. "If you want to know what's going on, *Joan,* just ask." I whispered so that visitors on vacation were not drawn into our little drama. The red-faced volunteer chewed on her pen and shrugged.

Zak returned to his office while Sarah and I marched out of the display area, across the deck, and down the stairs. We were halfway up the hill when we heard Zak's call.

"Wait up!"

He stood at the deck railing, waving a paper. He bounded down the steps and caught up to us. "Deborah left this in my inbox. Read."

Sarah read aloud,

> *A reliable source informed me that Sara Rochon was spotted stuffing the missing canvas bag in the backpack stowed under her cot. Check it out.*
> —*Deborah Mitchell*

"Who does she think she is? Telling me to do her dirty work." Zak sniffed. "She's a civilian employee, and certainly not my superior."

"She spelled my name wrong." Sarah reached for the note. "I'd like to know who this *reliable source* is." She turned the paper upside down and over, looking for a hint. I could see her mind running down the list of volunteers with whom she shared the dorm.

"How did you get this note, Zak?" I took the paper from Sarah's hands and scrutinized it. "I thought Deborah's been on the trail for two or three days. You said so in the note Taylor delivered to me."

"Yeah, that's right," Sarah confirmed. "How'd she leave the note?"

"Don't know. Maybe it was in my piles of stuff all along, and I missed it." Zak shifted within his baggy uniform shirt. "Anything's possible, but I should've spotted this over the last few days."

* * *

Thanks to the note, we knew exactly where to look for the canvas bag. Sarah dragged her backpack from beneath her cot and dumped the contents on the floor. Tent, rain gear, stove, fuel canisters. She unzipped the side pocket. Tissues, a lighter, headlamp.

"No bag in here." Sarah plopped herself on the floor and leaned against a roommate's bunk. "Now what?"

"All these cots look alike." I pointed to the six cots around the room. "What if..."

Sarah rolled onto her hands and knees and scanned beneath the cots. "That one has a pack underneath." She crawled to the cot and reached for the pack.

"Wait," Zak said. "You can't search someone else's stuff."

"Joan won't mind." Beneath Zak's frown, Sarah stopped and rolled her eyes. "Okay, we'll ask her. Amy would you mind running down to the visitors' center… Never mind. Joannie, I see you."

"What?" The woman with the pen in her mouth strolled into the dorm. "I was just coming to get a jacket."

Her high-pitched voice grated on my nerves. Joan was the type who took gossip as gospel and fell in love with soap opera stars. She should have been attractive, but her asymmetrical features made me uneasy. I tried to be charitable, but the stealthy way she moved brought out the worst in me.

With a sweep of his arm, Zak welcomed the dull-eyed woman into the dorm. "Joan, we lost something. Would you mind looking through your gear?" He motioned to her pack.

She cooperated, though robotically, and was the only one surprised to find a red canvas bag among her possessions. Her befuddlement was proof enough for me that she hadn't known the bag was in her pack. She didn't seem intelligent enough to be a good actor.

"That's not mine," Joan whined. "I don't know how that got there."

"We know, Joannie." Zak examined the empty bag, turning it over and over and working the zipper. "Nothing to find here."

"We weren't expecting the money to still be inside," I said.

"I didn't steal it!" Joan said in a panic.

Zak dismissed her with a flick of his hand. "Why do you assume there was money?" he asked and tossed the bag on the cot.

"Deborah accused Sarah of stealing her money, not just the bag," I said, "but if she had time to leave the note, why wouldn't she dash in here to grab the money herself?"

"Because she knew it was empty," Sarah said. "The bag's only purpose now is to frame me." Sarah sat dejected on the floor, her elbows on her knees and her chin on her forearms.

Joan listened to our discussion but feigned disinterest. She stalled, collecting her belongings in slow motion and returning them to her pack one by one.

"Joan, you seem to have a good sense of what goes on around here," I said, trying to win her over with a compliment. "Have you ever seen this bag before?"

"Sure, it's Deborah's. She keeps it in a locked file drawer."

"Have you ever seen it anywhere else?"

"Well, she carries that bag with her whenever she goes to the mainland," Joan said. "It usually has a little lock on the zipper."

"Any idea why she has money stashed away? Does she hold it for someone else?"

"How should I know?" Joan hid a blush by turning to push her pack beneath the cot. "I gotta get back to the center. No one is staffing the visitors' desk." She rushed from the room, forgetting her jacket.

Sarah watched Joan's departing figure. "Reminds me of a pet ferret I used to have, always slinking around."

"Sarah!" I scolded and held out my hand to help her up from the floor.

She brushed dust from her pants. "I'm just saying."

"I was thinking more of a mole with beady little eyes."

"Mmm. You could be right." Sarah stroked her chin. "But a mole for whom?"

"You lost me." Zak stared at us, perplexed. "What are you talking about?"

"The pieces haven't been put together yet, Zak, my buddy, but Amy's working on it." Sarah clapped the young ranger's thin shoulders and led him out the door.

* * *

On the way back to the visitors' center Sarah, Zak, and I guessed at Deborah's motives for planting the money bag and pointing the finger at Sarah. "Maybe she knows the thief but wants to deal with him herself," I said. "Maybe she plans to goad you into repaying the money."

"Maybe she's delusional." Sarah curled her lip in distaste.

"I don't believe Deborah left that note," Zak said. "I'm not blind enough to miss a note on my desk for that long."

Sarah threw up her hands and shrugged. "Who else would care?"

Zak thought for a moment. "Maybe the guy who hit Deborah wants us to blame you."

"Maybe, but wouldn't you have seen someone like that lurking around?" I asked. "How would he get past Joan at the desk?"

Sarah shook her head. "The public isn't typically allowed behind the counter or in the offices."

"I've been behind the counter," I pointed out.

Sarah jostled my shoulder playfully. "You're not exactly typical."

"He probably blends in." Zak rubbed his bony, hairless jaw. "We have sixty people filtering through Windigo every day: hikers, boaters, kayakers, day trippers."

"Maybe Joan let him in."

Sarah and Zak stopped in the middle of the path, waiting for my explanation. "If the guy who hit Deborah is the same slick guy who tried to bully us out of the shelter at Siskiwit, he's smooth enough to worm himself into your office. Joan looks like she might fall for his line of bull."

"I'll ask Joan about him, but what happened at Siskiwit?" Zak asked.

He listened to my story, but somehow my words didn't do justice to the fear I felt the day before.

"Fill out a report, will you?" Zak asked. "We don't want people like that on the island."

* * *

Joan was at her station behind the counter showing a hiker the trail map, so we stood off to the side rather than descend on her like vultures. When the customer wandered off, Zak handed me an incident report form and asked Joan to join him in the office.

He had taken on his official ranger voice. "Sarah, will you watch the desk for a few minutes?"

I leaned over the visitors' side of the counter and picked up a pen to fill out the report. The plastic cap had been chewed, so I tossed that pen to the side. The ink in a second pen was dry, so I looked for something to scribble on and reached for a note pad next to the phone.

I held up the pad of paper. "Look at this, Sarah."

She shrugged. "Yeah?"

"It's the same paper as Zak's note, same size. I wonder if…" I held the pad up to the light. Faint words were pressed into the top sheet of paper.

Sarah snatched the pad from me and rummaged through the drawer for a pencil. "I saw this on reruns of Dragnet." She gently shaded the paper with the side of the lead tip. "Look. It works."

Parts of words appeared in contrast, white against the gray of the lead; other words remained indistinct.

"*Reliable*… something," she read, squinting. "*Rochon*. This is the same note."

"Do the bottom line," I urged.

Sarah strained to decipher more. "*Deb… Mitchell*." She sat with a plop in Joan's chair. "So what does this mean?"

"I have an idea Joan may be able to tell us."

Sarah leaned back and peeked into Zak's office. "They're coming out."

Joan walked out of the office, ducking her head as if trying to appear smaller. Zak followed her, caught Sarah's eye, and gave a little shrug and shake of his head.

"Zak, may I look at that note you got?" I asked.

His brows rose in a question, but he found the folded paper in his pocket and handed to me. I smoothed the wrinkles from the note on the desk in front of Joan. Her eyes widened. She stared at the paper as if it contained pestilence.

I darted my eyes toward Joan, asking Zak for permission to speak to his clerk. He frowned as if he had a headache, but nodded.

"Joan, would you please write down the Volunteer Coordinator's name for me?" I smiled and handed the woman her chewed pen. "And her phone number, in case I have to call her."

"Deborah?" Joan hesitated. "Sure, I guess." She searched for a pad of paper, looked up a phone number, and wrote 'Deborah Mitchell' below the number. She handed me the slip of paper with a question on her face.

"Thanks." I took the note. "Zak, can we talk in your office?"

The beleaguered young ranger led me into his office. He sat in his swivel chair and pointed for me to sit in the visitor's seat. "What was that all about?"

I reached across his desk to place two pieces of paper in front of him. "Compare the note you received to this rubbing Sarah made a few minutes ago."

Zak hunched over, peering at the pencil imprints. "I can't quite read the entire note, but Deborah's name is clear." He slid the papers back to me. "Where did you get the rubbing?"

"From a pad on Joan's workstation." I handed him the slip of paper with Deborah's name and phone number. "Now compare the handwriting on Joan's note to Deborah's name on the other two."

Zak studied the notes. "So Joan wrote the note and may know about the conspiracy to frame Sarah." He sat back in his chair and groaned.

I had led him this far and figured he would draw his own conclusions, so I sat back and raised my shoulders to my ears. Only the woman who had written the notes could fill in the rest of the blanks.

"Joan, will you come in here a minute?" He raised his voice enough to be heard in the adjoining room. We waited. No one appeared in his doorway.

"Joan?"

Sarah burst through the entrance to the visitors' center, breathing heavy and red in the face. She threw up her hands when she saw us. "I lost her."

"You mean Joan?" I asked. "We're looking for her."

"Yeah." Sarah filled a paper cup with water and drank before explaining. "She bolted when I went to the bathroom. I spotted her headed for the marina, but she disappeared before I got there."

"Why would she run off and leave the desk unattended?" Zak asked.

"Hard to believe." I shook my head at his naiveté. "I'll bet she stood outside the office door eavesdropping while we discussed the notes."

Zak frowned. "She can't stay gone long. I'll talk to her when she comes back."

Two hikers clomped across the deck outside and rushed in, asking to see a ranger. Zak moved behind the counter to answer their questions. Sarah and I wandered to the library section to discuss Joan's guilty actions.

"Could Joan have been Deborah's attacker?" I absentmindedly leafed through a wildflower guide.

"I thought you decided Brad attacked Deborah." Sarah took the book from my hand and gave me another. "This is a better guide." She tapped her finger on the title. "Besides, Joan and Deborah are buddies."

"I'm still pretty sure it was him, but she's guilty of something." I scanned the pictures in the recommended guide and promised myself to buy a copy for my library. "In any case, the investigator will have someone besides you to question."

"Joan's suspicious behavior probably helps my case—if the investigator is a logical guy." Sarah leaned against the bookshelf. "I'll be glad when this mystery stuff is over."

"I wish there was more I could do, but I've got to get back to Siskiwit. I'm nervous about Meagan being alone. Valerie will have taken the dog away by now."

"You were a big help today." Sarah draped her arm over my shoulders. "You've got a long walk back. If Zak doesn't need me, I'll walk you as far as the Greenstone."

Zak's voice from the counter area took on a tone of urgency. He spoke into a radio while the two hikers waited. "Those are the GPS coordinates, just east of Siskiwit. The boat patrol will meet you there with a stretcher. I'll have the float plane pilot waiting."

"Siskiwit?" My skin went cold.

Sarah and I edged closer to the conversation.

"What's going on?" Sarah asked the hikers.

"A girl near Siskiwit fell and cracked her head." The young man raised his hand to the back of his head. "She was unconscious. The leader of a youth group asked us to hurry here to report the accident and get help."

Zak came over and put his hand on the young hiker's shoulder. "Thanks, man. I radioed the work crew at Island Mine to send their first-aider to the scene, and we'll send a boat up with a stretcher to meet them. They'll radio back if she needs to be airlifted to Thunder Bay."

The two rangers rushed into the room before I could ask questions. Zak thrust the hikers' report at the uniformed men, and they were out the door.

Sarah gave me a shove. "Go with them."

"What if it's Meagan?" I gasped.

"I know. Go," Sarah ordered. "Zak, Amy needs to get back to Siskiwit, let her go with the patrol."

Harried, Zak waved his hand. "I don't care. If you can catch them, go."

I was out the door and running across the deck before I knew what I was doing. I heard Sarah's shrill whistle pierce the air over my head.

"Hey, Matt, Cody!" she shouted.

The two rangers, in a run toward the marina, glanced over their shoulders.

"She's coming with you!" Sarah made an exaggerated point at me, and the two men waved, but didn't slow.

The steep downhill gave me speed. I had to concentrate on my feet keeping up with the momentum. "Thanks, Sarah," I yelled back, but didn't dare turn to look at her still up on the deck.

I scrambled aboard the park service patrol boat just as one of the rangers threw the mooring ropes onto the deck and hopped on. Trying to catch my breath, I sagged onto a gear box behind the enclosed pilothouse and hung on. The huge outboard motors roared and the patrol boat surged forward.

The dark-haired ranger handed me an orange life vest. He shouted over the deafening engine noise, introducing himself as Matt, and insisted I tighten every strap. I begged him for information while fumbling with the buckles.

"My daughter's in Siskiwit," I yelled. "What do you know about the injured girl?"

Matt pulled out the report and held the paper tight against the wind. He braced his feet on the heaving deck and tried to read. "Fifteen years old. British."

What a relief. Fear for my Meagan left me, but worry niggled at the back of my mind, perhaps out of concern for the injured teenager. Before I could ask about the girl's condition, Matt turned away to gather mooring ropes.

I staggered to a seat. My maternal instincts remained on edge, so I sent a prayer up for the girl and her British mother. Images of

Meagan in trouble flashed in my brain. I tried to ease my anxiety by watching the capable intensity of the reedy, blond ranger at the helm.

He glanced at me over his shoulder. "Cody," he shouted, pointing to himself. "Hang on!"

We sped out of the marina, thumping over the wake of a double-decker yacht. Its captain waved and the three of us returned the greeting. I wondered if boat-waving was universal. My gaze followed the pleasure boat as it slid into the marina. "Spending Their Inheritance" was emblazoned across the stern. The clever meaning relieved my pent-up tension, until I realized where I had seen that phrase before...one of the song titles listed on Deborah's computer. Why would she keep a list of boat names? Was it part of her job?

In the distance, Sarah stood on the display room's deck. I frantically pointed at *Spending Their Inheritance* and tried to shout the name over the roar of the engines and into the wind. Sarah waved good-bye and walked inside the building.

11

Siskiwit 911

A mile of Isle Royale's rugged shoreline passed before I relaxed and explained to Matt why I had hitched a ride on their mission of mercy. Yelling over the roar of the engines made real conversation impossible, and Matt didn't ask questions. I got bounced around in the stern while he took inventory of an impressive array of emergency medical supplies. Meanwhile, Cody steered the boat, his eyes constantly scanning the horizon.

After an hour of hull-pounding through endless waves, Matt shouted, "Siskiwit Bay!" and pointed to the left ahead of us.

I loosened my stiff fingers from the gunnel and shaded my eyes against the glare reflected off the water, hoping to see Meagan on the pier or basking in the sun on the beach. The two quiet shelters perched on a hill above an empty shore. Only the wind moved through the flowing grasses and yellow and white wildflowers. No scouts. No daughter.

Matt's short, muscular legs propelled him onto the cement pier a second before a slight bump announced that Cody had expertly docked the vessel. Matt looped ropes around dock cleats to secure the boat, fore and aft. Cody cut the engines and locked the pilothouse door. They grabbed the backpack labeled "Emergency

111

Supplies" and a wheeled stretcher and ran from the dock onto the trail leading away from the beach.

Their speed and single-mindedness made my head spin. "Good luck!" I called after them, wishing the British girl well. Matt pushed the metal stretcher ahead of him for a short distance and then hoisted the basket-like contraption onto his shoulder and continued to run. They disappeared over a rise in a matter of minutes, and I was left on the deserted pier, proud that I had known them for an hour.

I scrambled up the hill toward our shelter. "Hello!" Our sleeping bags fluttered from the rope strung from the shelter eave to a nearby tree. "Meagan, hello!" Her backpack was propped against the wall next to her boots in the corner. Remington was gone, of course, but his water bowl still sat on the floorboards. Clothes were strewn on Meaghan's sleeping pad. Something wasn't right. My organized, CPA daughter had left the place in disarray.

What if that yacht captain came back to corner Meagan? I fought down a bilious fear and hurried from our shelter to the one occupied by the scouts to get information from Mr. Domkowski. No boy-noise disrupted the peace. Instead, two young women watched me wade through the grasses toward them. Newcomers. I hoped Meagan was there to greet them.

"Hello. Excuse me. Have you seen the woman camping next door?" I pointed back toward our shelter.

The girls spoke to each other in what sounded like French before the one with flowing black hair stepped forward, frowning. *"Non, madame, no one is in la cabane."* She formed her words carefully, trying to make herself understood through a heavy accent. The second girl held up her finger to stop her friend and spoke in rapid French.

"Ah, *oui*," the black-haired beauty said in halting English. "We saw *une femme*, um, a woman *marchant il*, um, walking." She motioned to the far side of the bay and tapped binoculars suspended from a strap around her neck.

Real conversation proved too difficult. I thanked the pleasant women and returned to our shelter to wait for Meagan. I kept worry at bay by cleaning up the place and removing the sleeping bags from the clothesline. Between tasks, I scanned the curve of the beach and squinted toward the opposite shore. I sat on the wooden steps with my elbows on my knees, waiting. No Meagan. Fretting was useless; I had to find my daughter.

On a mission, I tromped down the hill toward the beach and headed west along the long, lonely stretch of sand. Hundreds of yards down the pristine beach, a set of fresh footprints angled away from the bordering vegetation and through the deep sand to the edge of the water. I quickened my pace. Did another set of prints follow in pursuit? I held my breath while studying the area until satisfied that only one person had passed that way.

"Meagan!" I yelled.

The footprints had to be Meagan's running shoes. I measured the prints and the long stride against my own. She must have jogged along the lake. With her speed she could be anywhere. I regretted not leaving a note for her in the shelter. I glanced back at Siskiwit, but saw no one on the pier or beach and kept walking—past the firewood I collected two days ago, past the spot where Remington floated ashore. Meagan's shoe prints left the wet sand and headed inland. I followed until Siskiwit Creek blocked my progress. The ankle-deep water flowed over the beach, fanned out, lost its depth and merged with Lake Superior. Meagan's trail disappeared.

I backtracked to find a narrow path through the thick vegetation. A puncheon cut through the reeds and led to a heavy-duty bridge that spanned the creek and gave me a good view of the area.

"Meagan!" I called into the wilderness. The wind blew my voice out over the lake. Frustrated with the lack of volume, I searched my fanny pack to find my whistle and blasted on it twice. A squirrel ran for its life along the length of the iron railing. I listened to the deep woods.

Nothing disturbed the sounds of nature.

I walked further into the forest, calling my daughter's name, until I spotted part of a shoe print to the right of the trail. Maybe Meagan tried a shortcut. The thick foliage had been beaten back and moose prints rutted the soft ground. If she went that way, I would, too.

The path followed a meandering route with no apparent destination, except deeper into the wilderness. Determined to explore every possibility, I fought through thickening reeds. Trees grew taller. Humidity weighted the air. Boggy earth sucked at my boots. The path petered out. Disgusted with myself for leaving the main trail, I turned around to retrace my steps, but a wall of reeds penned me in. I pushed forward, but soon stopped, unsure of my direction. I looked for the sun to get my bearings, but the thick canopy shaded the woods. I thrashed through the weeds to what I thought was the south for several minutes before realizing I was headed west, or maybe north.

My thoughts raced and my heart beat too fast. With a start I realized that I wasn't thinking clearly, and was in danger of getting myself lost. I fought down panic and took several deep breaths, then tried to take stock of my situation and location. Being lost myself would not help my daughter.

My training told me to go back to the last place I recognized—the main path, the iron bridge, the beach. But how?

I stilled myself and opened my mind to my surroundings. The vast expanse of water seemed to lie to my right. Blue sky filtered through the trees in that direction. I fought through the foliage for twenty paces, reoriented myself, and fought another twenty paces.

114

I stopped and listened. Fresh air from the lake. A mechanical sound. An engine. I made a beeline for the sound. The foliage thinned. Trees gave way to blue sky. I spotted a small plane rising into the air. It had to be the float plane taking off from Siskiwit with the injured British girl. That gave me my bearings, and I beat my way through the shrubbery.

Finally, I broke through onto the beach. Weak with relief, I sank onto the rocky shore and let myself breathe. As if the whole world had opened up to the light, I could see for miles. The distance I had come surprised me. On the opposite shore of the inlet lay Siskiwit like a miniature diorama with a toy boat moored at the dock.

The patrol boat was still there. Matt and Cody would help me find Meagan. I jumped to my feet and ran along the sand toward the pier. My lungs soon gave out, so I stopped and yelled with what breath remained.

"Wait!"

Wind and waves absorbed my plea and the rangers puttered away from the dock, oblivious to my shouts. Cody's engines roared and the boat jerked forward, leaving a trail of white foam in its wake.

My hopes for building a search party to find Meagan receded along with the boat gliding out of sight. Exhausted, I stopped my useless running and shouting. Nature's quiet settled over Siskiwit Bay, but the silence gave me no serenity. I trudged through the sand toward our camp. *Maybe she heard about the British girl,* I thought. *She went to help, and is back by now.* The possibility quickened my steps.

A familiar tone drifted on the wind and caught my attention. I stopped breathing and cocked my ear.

"Mom!"

I jerked my head toward the faint hint of her voice and spotted her golden hair emerging from the bushes about a hundred yards ahead. "Meagan!" I waved in celebration.

The sand dragged at my feet, slowed me, but she ran like an Olympian to close the distance between us.

"Mom!" She wrapped me in a desperate hug. "I thought you were in Windigo. What are you doing here?"

"I've been looking for you for hours. Where…"

"How did you get back so fast?"

I stepped back and looked at my daughter, confused by her demanding questions. "I hitched a ride with the rangers…"

"Was that a ranger boat?" She shot a frown toward Lake Superior. "What did they want? Did they…did they find something?"

"Settle down, Meagan," I said. "The EMTs rescued a British girl with a head injury." I held both her hands in mine to still them. "First, I thought you had been injured, then I thought you went to help her."

"No, I…I saw that rescue plane and I came back. Oh, Mom." She looked like she wanted to cry. "I was upset and needed to get away. I just ran through the woods, for hours…" Her words trailed off.

"I'm sorry, Meagan. Were you upset over the dog? I told Valerie about Remington back at Windigo. Was she nasty?"

My daughter's face clouded over. "No, she was fine, nice even, but that…"

"Well, we did the right thing. She loves that dog." I stroked her arm. "I'm just so glad you're safe. I was worried sick that something had happened to you."

She burst into tears. Shocked by her emotional state, I gathered her in my arms and comforted her as best I could. "What's wrong, sweetheart?"

She pulled away and straightened up. "Nothing."

"Come on, Meagan. What's the matter?"

"Really, I'm fine. Sorry. I'm just emotional." She clenched her teeth and sealed her lips.

The rejection stung. Confounded by her refusal to talk, I took the easy way out. "Let's walk, honey. We'll get back to the shelter, build a fire, and get you some dinner. You'll feel better."

Meagan nodded, her face still scrunched and wet with tears. We followed the long curve of the beach back to Siskiwit campground. All the while, guilt for not knowing how to talk to Meagan hung like an anchor around my neck. I wracked my brain for answers. *What's going on with my daughter?*

12

Day 6 - Island Mine

Island Mine was our morning destination. For 150 years nature has worked to reclaim Island Mine—or so said the pre-trip internet search I did on the history of Isle Royale. The last copper was extracted from the mines in 1876. Most of the people then moved to the mainland and left behind mine shafts, broken tools, stone wells, and other evidence of human occupation that the forest has camouflaged, entwined, and overgrown. Slag heaps dot the hills and valleys. Their steep mounds crop up in an otherwise predictable landscape. The mining detritus is barren, but a hundred years of windblown dust and dirt layered with a century of leaves has created a thin soil in which intrepid maples have taken root.

I suspected that the unobservant typically trek through the area as if in any other northwoods forest and that hikers seldom stop, but continue on to anywhere else. Something isn't quite right about Island Mine. The air is uncomfortable, humid and abuzz with mosquitoes. Eerie. The earth still suffers from its wounds.

Designated campsites at Island Mine were bare spots in the thick woods on the convenient route to Windigo. I intended to dawdle, spending valuable time with my daughter. Meagan had been quiet and withdrawn since her run yesterday. She bristled when I questioned her and gave me no clues to what had upset her. I was afraid to intrude on her silence—afraid she'd reject my offer of support.

Each with our own thoughts, we set up our tent at a high point in a clearing at the juncture of two trails; one the main route from Siskiwit to Windigo and the other connecting the group site with the permanent camp used by trail maintenance crews. Tall trees hemmed us in and blocked the view. Meagan seemed on edge.

"Mom, why don't we keep going to Windigo?" she said. "It's not that far."

"Because we agreed not to rush, to spend more time together. Besides, we can explore the area, maybe find the mine shaft."

Meagan looked over her shoulder as if ghosts might be hidden in the shadows. "But I didn't know this is where you intended to stop."

"What's troubling you, honey?"

Her eyes darted at me, and I regretted my intrusive question.

"Nothing." She pursed her lips. "This camp will be okay."

The repairs made to our relationship at Feldtmann Lake continued to unravel. "We'll relax once we settle in." I grasped at that small hope. "Come on, let's filter some water."

Meagan hesitated but followed me down the hill to a shallow stream. We slid in the mud on the steep bank. I straddled the shallow stream, scooped the orange water, and pumped it through our filter. The basic task relieved my tension—brought back a bit of normal.

Meagan made a face. "This doesn't look drinkable."

The water remained a murky yellow. I worried that the rainwater leached metals from the mines. "I wonder if it's safe." The sample I sipped left a metallic tang on my tongue. "Let's scout around for another source."

We packed away our filter and bottles and headed up the next incline toward sunlight piercing through the leafy canopy. While concentrating on getting up the steep hill, I cocked my head to identify a sound. Heavy metal clanked against rock. We drew closer to see a group of sweaty young men in tee-shirts and yellow hard hats laboring on the trail. Looking closer, I saw that several of them were girls with great biceps. Meagan and I stopped to watch the work. The crew's apparent task was to shore up the hillside with unearthed boulders and reshape the trail using pickaxes, crowbars, and brute strength.

"Looks like you're doing a great job," I said. None of them looked up. Meagan and I exchanged glances and shrugged. "I guess we'll have to wade through the bushes to get around them."

We moved forward and startled the nearest worker. He smiled and put his hand out to stop the others' work. They seemed happy to lean on their tools and allow us to continue up the trail.

"Do you know if there's water up ahead?" Meagan asked. Each of them smiled and bobbed their heads. We waited for an answer. A thought seemed to dawn on one of the bronzed young men. He raised a dirty finger as if to say, *Just a minute*, and whistled.

A young woman appeared further up the hill. "Hello!" she called and marched down toward us, swinging her arms. About thirty-five, she had a solid build and wore a neat chambray shirt. A blue hard hat with the letters *MCC* emblazoned across the front perched upon her head. "Hi. I'm Linda." She wiped her hands on her heavy twill pants before offering a handshake. "Did you ask the crew something?"

Her strong, calloused grip impressed me. "Yes, we wondered if there is water anywhere—other than back down that hill."

"I'm afraid not. That sorry little stream is all Island Mine has to offer." She smiled broadly and crinkled up her nose. "It takes some getting used to."

One of the crew members grunted, trying to pry loose a stubborn rock. Linda paused, watching the effort. A soft look of approval spread across her face.

"What are they working on?" Meagan asked.

"Erosion control. The rain runs through here so fast, it washes out the trail." She swept her arm up and down the hillside, proud of the work. "I'm the supervisor and interpreter for the crew."

"Is this a volunteer group or something?" I didn't want to stare at them, but every one of them was what youth is meant to be: lean, muscled, and healthy. "What does MCC stand for?"

"Minnesota Conservation Corps."

"Ah. I should have been able to figure that one out."

The woman chuckled at my discomfort. "The MCC gives youth groups, especially the hearing impaired, a chance for summer work." She signed something to the group, and they all reached for their water bottles and took a break. "We've been here all summer, staying at the group site at Island Mine. We've gotten used to the water, I guess."

Linda removed the hard hat and dragged her sleeve across her forehead. She wore a no-nonsense, close-cropped hairstyle, perfect for living in the woods. I asked her about life in the wilderness. Her description of the crew's hard work made me view the 165 miles of trail on the island with a new perspective. The three of us stood, each with one foot uphill and the other down, chatting amiably. Without a word from Linda, the young workers took up their tools again—our signal to leave. Linda promised to visit that evening. We thanked the crew with a wave before we headed back toward our campsite and the orange water in the stream.

Later, after lunch with our chores done, my daughter and I settled in. Island Mine felt safe and homey. Meagan propped herself against a log and hid behind a mystery novel. No chance of bonding there. I pulled out my field guide and roamed the area looking for wildflowers. After circling our perimeter and noting only a few late summer specimens, I ventured down the path toward the work crew's permanent camp. Nosy, I guess. I wondered if they lived in tiny backpacking tents or in room-sized cabin styles. They hadn't yet hiked back from their work site and surely wouldn't mind if I took a peek.

Though certain that the place was deserted, I listened as I walked down the shaded lane. Their camp hadn't yet come into view when I heard metal clinking. I stopped in mid-stride. My face reddened. One of the crew must have been left in camp. Not wanting to be caught snooping, I scurried back to Meagan.

Her paperback lay in her lap. Lost in thought, she barely noticed when I took a seat on the log near her. I tried to appear innocent of being a nosy neighbor, but soon felt antsy. I grabbed my fanny pack from the picnic table and tried to interest my daughter in our surroundings.

"Let's explore a little and take pictures. Maybe find that mine shaft."

Meagan sat up straight. "I don't want to go out there. I'm reading." She fanned through the pages of the book. "Maybe you should stay in camp and rest."

"I'm not tired, honey. We can make the search fun." I spotted a small opening in her armor. "Are you worried about something? Do you want to talk?"

"No, but..." She bit her lip and hesitated. "You should stay here."

The steady drum of footsteps interrupted us. We turned to see a row of bobbing yellow hard hats through the shrubbery. The work crew's tools were strapped to backpacks or slung over their shoulders. They walked in silence, but at second glance, their hands flew in a language all their own. We raised our hands in greeting to the crew shuffling toward their camp hidden down the path behind our tent. Linda, under her blue dome and with a sheaf of papers tucked in the crook of her arm, brought up the rear. I met her at the intersecting trails.

"End of a long day, huh?"

She shrugged good-naturedly. "Every day is long!"

"So does someone stay in camp to fix dinner for you?"

"Ha. I wish." Linda's laugh could brighten any day. "Nope. Cooking is next on the agenda."

Maybe a raccoon had rummaged through their cookware. I kept my snooping a secret and changed the subject. "Are there any historical sites nearby, Linda?" I held up my camera. "Mine shafts, old buildings?"

"Hmmm." She stroked her chin, leaving a smudge of dirt along her jawline. "The map shows several old copper mines on the island. People talk about one out beyond the stone well, but I've never seen it." She pointed to the east. "There's no sign, but you'll find the well twenty feet from the trail, if you look."

"Great. We'll check it out." I thanked her for her information and invited her again to stop by after dinner for tea and conversation.

"Maybe I will," she said, but she looked worn out. I doubted she'd pay us a visit.

I waved good-bye to Linda and motioned to Meagan. "There may be a mine down this way. Let's go for a walk."

"No, thanks." She stood, idly thumbing the pages of her paperback. "You go, Mom. I'll stay here."

"Come on, honey," I teased. "Maybe we'll find a lost mine and buried treasure."

She rewarded my attempt to lighten the mood with a wan smile. "Enjoy yourself. I'll be right here with my paperback."

"Well, okay. I won't be gone long," I said. "Linda and the crew are right down the path, if you get nervous."

My daughter straightened her spine. "I'll be fine, Mom. I'm worried about you."

I appreciated her concern, but waved it away. *We must be bonding better than I thought.* I smiled to myself and went in search of the mine shaft.

Ten minutes later, after walking and scanning the sides of the trail for something out of the ordinary, I spotted a casual path off to the right. Several slag heaps in the distance marred the woodland scene. *This must be the place.* Before I could veer off the main trail, a middle-aged couple, husband and wife, I assumed, strolled down the hill holding hands. I greeted them. They nodded and their eyes followed mine down the narrow path to a tiny clearing.

"What's down the path?" the man asked, ready to explore.

"Don't know for sure, but I've been told there's an old stone well and maybe a mine shaft beyond that."

"Really?" The woman reached for her digital camera, and my hopes for quiet reflection on the area's past vanished. They followed me fifteen feet to the clearing where a circle of flagstone rimmed a hole in the ground. The remains of a small split-rail fence lay scattered like Lincoln Logs.

"Someone could easily walk through here and fall right in," I murmured and made a mental note to mention the needed repair to the work crew.

"Any water in it?" the man asked.

I've always loved natural stone fences and limestone buildings, so the structure of the well interested me enough to investigate. Long ago, a stonemason had layered neat slabs of rock to form the smooth inside wall—a master of his craft. I crept nearer to the edge and peered into the depths of the well. I blinked, refocused, and grabbed for my flashlight to clear away the shadows.

"What do you see?" The couple crowded next to me and looked into the hole. The woman jerked backwards, colliding with her husband's chest. She screamed and ran to the main trail, her hand to her throat. She screamed until the man was at her side with his arm around her shoulders, shocked and ashen himself.

My knees failed me, so I sank to the ground at the edge of the well and forced my eyes to see what the light beam had illuminated. Nine feet down a man sat slumped against the wall in the cramped hole, his knees bent and splayed apart. A large rock lay in his midsection. Red pulp filled the cleft in his skull. Blood in dry rivulets streaked his face and had pooled into a rusty stain in the grit beneath his elbow.

My breath left my lungs as I gaped.

Meagan was the first to come running in response to the screaming. She grabbed my arm and tugged me to my feet. She stared at the scene in the well and gasped. "Get away from here," she demanded. I tripped over my feet as she dragged me, urging me to hurry.

"Stop, Meagan. Stop." I pulled my arm free and leaned over with my hands on my knees to catch my breath. "We have to think. We have to do something."

"Let them do...whatever!" Meagan motioned to where the couple had stood. They were gone, running away toward Siskiwit.

"We have to go..." Meagan continued.

Linda had also heard the woman's screams. She and her crew charged down the trail. The young men and women stopped in front of us, signing and asking questions with their eyes and facial expressions. All I could do was point to the well. My daughter blew air from her cheeks and stepped aside.

Several of the crew filed toward the well, looked in, and gasped. One by one they returned to the trail, shaken. Two of the girls hung back with their leader.

"Don't look," I warned Linda, but she didn't believe the scene her crew described to her.

She disregarded my advice, looked into the hole, and returned to my side with a pinched face and tears welling in her eyes. "What happened?"

"I don't know." I put my arm around her for a moment while she pulled herself together. "Is he one of your crew?"

Her shoulders shuddered as she jerked away from me. "No, oh no." But she scanned the young people around her, counting. "We have everyone." She closed her eyes and sighed. "Should we pull him out of there and run for help?"

"Let's not touch anything," I whispered. "The rangers will want to see the scene as it is. Why don't you call them on the radio?"

While Linda contacted the Windigo ranger station, I went to Meagan who had wandered up the trail, away from the grisly scene. "Are you okay?"

"Not really," she said, shaking her head.

I hugged my daughter and sat her down on a log. "Stay here for a few minutes. I'm going to talk to the crew."

"Please don't get involved, Mom," Meagan pleaded. She kneaded the spot between her eyebrows.

"Don't worry, sweetheart. I'll be right back."

"Mom!"

I motioned for her to stay calm. "This will take only a minute. Then we'll wait for the rangers back at our camp."

* * *

Linda stationed two crew members on the trail to prevent unsuspecting hikers from stumbling into the scene at the well. She and her work party milled around our campsite at the intersection of the two trails rather than sequester themselves back in the group site. People need other people while trying to make sense of a tragedy. I did my best to keep hot water boiling for coffee and tea.

"Hello in the camp!"

Meagan and I turned toward Taylor Lorenz's familiar voice. The wolf researcher loped up the trail from the west. "I heard on the radio that there had been an accident," he said. "Is there something I can do?"

We stood to greet him and introduced him to the others. We told Taylor what we had found, but he declined to view the body.

126

The news subdued him, put a pall over his easygoing nature. Along with a cup of tea, we shared with him our descriptions of the horrific scene.

The presence of a newcomer, someone who hadn't seen the blood, seemed to calm everyone. The female crew members, probably drawn to Taylor's good looks, seemed to take comfort from his presence. As a group, we distracted ourselves with small talk while waiting for the rangers to arrive.

"You're a good, strong runner," Taylor said to Meagan. "Do you run in marathons or just for the exercise?"

"What?" Meagan stumbled over her response. "Oh, sure, I do marathons."

Her hesitation caused Taylor to frown in confusion. "Wasn't that you I saw east of here yesterday zipping up and down the hills?" He smiled, trying to give her a compliment.

Meagan darted a look at me. "Maybe it was. I did go out for a run after noon."

"I thought so." His grin widened. "I'm a runner myself. Did two Iron Man events—Louisville this year and Madison last year."

Ordinarily, Meagan would have jumped into a conversation about the races, the finish times, the training, but she said, "Good. That's great." Her eyes met mine and glanced away.

I tried to cover for her lack of enthusiasm by asking about the swimming portion of the Iron Man. Taylor sensed I was struggling with the subject and changed topics, asking Linda about the conservation efforts of her crew.

"Meagan," I said, "let's go down the hill and filter more water." I stood and let her know she had no options. I was done being the soft-spoken, understanding Mom. *She's almost thirty years old, for Godsakes. If she's going to act like a hormonal teenager, I'll treat her like one.*

My daughter screwed up her face, sighed, and rose from her seat on the log. "Okay, I'll get the bottles."

Once we were away from the campsite and in the seclusion of the ravine, I took my daughter's elbow and turned her toward me. "I've had enough of this, Meagan. There's something you're not telling me, and I want to know what it is. Now."

She stood with slumped shoulders, her mouth turned down. "Mom, I tried to tell you, but some things are just hard to talk about. I didn't know it would turn into a big deal." Meagan wrung her hands. "Now it's a mess."

"Back up, Meagan," I demanded. "Start from the beginning."

I bent over the little stream, pumped yellow water through my filter and waited for her to speak. She squatted next to me to take me into her confidence.

"That Valerie woman came to get Remington. I was upset, so I went for a run. I didn't know I ran this far, and I didn't know this place is called Island Mine." Meagan seemed defensive and—fearful. "I guess Taylor saw me."

I stopped pumping. "Go on."

"That man was here—or he followed me. Brad, the one from the yacht."

I grabbed her arm and shook her. "That happened yesterday, Meagan. This is ridiculous!" My anger rose, and I stopped listening. "You waited this long to tell me that a man, that jerk, is stalking you?" My rant might have gone on, but I saw her expression turn to misery. I took a deep breath and softened my voice, got it under control. "What happened, Meagan? Did he harass you?"

"I did it, Mom."

"Did what, Meagan?"

"I killed that man."

"What?" I felt color run from my cheeks. "That's impossible. Of course, you didn't."

"I did."

"Meagan, what are you talking about?" Suddenly, the shirt at the bottom of the well looked familiar, the blond hair caked in blood. "Are you telling me the man in the well is Brad Olson?"

She nodded, hiding behind her hands. Her shoulders shook. I pulled her hands down and, in my panic, wanted to slap her for putting herself in a dangerous situation, but stroked her cheek instead. "Meagan, tell me what happened."

"I killed him, Mom. He followed me—I spotted him and ran faster. I thought I lost him. I stopped at the stone well to stretch against that little fence." Her tone was dead. "And then he was there—behind me. His arm went around my neck and he covered my mouth. He grabbed me. His awful hand—slid all over my body.

Meagan's fingers moved down the front of her shirt. Her mouth twisted as if to gag. She stared at the muddy stream at our feet. "He touched me, Mom—where my baby was."

She sagged onto the side of the hill. I wrapped my little girl in my arms and rocked her while she sobbed.

"Meggie, Meggie," I crooned and kissed her golden head. A breeze blew wisps of her hair across my cheek. A dry leaf tumbled into the water and floated downstream. How was I to comfort her? A mother's job is to protect. I had failed again. I wiped my nose on my sleeve, coupling my grief to hers while she mourned her baby.

In time she lifted her head. "What should we do?"

"You and Ed can try again. You're young," I said.

She laid her hand on my arm and looked at me with real love in her eyes. "I mean about the dead guy."

Meagan straightened her back, and I took strength from her recovery. I rearranged my thought process and adjusted my cap. "Tell me exactly what happened. I'm certain you didn't kill him."

"I think I did. When he touched my...my..." Her hands cradled her lower abdomen. "I was so angry, kind of crazy. I think I flipped him over my back. He fell in that well and screamed like he was dying."

Horrified at her close call and proud of her survival instinct, I stared at her in shock. "Meagan, what were you thinking? Why didn't you tell me?"

"I don't know." Meagan hung her head. "I didn't want you to worry about me, I guess. That guy had done enough to ruin our vacation, and I didn't know that I'd killed him. I thought he'd climb out of there and chase me down."

"Meagan, you didn't kill him. When you left him, Brad was alive, right?" I prayed there wasn't a law against running away from your attacker; that she couldn't be accused of leaving an injured man to die.

"Yeah, he was. He screamed obscenities at me." Meagan wanted to believe she hadn't caused the man's death, but she covered her face with her hands and shook her head. "Will they arrest me?"

"Of course not. You shoved him into the well in self-defense." My words were weak and whispered, but I vowed to keep her safe. I needed the new trust she placed in me and would not fail her.

"That rock…" She shook her head in horror.

"We'll find out what really happened," I assured her. "That guy was scum, and there must be more going on here than we know."

Awful scenarios played in my head. *What if someone pinned the murder on her and she goes to prison?* I pumped water mechanically, fiercely. The overflow spilled onto my boots. Meagan put her hand over mine to signal a stop.

"The rangers will ask questions," I told my daughter. "Answer them truthfully, but don't give extra information—or your opinions," I said. "If they know you fought with Brad, they'll stop looking for anyone else. We need to figure out who was here after you ran back to Siskiwit."

My daughter nodded, as if my advice contained wisdom.

After several minutes of reviewing possible scenarios, I splashed water from the stream onto my face, patted it dry, and passed my bandana to Meagan. We capped our water bottles and trudged out of the muddy ravine. We crested the hill in time to see Taylor and the MCC group trot down the trail toward the well.

13

The Man in the Well

Matt and Cody must have run to their patrol boat immediately, as they had the day before when rescuing the British girl. The rangers' response today was rapid—less than two hours. I hoped yesterday's mission of mercy had a better outcome than this incident.

I spotted tall, blond Cody and stocky Matt cordoning off the area around the well with yellow tape. They moved with strength and confidence. In a moment of weakness, I wanted to tell them Meagan's story, to transfer the weight of her admission from my shoulders to theirs. Could I trust the rangers to find the real killer or would they blame her? Would her involvement spiral out of control and into a prison situation? I couldn't risk her future to those young men. I set my mind against them.

A third NPS uniform appeared on the trail, just arriving. My confidence level soared as Sarah bounded toward us. She grabbed Meagan and me in a double bear hug, and we did not resist.

"I couldn't help it. I heard your name on the radio and figured you were in some sort of trouble. My buddies let me hitch a ride. What's going on? We got here as fast as we could and ran all the way from Siskiwit. I almost didn't make it!" She was flushed and out of breath.

"Take a breather, Sarah," I said. "We're fine. You didn't have to worry, but I'm so glad to see you." Already some of my anxiety had left me. I had an ally. The three of us stood off from the crowd at the crime scene and I told her I had found the body. "I think it might be that Brad guy—the one who harassed us at Siskiwit," I whispered. "Same sort of shirt and pants."

Shock took over Sarah's face. "You're kidding. What happened?"

Meagan cringed and shot a look of fear at me. I'd trust Sarah with my life, but not with my daughter's secrets. Our newly repaired mother-daughter relationship was too fragile, too important to me.

"We don't know exactly," I said. "Either he pulled a rock down on himself, or someone threw a rock in after he fell."

Sarah cocked her head. "That's—really odd." She nodded her head in thought. "He must have bullied the wrong person."

Taylor approached to greet Sarah, and they thumped each other on the shoulders like old friends. The four of us joined the activity near the well where Cody stood apart surveying the scene, taking pictures from various angles. Matt moved among the assembled MCC group with a clipboard. He took statements from everyone with Linda at his side, interpreting. He approached the job with gentle concern, and the crew talked with him openly, each telling the same story. I listened, trying to catch clues that would prove to the rangers, and to Meagan, that someone else killed Brad.

Matt approached me, taking his pen from behind his ear. "May I take your statement?"

Sarah came to stand at my side. Strength and confidence transferred from her body to mine. I stood up straighter and nodded to Matt. "Sure. What would you like to know?"

"Linda tells me you discovered the body." His pen paused above the paper on the clipboard.

"That's right. I had just gotten to the clearing when a couple arrived, a man and a woman. They ran off toward Siskiwit after seeing the body."

Matt nodded. "They hailed us on the trail and reported what they saw." He paused and looked directly at me from beneath raised eyebrows. "Were you here yesterday?"

I answered the ranger's every question with care and truth. He might have asked more probing, more specific questions, but didn't, and I didn't volunteer extra details. Sarah listened closely, her arms crossed and her knuckles pressed against her lips. Meagan stood nearby, zipping and unzipping her jacket, waiting her turn.

Cody tapped Matt on the shoulder. "Finished with pictures," he said. "Let's get him out so we can get back to Windigo before dark."

Matt nodded, but made a few more notes, looking at Meagan, Taylor, and one of the crew members not yet interviewed. "Thank you," he said to me as an afterthought. Then he turned to Cody and began to discuss, in low, serious tones, ways to retrieve the body from the narrow well.

Cody rubbed his jaw as he eyed the rescue stretcher and shook his head. He donned a surgical mask and gloves, and directed several of the MCC crew to line up on the end of a sturdy rope and hold it taut. The thin ranger then paused at the edge of the well, grasped the rope, and lowered himself below ground level.

Sarah added her strength to the line, while Matt readied the basket stretcher at the rim of the well. Taylor hovered nearby, glanced into the hole, and backed away. I felt rooted to the ground where Meagan and I stood out of the way, near the fallen split-rail fence.

After several minutes Cody's muffled voice sounded from the well. "Throw down a towel."

Matt unzipped the supply pack, unwrapped a package, and dropped a white cloth into the well.

A minute later his partner signaled his readiness. "Okay, pull him up!"

From the top of the well, Matt motioned to the crew to grasp the rope and walk backwards. Dust and bits of stone flew up as the rope scraped over the edge of the limestone rim. On his knees, Matt reached down to receive the body. He grasped Brad under the arms and struggled with the dead, rigid weight.

"Oh." Meagan groaned and turned away.

Before I knew what I was doing, I rushed to Matt's side. I grabbed Brad's belt and reached for his bent legs. A garbage-like odor stung my eyes. I held my breath and narrowed my vision until I focused only on his Italian shoes. Finally, we wrestled him onto flat ground.

"Okay." Matt motioned for a stop.

The crew let the rope go slack. Most of the volunteers stared at the stiffened, bloodstained body. A few of them covered their eyes. Some, their noses. The pure, white towel hid Brad's damaged skull.

At least that image won't be part of their nightmares, I thought, hating that my dreams would feature the blood. I wished my daughter had been spared the sight. I backed away from the misshapen body and slipped my arm around Meagan's waist, holding the back of my hand to my nose. She bent into the shrubbery and vomited.

Matt loosened the knot, slipped the rope from beneath the dead man's armpits, and threw the looped end into the well. He signaled the crew. "Hold it taut."

With grim expressions, they pulled the rope tight. Cody hauled himself up and crawled over the edge of the well.

Within minutes the rangers had Brad's body wrestled into a plastic body bag and strapped into the metal basket-weave stretcher. Sarah bundled up the rope, handed it to Matt, and came to my side. I stood, trembling.

The presence of death took away all sound. The young work crew, Taylor, Meagan, Sarah, and I all stared at the neatly zipped body bag until Cody spoke. "Thank you, everyone, for your help."

We needed to hear that we had done a good thing.

"This appears to be an accident," he said. "It looks as though this man fell into the well, between twelve and twenty-four hours ago. He pulled a rock down on himself while trying to climb out."

Yes. An accident. I wanted to believe it, but I had seen the rock that caved in his skull. It was a jagged, irregular shape. The well was made of chiseled limestone slabs. It was possible, though, wasn't it, that one odd rock had been on the edge?

The assembled group nodded soberly at the ranger's pronouncement. They stared at the black body bag as if remembering the grotesque thing Brad had become.

Cody snapped the emergency supply pack closed and hoisted it to his back. "If you hear or see anything that should be included in the report, please stop in the office at Windigo."

Matt spoke up then. "I missed interviewing several of you. Please come see me before leaving the island." He added a smile. "Sarah, you coming back with us?"

"I'm staying," she announced.

Matt nodded. "Thanks, everyone." He picked up the wheelbarrow-type handles, as if the laden stretcher weighed nothing, and heaved the contraption forward on its one wheel, bumping over the rough terrain toward Siskiwit. The garbage-like smell wafted in his wake. Within minutes the two rangers were out of sight.

I was relieved to see them go. Relieved for the air to clear. For that body bag to be hauled out of the wilderness and shipped off this beautiful island. Maybe I should have at least told Matt the dead man's name. Maybe the rangers should know Brad wasn't a good guy—that he was a bully. I wondered if withholding evidence could mean jail time for me.

I sighed and promised myself to tell the whole story before I left the island for home. But first I'd try to find out what really happened and make sure my daughter wasn't a suspect. Meagan's version of events need not be told for a day or two. In the meantime, maybe a witness would come forward and the rangers would solve the crime. I could hope.

Eager to get away from the scene—especially the lingering odor—Meagan, Sarah, Taylor, and I shuffled along the trail toward Island Mine as silent as Linda's youth group ahead of us. We followed them, each lost within our own thoughts, not speaking until the air was clean, breathable.

Meagan still looked shaken and pale. She dabbed her face with a wetted, pink bandana as I walked at her side.

"That's something I don't need to see again," Taylor said from behind us.

"Whew! That smell," Sarah said in disgust. "I hate blood."

"Which makes me all the more surprised you ran here to help." I turned and gave her shoulder a gentle shove. "Thanks. Where's your stuff?"

"Stuff?" Sarah was caught off guard. "Oh, I grabbed my daypack. There's probably…"

"You weren't planning to stay, were you? You rushed here to support us and didn't think to bring gear."

"I must admit staying was a last-minute impulse." She shrugged and dismissed the problem. "Maybe Linda will have extra gear."

"We'll fix you up." I smiled at her. "Thanks for coming."

Meagan and Taylor settled themselves at our campsite's only picnic table. They talked quietly—about wolves, I suspected—about anything but the body on its way to Siskiwit. Most of the MCC crew returned to their own campsite, and Sarah wandered in that direction to ask Linda about an extra sleeping bag.

Normal began to return, but the smell of death clung to me. I needed to wash my hands.

* * *

I returned from the creek, waving my hands to dry the excess hand sanitizer. Meagan spotted me and stared at her own hands as if they suddenly offended her. I tossed her the sanitizer and she rushed down the hill.

"The water is still hot," Taylor said, motioning to the pot on the little camp stove. "Do you want tea?"

"Hot chocolate sounds like a better idea." I dumped cold tea from my mug and rummaged through the food sack for a packet of cocoa. While Taylor poured boiling water into my cup, I wondered about the handsome young biologist. What did we really know about him? Sarah had vouched for Taylor, but she'd just met him, too. Did he and Brad have a history? Maybe he heard Brad yelling from inside the well and settled an old score? Did Taylor have a passion that might drive him to violence? *Maybe if I catch him off guard*, I thought, *he'll let something slip, and the rangers will have someone else to investigate besides my daughter.*

"Did you know the man in the well?" I asked.

"No. Poor guy." Taylor sighed and shook his head. "I don't know anyone on this island except the rangers and a few volunteers. My work keeps me in the field, mostly alone." He spoke low and respectfully, as people do at funerals. "Unless he was a backpacker. Occasionally, a hiker goes off-trail and stumbles across my camp."

I thought of the yachtsman's expensive shirt and Italian shoes. "Brad was no backpacker."

Taylor nodded solemnly. "So they found I.D.?"

"What?"

"You said his name was Brad."

How stupid of me to drop the dead man's name like that. I shook off my blank stare and fumbled around for words. "Yeah, they think his name is Brad—and he's not a backpacker. He wasn't wearing hiking clothes or boots."

Taylor frowned and narrowed his eyes. "You helped drag him from the well. I guess you noticed more details than most of us."

To cover my gaffe I stirred my hot chocolate and blew the steam off its surface. "Were you in Island Mine yesterday?" I said from behind my cup.

Taylor sat up straight. Had I touched a guilty nerve?

His fingers curled into fists on the picnic table in front of him. "Not in Island Mine, but *as I said earlier,* I was east of here." He enunciated each word as if underlining them with a sharply pointed pencil. "Where I saw your daughter running."

I flinched and felt my face go white. I had offended him. Was he threatening to report Meagan? Beneath his long, thick lashes Taylor's gray eyes showed more hurt than anger. I realized I'd been flailing about for any other suspect, someone to shove under the bus—anybody other than my daughter. I let out a long breath and held out my bag of trail mix toward him as a peace offering. He waved it away brusquely.

Okay, Taylor wasn't the murderer, but did he know who was? I persisted. "Besides Meagan, did you see anyone?"

He shook his head in exasperation. "Amy. You're a terrible interrogator. You can't think I had anything to do with that man's death?"

I slumped against the table and groaned, disgusted with my inept attempt to play detective. "Sorry. Of course not, but I'm worried sick. Meagan was near the crime scene yesterday. The rangers investigating the death will question her."

"And they'll question me, too." He watched me more closely. "That doesn't mean either one of us is involved. Stop worrying."

An angelic face like his couldn't be guilty of murder. I believed his declaration of innocence and decided I owed him an explanation.

"The rangers said the man probably pulled a rock down on himself, but it looked to me like the rock was thrown down with

139

some force. So I wondered who, besides Meagan, was near the well. Maybe you saw someone?"

"I didn't see anyone near the well." A hint of worry darkened his expression. "There's no reason for the rangers to think it was Meagan…or me."

Except that she might tell them her story.

"Let me think," he said. "Yesterday I hiked here to bum fuel off the volunteer crew." He jerked a thumb toward the group site behind us. "Linda refused money for the canister, by the way, so I owe her."

I appreciated his attempt to lighten the mood. He scrunched up his face, remembering. "Very few people were on the trail on the way back to my camp, but I ran into a French woman about a mile from here. She had twisted her ankle, and I wrapped it for her." He patted his daypack at his side. "Always prepared."

"French?" That was a clue. I leaned forward to pounce on the details. "Was anyone with her? Did one of them have long, jet-black hair?"

Taylor rolled his eyes, irritated. "There was only one woman. Her hair was about this long." He gestured with his fingers at shoulder length. "Brownish, I think, sort of like yours, but more red. She said she was hiking to Siskiwit." He almost smiled. "She pronounced it—See-skee-weet."

I tried to picture the French girls at the Siskiwit shelter. The long-haired beauty stuck in my mind, but the petite girl was a blur. How would they even know Brad? Unless he cornered them, too, and they took their revenge. Did either one of them have a bandaged ankle or a limp? I couldn't remember.

"Was she upset or maybe even bloody?"

Taylor endured my interrogation. "Only from her fall. Not upset, maybe in a hurry. She was a small woman and couldn't have shoved that big guy into the well in any case, if that's what you're thinking."

I nodded as if agreeing with him, but thought him naive. A young man who sits in the woods all day observing wolves wouldn't understand the pent-up rage a violated woman might harbor, the strength her anger might give her. My adrenaline spiked just thinking of Brad fingering my buttons. There was no guessing how many women that pig had harassed and bullied. My ex-husband once confided that all men are pigs. That unhappy memory did nothing to settle my adrenaline.

Not all men, though, I thought. I glanced at the young biologist next to me. Bookish, reserved, so downright handsome he was beautiful. Was Taylor too good to be true?

* * *

Sarah returned from visiting the work crew's camp with a sleeping bag under her arm. Taylor met her on the trail and stopped to say good-bye. He motioned back at me. Sarah raised her eyebrows and put her hand on his shoulder. He likely told her that I had tried to pin the murder on him. I felt as though he was tattling to my mother. I poured myself another mug of hot water and waited for Sarah's lecture.

"That Linda is real cute," Sarah said, sitting down at the picnic table. "And nice, too. She lent me her own sleeping bag. Says she'll be warm enough tonight inside her tent with just her liner." Sarah unrolled the bag and held it to her cheek. "Goose down. I'll be fine. We're not expecting rain, are we?"

"Not that I know of."

"Good. I'll sleep under the stars over there." She pointed to the edge of the clearing. "Close enough, if you need me. Far enough away so you and Meagan don't hear me snore."

"You weren't so bad." I smiled at Sarah. "Though I did stock up on earplugs after our trip to the Grand Canyon."

She laughed with me, but then stopped and sighed. "You know, Taylor's a good guy. Why would you think he had something to do with the body in the well?"

"Because he was here yesterday."

"So everyone who was here is a suspect?" She looked at me from the corner of her eye. "The work crew? Linda?"

"Who knows." I shrugged. "I want to figure it out, so I'm asking questions. That's all."

"Cody said it was an accident. That's good enough for me."

"Not for me."

Sarah turned in her seat to face me. "When you gave your report to Matt, you left out a few details. What else do you know?" She cocked her head to the side. "What were you trying so hard not to say?"

"I answered every one of his questions," I insisted.

"You're hiding something." Sarah talked friend to friend, but I felt trapped.

She pressed on. "It has to do with Meagan, doesn't it?"

"No. Of course not." I know I should have looked Sarah in the eye, but I stared at her shoulder, then the table and the trees beyond. "How can you even think Meagan could kill a man?" I jumped up, feeling the need to fight.

"Taylor said…"

"So he's trying to incriminate my daughter, and you believe him?"

"Relax, Amy. I didn't say that, and I don't think it." Sarah took my wrist and pulled me back into my seat. She took a granola bar from her shirt pocket. "Here. Eat. You'll feel better."

I grabbed the granola bar and threw it to the ground. "Don't you patronize me! I expected help from you to find the killer. Instead, you've practically accused Meagan."

"I said it was an accident." Her words came at me hard and direct.

"But you listened to that friend of yours. Taylor." Fear for my daughter kept me ranting. "Instead of believing me, you listened to that…that…biologist!"

Sarah laughed out loud.

Her grin, hidden behind her hands, did nothing to relieve my tension. Fueled by embarrassment, my anger grew, taking control of my arms and legs. I clenched my fists. I wanted to scream my fear and anxiety at her. Instead, I stomped away. Before making my escape, I spotted Meagan at the edge of the campsite, her mouth agape. She stared at the spectacle that was her mother.

14

Crash Landing

Neither Meagan nor Sarah followed me. They must have known that I needed to burn off my adrenaline and clear my mind. My ridiculous tirade was now only an embarrassment, and my pace eventually slowed to a walk. I didn't hike far, but backtracked over the same section of trail three or four times; saw the same trees, the same slag heaps. I passed the same casual side-path and kept coming back until I was ready.

I had avoided going to the well, the place most likely to give clues to the murder. I envisioned evil spirits spewing from the well, like a geyser. Yet the scene was serene, pastoral—as I had first seen it. I ignored the trampled vegetation, the fallen fence rails, the memory of the bloody body, and willed myself to see small things, possible clues.

I stood still, feeling the history. A maple branch shadowed the edge of the small clearing. Brambles crowded in, waiting to engulf man's handiwork. Grasses grew tall. During the well's useful days, had there been more than the flat ring of limestone slabs? An oaken bucket and rope? A wall on which to rest the bucket?

Not ready to inspect the deep well, I circled around. Thick grasses, interspersed with toadflax, carpeted the area along with fallen branches and chunks of rock. Nothing human.

The well was a mere hole in the ground bolstered by a wall of limestone. I knelt at its edge and peered inside. No seepage, no moss. Dry. *How ironic. Isle Royale is surrounded by the largest lake in the world, and Island Mine has a dry well. Did the water seep away when the mines were dug?* I suspected the place had always been unlucky.

The beam of my headlamp lit the depths of the well, the stony bottom, the layered walls, the large rock. A brown stain marked the spot where Brad had met his end. I shook away the ghastly image and searched for other smaller pieces of information. My LED light revealed a bit of white. The white was at odds with the gray dirt and deep shadows. A shard of limestone? A piece of paper?

I lay on my belly and hung my arms over the limestone rim with the zoom lens of my camera extended toward the bottom of the well. The faint odor of garbage crawled up my nose. I held my breath and backed away from the edge when the shutter clicked. The digital image showed the spattered blood on the rock in good contrast, but the white item was still too small to identify.

Why hadn't the rangers seen the bit of evidence? Maybe it wasn't evidence at all, but something Cody dropped. *But if the scrap is evidence,* I argued with myself, *it could prove Meagan's innocence.*

"Don't be stupid, Amy," I said out loud, but I knew what needed to be done. I had to get into the well to check out that rock and see if the white scrap held any clues to the killer. Already, in my mind, the white thing was a paper—maybe an I.D., a torn photo, a receipt.

A rope would be useful. Heck, why not wish for a ladder?

The split-rail fencing lay scattered in the clearing looking a lot like a rungless ladder. *Worth a try.* I dragged one of the seven-foot rails to the well and tipped it over the edge. It hit bottom with a thunk. The rail leaned against the inside of the well, like a straw too short for a soda bottle. Undeterred, I heaved a second rail over the rim. *Not bad.*

The plan was to slide my boots along the rails and gradually lower myself into the well. I planted a foot on the rail and felt it bow beneath my weight. I bounced a bit and the rail held, but prickles of fear irritated the nape of my neck. Suddenly, my boot slid, and I grabbed for the rocks lining the edge of the well. I darted a glance around the clearing. Thankful no one had witnessed my embarrassing slip, I dabbed sweat from my upper lip and steadied myself.

I ignored the pain in my elbow and tested the makeshift ladder again. With one hand on each side wall, I balanced my feet on the wood and inched my way down. *This should be easy,* I thought. As a kid I could shimmy up between door jambs like a monkey.

I was no longer a kid, and my shoulders quivered with exertion. My boot slid down the slick railings and my arms gave way. Gravity took over, and I crashed the last five feet to the bottom.

"Stupid!" I leaned against the cool stone wall to catch my breath and take stock of my body parts. The wood had broken my fall, but my hip and elbow had taken a beating. My foot, wedged between the two rails at an odd angle, gave me a scare, but I was more irritated than hurt. I switched on my headlamp and struggled to my feet to brush myself off. The smell nearly knocked me down again. I pulled my shirt over my nose.

Pain stung my hands. Splintered wood was embedded in my fingers, and I picked at them while glancing around the narrow space. The paper had disappeared. I looked up to get my bearings and shuffled my boots in the dust and bits of limestone. The paper I had risked my life to retrieve was nowhere to be seen. I turned in circles, shining my light over the hard-packed ground. My eyes must have played tricks on me. I looked for stones or leaves that might have mimicked paper. Nothing.

Like an elephant in the corner, the bloodstained rock—the size of a squared-off bowling ball—sat to one side. I bent to study it. My light reflected off tiny flecks on the surface. Definitely not limestone, maybe quartz or granite, like those hidden in the tall grass up there. I took pictures from several angles, but would have to leave the murder weapon for the rangers to retrieve.

Exasperated with the phantom paper, I prepared to go back up. The splinters in my hands burned with each touch, but I repositioned the rough wooden rails at less of an angle to give my boots better footing.

I kicked the end of the length of wood to wedge it against the wall. A bit of white caught my eye. The fragment of smudged and ragged paper must have been beneath the rail, driven into the dust when the rail hit the bottom of the well. I snatched up the scrap as if it might get away again.

* * *

With the evidence that could save my daughter tucked in my pocket, I mounted the broken rails to save myself.

But no matter how I stretched and jumped, the rim above remained more than two feet beyond my fingertips. Again and again, I braced my arms between opposite walls and dragged my weight up only to have my arms give way. I jumped down, clear of the wood and the rock, and stood exhausted at bottom of that hole, staring up at the other world, the circle of blue sky. My shoulders ached. My fingers smarted.

"Hey! Anybody out there?" The shouts bounced around the inside the well. After the echo died, I listened for footsteps or an answering call.

"Fire!" I yelled, having read that people can hear the word "fire" more clearly.

"Help!" That didn't work either.

Unless a hiker happened to be near the clearing at that moment, shouting was useless. I balled up my fists and tried good lusty screaming until the veins in the side of my neck bulged.

Meagan and Sarah would wait at the campsite until dinner time before they worried enough to search for me, but where would they look? Had I known my destination, I wouldn't have told them anyway. I kicked myself for the tantrum that made me stalk off. I should have at least left my bandana or fanny pack on the trail as a signal.

Fanny pack. I unbuckled it from my belt and rummaged through the miscellaneous clutter inside, hoping I hadn't left my emergency supplies in my main pack. Duct tape, lighter, first aid—whistle. I took a deep breath and blew. The shrill blast in the concentrated space made me wince. I covered my ears and whistled again. And again.

I trained my eyes on the blue sky and listened for voices. The sound of my heartbeat ticked off the seconds. Every few minutes I blew another series of SOS tweets until my mouth went dry, and I began to wish the well hadn't dried up years ago.

"Don't panic," I told myself. "They'll come."

What if they didn't? Darkness was two or three hours away, and the thought of spending the night in that stinking grave sent chills across my shoulders. I blew the whistle until dust collected on my tongue.

Needing a break, I sat on the bloodstained rock and forced myself to wait. *Patience is a virtue*, my mother had quoted. What would she do? Stay busy, that's what. The slivers in my fingers needed tending, so I switched on my headlamp and poked at them with tweezers from my first-aid kit. Several of the splinters were large enough to grasp, others were too embedded.

A pebble fell on the bill of my cap. I looked upward and caught a glimpse of a shadow disappearing from the rim of the well.

"Hello!" I jumped to my feet. "Help! I'm down here!"

I heard only faint movements. Maybe an animal had wandered by—a raccoon? No, bigger. Maybe a curious wolf had picked up the smell of death, sniffed the well, and run off. Maybe a moose grazed in the grass.

"Hey!" I blasted the whistle again, probably scaring the poor moose away from his meal. My stomach rumbled. I sat down on the rock, disheartened, and regretted that I had thrown Sarah's granola bar to the ground.

I found the tweezers in the dirt and settled myself to resume picking at my inflamed fingers. Suddenly, sound crashed around me. Panicked, I wanted to run, but didn't know where to or what from. The fence rails bucked and jumped as a large rock ricocheted off them, against the stone wall, and landed at my feet.

"Hey!" I screamed. "What are you doing? You're going to kill me!" With a start, I realized that was the intent. I stared at the new chunk of granite in disbelief and then up at the mouth of the well. Dust hung in the air and stung my eyes. I froze, listening. *Good God. He's going to throw another one!*

I hefted the bloodstained rock above my head to protect my skull, then crouched against the wall and beneath the wooden rails. Seconds later another hunk of granite hurtled into the well, careening off stone walls. I cringed, waiting for pain.

Wood splinters flew. Debris rained down.

All went silent. I should play dead. Easy. Beneath the broken rails I let my body slump with Brad's rock resting on my head. It got heavier by the moment. I held my breath.

My life passed in front of me while I played dead; my kids, my friends, even my ex-husband at my funeral, the lovely eulogy. An eternity went by. I warned myself that the silence might be a lure. I tried to stretch an eyeball toward the entrance of the well without twitching a muscle lest he was there—like a deer hunter in a blind, watching and waiting to snuff out signs of life.

Scraping sounds came from above. I stopped breathing. Bits of dirt and grit sifted down. I was certain he could see my pulsing veins.

Horrible screams clawed through the silence. It sounded like a woman being murdered. Like my Meagan being... My eyes flew to the top of the well. No one was there, but the screaming continued.

"Meagan!" I shoved aside the heavy rock and sprung from beneath the pieces of wooden rails.

"Meagan!" I had to draw him away from her. My hysterical anguish filled the dusty air. I wanted him to hear me. I wanted him to throw more rocks. I dug my fingernails in, trying to scale the rocky walls.

"Meagan!"

"Amy!" Sarah's voice reached through my hysteria. "It's me."

I stopped clawing the wall and looked up. Sarah's face was silhouetted against the blue sky. "Where's Meagan?" I shrieked.

Sarah turned away and drew my daughter to her side. "Look." Sarah pointed down at me. "She's alive."

Meagan peered over the edge with her knuckles pressed into her cheeks. "Mom!" She bawled. Her tremors almost toppled her into the well. Sarah embraced her, held my daughter, made her safe. I leaned back and slid down the wall, exhausted.

"Mom." Meagan's voice was a mere whisper. "Are you hurt?"

She lay at the top of the well with her arms stretched down to me. I stood up and reached for her hand. Our fingertips were still more than a foot apart, but it felt good.

"Well, I have splinters in my hands, but otherwise I'm fine."

"You were lying still with a bloody rock on your head. I thought you… You looked like him. Why are you down there?"

I'd save most of the story for later. "Evidence," I said and waved the scrap of paper up at Meagan. "Ask Sarah to help me get out of here, will you? I've been here long enough."

"We'll get you out." Meagan hid her nose in the crook of her elbow. "Sarah ran to the work crew's camp to get a rope or something."

"Sarah's not up there with you?"

"No, she went to get help."

"Meagan. Stand up and make sure no one is around. Get your knife out and don't let anyone get near you."

"You're scaring me, Mom."

"Just do it."

Meagan stood guard. I imagined her up there with her blade in one hand and a stout stick in the other. We called words of encouragement back and forth as she paced around the clearing, waiting for reinforcements. With help on the way and Meagan on alert, I thought about what had happened.

Why would someone want to kill me? Obviously, there was a connection to Brad's death. The similar circumstances could not have been a coincidence. Because I asked questions? Did the killer think I knew more than I did? The killer obviously heard me screaming and used my predicament to end my questioning. But why? Who knew I was asking questions? Who was in the area? Taylor. Linda and her crew. Maybe the French women hiked back this way.

The questions swirled around, sending chills through my veins. "Meagan?"

"I'm here."

"Honey, do you have a jacket? The cold is getting to me."

"Sorry, Mom. I don't. You'll be warm when we pull you out of there." She stood at the rim of the well with her knife in her hand. "Are you going to tell me what happened? From whom am I guarding us?"

"Stay on alert, Meagan." I pointed my finger up at her. "I don't know who, but someone heaved these rocks down at me. It was no accident. Whoever it was tried to kill me just like Brad was killed."

Meagan's mouth dropped open. She put a hand to her forehead and closed her eyes. "This is all my fault. I started it."

"Stop it, Meagan," I scolded. "All you did was protect yourself."

"I know." She bobbed her head slowly. "You don't have to try to keep it a secret any more. After I saw you and Sarah arguing, I told her everything."

Relief eased my mind and warmed me. "Thank you. I'm not good at dancing around the truth. What did Sarah say?"

My daughter almost laughed. "She sounded just like you."

"Good advice then, huh?" I smiled up at Meagan's silhouette. "Now get back on guard so whoever tried to kill me doesn't try again."

Her head jerked up and she raised her jackknife. "Someone's coming," she hissed.

Meagan disappeared from the mouth of the well, leaving me alone with my worry. I bit my lip and listened.

Thirty harrowing seconds later, my daughter reappeared. "They're here." Even nine feet below ground the relief in Meagan's voice reached me.

Seconds later, Sarah knelt at the edge of the well with her hands on her knees. "What are you doing down there?" she asked with an amused smirk.

"Someone tried to kill her," Meagan snapped.

Sarah jumped to her feet. She and my daughter drew away from the edge while Meagan summarized my story.

Linda listened, but stayed with me. She signaled to her silent crew. Soon the end of a rope came over the edge.

I grabbed for the lifeline. Sarah's angry face appeared above me and urged me to knot the end around my boot. Linda signaled the crew to pull the rope taut.

I tested my footing. "I'm ready."

Careful to avoid pinching my finger between rope and rock, I allowed myself to be hauled upward. The lifeline lurched, lost ground, and lurched again. I imagined Linda's group above— young people straining at the rope as if they were in a high school tug-of-war, but solemn and earnest. Embarrassed by my weight and the trouble I'd brought upon them, I tried to help by searching for a toehold. I succeeded only in twisting around and banging my shoulder against the wall.

Friction sizzled and frayed the rope against the sharp limestone edge as I hung like a giant carp being lugged into a boat. Dirt and bits of stone rained down. Unable to shield my eyes, I ducked my head and waited.

At the rim, Sarah and Meagan yanked at my arms and dragged me by the seat of my pants across the lip of stone. Sharp rock bit through my thin nylon slacks. To mask a cry of pain, I grunted as if in the exertion of getting my body over the edge.

Finally, I rolled on my back on flat ground. The cramped circle of sky, which had been my view for an hour, spread into a vast and wonderful canopy. My bones ached from the fall, abrasions marked my elbows, thighs, and shins, but the air smelled sweet. Giddy with relief at being free of ropes and rock walls, I laughed at the absurdity of the situation. The simplicity of my release was staggering when compared to the terror I had experienced.

Meagan's frown of concern turned into a wry grin, and she hauled me to my feet. She trembled within my embrace, while Linda and her crew smiled and stepped forward to pat my back. One young man stood to the side, reeling in the rope.

"Where is Sarah?" I asked Meagan.

"She ran off that way." She pointed toward the nearest slag heap, beyond the gaggle of teenagers. "Probably looking for whoever did this to you. If she finds him, he's dead."

I had no doubt an enraged Sarah would be a formidable opponent in a fair fight, but what if the coward ambushed her with a rock—or had a gun? I scanned the woods. Thick foliage gave ample cover to wolves, lost mines, and stalkers—to Sarah.

Should I go after her or stay to protect my daughter?

My decision was made for me. Sarah's angry voice broke the forest silence. "Coward! You come near us again, and I'll beat the crap out of you!"

Linda's head jerked toward the sound. She flashed a signal to her work crew. They froze in place, like deer caught in open field. I

153

riveted my eyes in the direction of Sarah's threat, listening for a response, ready to run to her aid.

Meagan grabbed my arm. "Stay here."

We heard the distant cracking of branches.

"Sarah!" I yelled into the thick woods. "Are you okay?"

As the sound of snapping twigs and rustling leaves came closer, I stepped in front of my daughter and scanned the edge of the forest.

"Yeah." A frustrated Sarah broke into the clearing, breathing hard and red in the face. "I'm fine."

Relieved to see her alone, I met her in the knee-high grass. "What's going on?"

"There was movement back there." She stood with her hands on her hips, still glaring into the deep woods. "We could all fan out and track down the guy." She turned to look at the work crew.

"Oh no," Linda said. "These kids are my responsibility. I can't put them in danger." She positioned her body between Sarah and the youth group as if to protect them with her life.

Sarah raised her hands in surrender. "No, of course not, but a guy who'd throw Amy into the well is a danger to everyone." She draped her arm around the group leader's shoulder. "But you're right. Keep your group together, and they'll be safe."

Linda relaxed, released herself from Sarah's friendly hold, and went to round up her anxious charges.

"What'd he look like, Amy?" Sarah asked while watching Linda sign to her young workers. "Did you ever see him before?"

"I never saw him at all," I said. "And, for the record, he didn't throw me in the well, I climbed down."

"Are ya kidding me?" Sarah threw open her hands and gaped at me.

"I thought I could do it." Hating to admit my lack of common sense, I fumbled for my excuse. "There was a scrap of paper down there, and I thought..." My weak explanation trailed off. I found the bit of evidence in my pocket and held it up. Most likely the paper was nothing but litter, and my climb into the well had been foolhardy.

"Evidence?" Sarah asked. "Shouldn't you leave a crime scene alone for the rangers to investigate?"

"They've labeled it an accident," I reminded her, defending myself with little enthusiasm. "I thought they were done with their investigation here. Besides, the next rain would have ruined this paper."

Sarah looked askance at the scrap. "What is it?" she asked, moving closer to get a better view.

"Someone tore off the end of an envelope." I ran my finger along the smooth edge of the quality stationery. "There's even part of a logo showing." The remains of the embossed picture appeared to be the tip of a hook, maybe the fluke of an old-fashioned anchor.

"Good find, Mom." Meagan nodded, staring at the design. "Maybe rich people have stationery printed for their yachts." She held out a tissue into which I placed the scrap.

I smiled at my daughter for her support and tucked the evidence into my shirt pocket. "Let's get back to camp. Linda already has her crew rounded up."

Sarah didn't move. Concentration put a frown on her face. "Why would anyone carry an envelope into the wilderness?"

"Exactly," I said. "And why would part of it be left in the well? Maybe Brad delivered a letter, his killer wasn't happy, and sent a rock down on him in response."

The three of us pondered the situation as we walked. Linda hurried her youth group ahead, and we quickened our pace to keep up. Safety in numbers. Whoever killed Brad wouldn't dare threaten such a large group. Or so I thought.

15

Group Camping

I recognized their noise before I saw them. The creaky voices of adolescents whose hormones hadn't yet decided what to do with them. Wyatt careened down the path, chased by a fellow scout, until he and his exuberance screeched to a halt in front of the line of silent work crew members. The chastened boys yielded the trail to the crew.

"Hello, Wyatt," I said as I came abreast of the scouts standing off to the side. The MCC group continued the trek toward their camp, but Meagan and I stopped to greet the boys like old friends. They didn't remember us.

"So who are these scrappy young men?" Sarah's hearty camaraderie caused Wyatt's friend to step backwards.

Trying to ease the boy's discomfort, I said quietly, "These are two of the scouts who came to our rescue and chased off the bad guy back at Siskiwit."

Wyatt's freckled face brightened with recognition and both scouts swaggered a bit. Wyatt's eyes searched the ground behind me. "Where's your dog?"

"Remington's sailing around on one of those fancy boats," I said and nodded in the direction of the big lake. "His real owner missed him."

The scout's disappointment didn't last long. He chattered on about the troop's hike to Daisy Farm and the moose they spotted at

Chicken Bone Lake. The young man might have talked our ears off if the remainder of his troop hadn't shown up to intervene.

"Hello again," Mr. Domkowski called from behind his group of teenagers. He waded through his boys with a big smile, and I introduced him to Sarah. While the scouts wandered further down the trail, the leader shook hands all around as if running for office or simply in love with his life. "Good to see you again. No more trouble, I hope."

The jovial man lost his good humor as we filled him in on the body found in the well and my near-miss less than two hours earlier. His thick brows joined above the bridge of his nose.

"Boys!" Mr. Domkowski bellowed.

Unused to a demanding tone from their affable leader, the scouts pricked up their ears and gathered around.

"No more exploring today," he told them. "We're headed back to camp. Conor, take the lead."

The scouts grumbled and groused, but turned toward the group site at Island Mine, unmindful of lurking danger. Their leader spoke in a low voice. "Maybe you should camp in our clearing."

I checked Sarah's and Meagan's reactions. "Don't worry. There are three of us and the work crew is nearby."

"Well, whistle if you need help." He increased his volume for the boys' benefit. "Come by for dessert at least." He herded his scouts up the trail, but he'd lost his carefree saunter. "The boys are making chocolate pudding," he called over his shoulder. "There'll be plenty—if you come early."

* * *

Sarah, Meagan and I stayed close together while filtering water at the creek and kept each other company while preparing our dinners. Peace had returned to Island Mine. Crimson maple leaves quivered in the mild breeze. Small birds, maybe junco or thrush, foraged on the forest floor. To the west, the MCC crew was a quiet bunch—no doubt worn out from their day's labor and their efforts to haul me up from the well. The boisterous scout troop to the east was too far away to disturb our tranquility. Lengthening shadows and quiet invited the eeriness of Island Mine to surface.

The three of us relived the day's events in near whispers. We donned jackets and sat at the picnic bench with mugs of hot tea in our hands, waiting for our packaged meals to rehydrate. Still, I shivered as I told and retold the details of my harrowing experience. Throughout the telling, my daughter kept contact with me—a light touch, her thigh against mine. Whether it was to comfort herself or to protect me didn't matter. I needed her near.

"I'm sorry, Mom. We should have started searching for you sooner. If we hadn't heard your whistle…"

"Well, you did and arrived right on time." I patted her knee. "Thank you."

The first of the evening's voracious mosquitoes buzzed around our heads. I slathered on the Deet, stinging my splinter wounds in the process, and handed the repellant to Meagan. "You didn't see anyone running away from the well?"

"Not a soul," Meagan said. She slapped at a mosquito on her cheek. "He probably heard us coming down the trail. He must have been right there." She shuddered and grimaced.

Sarah frowned while stirring her rice and chicken. "We should have seen him," she said. "I guess we were fixated on that dang well. I figured you were investigating again and had to have gone there."

We sat in silence for a while, perhaps reliving events—or conjuring new ones with more ghastly outcomes.

"I thought Brad was the bad guy," Sarah said. "Maybe he was just a jerk."

"Or one bad guy killed the other bad guy—and then tried to stop me from asking questions." I was depressed and had had enough. I wanted to hike back to Windigo and catch the next boat to the mainland. I held my tongue. Maybe my low blood sugar sapped all my energy and stole my resolve.

"So, someone else attacked Deborah," Sarah continued, "or it was Brad, and an even more vicious person cracked his skull." Sarah took her turn with the Deet. "The killer must have been thrilled to find Brad trapped in the well."

Poor Meagan sat with her head hung low. I darted a look at Sarah to squelch that part of the conversation.

"I'm just sayin'," Sarah said.

After dinner, more able to think with my stomach full, I pondered how the events of the past few days had started with the stapler attack on Deborah and with her computer list. "Hey, Sarah, when I jumped on the boat with Matt and Cody, did you know what I was trying to tell you when I was pointing frantically at the other boat?"

Sarah's blank look told me she hadn't a clue. "I thought you were waving."

"The boat pulling into the harbor was named *Spending Their Inheritance*. Where have we seen that phrase before?"

Sarah blinked twice before realization dawned. "Ohhh. On Deborah's list of—"

"Boat names," Meagan cried.

"Exactly."

We both looked at Sarah expectantly, but she screwed up her face.

I filled in the silence. "I had hoped you could survey other boats in the harbor to see if their names were on the list."

"Sorry." Sarah bowed her head as if she had disappointed me. "Zak kept me busy."

"Don't worry about it. We'll do a survey when we get to Windigo tomorrow." I patted her knee. "How about we wander down to the scout camp. I get such a kick out of those little guys. It'll be our evening entertainment."

"I'm in." Sarah perked up. "It's too early to even think about hitting the sack."

"I'm not staying here alone," Meagan said, getting up and shoving her eating utensils into her pack.

"Bring your spoon," Sarah said. "I hear there is pudding being served."

Meagan shook her head at Sarah's immutable humor and stuck her spoon in her pocket.

* * *

Our timing was impeccable. Conor and several of the older scouts had just returned from the stream where they had submerged several zip-locked bags of pudding to cool. Proud of their chocolate concoction, they offered us the first servings. We each took a spoonful and pronounced the dessert delicious.

While the boys doled out pudding to the troop, the two adult leaders invited us to sit at a picnic table. Domkowski and the other dad shot questions at us about the body in the well and the attack on me. When our story wound down, the usually cheerful leader frowned and stroked his heavy jowl.

"I wonder if the abandoned gear over there is connected somehow." Domkowski glowered as if imagining the killer had walked this very ground.

We all looked in the direction of his gesture, across the clearing at a haphazard pile of camping equipment amidst the row of neatly erected scout tents.

"Quality gear, just dumped there," the co-leader said. "It was here when we arrived late yesterday. We figured someone would claim it today."

"Do you mind if I take a look?"

"Be my guest." Mr. Domkowski heaved himself to his feet. "I have to suggest a competition to the patrol leader. The boys are getting bored."

Sarah was already on her way across the clearing, Meagan and I followed behind.

Domkowski was right. The backpack and other gear was name-brand stuff. It looked as if its owner had upended the pack and left the equipment where it fell. Beneath the large pack lay a blue tent, half constructed, its fiberglass poles disjointed like a collapsed skeleton.

A main strut caught my attention.

"I know this tent." I untangled the pole from an unrolled sleeping bag and ran my hand over the duct tape. "It belongs to Patrick Kinzler. Valerie broke this pole, and I gave him the tape."

Sarah whistled softly. "You mean, the husband of the woman with all the bling?"

"Yep."

Meagan shook miscellaneous gear off and picked up the empty pack. "This looks familiar, too." She was right. It was his, though the lantern and all the unnecessary luxuries that had dangled from the pack were gone.

"What is his stuff doing here?" I wondered aloud. "I thought that after their ordeal at Feldtmann Lake, Patrick and Valerie would never camp again."

"Maybe the gear was stolen from them," Meagan guessed.

"And then the thief dumped it here?" I didn't think so. I examined a pricey little water-sterilizing pen, fought off gear envy, and slipped it into a pocket of Patrick's pack.

Sarah read the manufacturer's wrapper on a technically advanced neoprene sleeping pad and shook her head. "Maybe the shrew kicked him off that fancy yacht, and he tried hiking back to Windigo."

"Then where is he?" I asked.

"I don't know." Sarah shoved the sleeping pad in with the other gear. "He got disgusted and kept walking without the stuff? Who knows."

"That sounds like something Patrick's wife would do," Meagan said. "Maybe she dropped this stuff here."

"Are ya kidding me?" Sarah sniffed. "That little princess couldn't have carried a fifty-pound pack."

I knew I couldn't carry that much weight—not the distance from Siskiwit, anyway. I sat on the ground staring at the pile of camping equipment as if it could send me answers to the questions buzzing around in my brain. Did the backpack prove Patrick was in Island Mine? That would place one more person near the well. One more person for the investigators to question about the body.

"Uh oh," Sarah said. "I can see you're hatching a plan."

"No plan," I said. "I was trying to figure why Patrick had been here. Could he have had anything to do with the murder? He seemed too mild-mannered."

"Big men can afford to look mild," Meagan said. "Their size is intimidating enough. Maybe Brad somehow met Valerie—they were both boat owners. He worked his smarmy charm on her, and Patrick tracked him to Island Mine in a jealous rage."

Patrick obviously loved his wife, was even cowed by the woman. But murder? That didn't fit the man I'd met. "And where's Brad's boat? It wasn't docked at Siskiwit when I came in yesterday." I looked at Sarah for confirmation.

"No big, white yacht in the bay this morning either," she said, "though I was in a rush to get here and may not have been at my most observant."

"He could have left it at Rock Harbor or Windigo and hiked to Island Mine," Meagan suggested.

My daughter's explanation was plausible, but I shook my head at the unlikely idea of Brad's fancy shoes surviving such long treks. We had run out of ideas, so we stuffed Patrick's tent into its sack, rolled the sleeping bag, and crammed miscellaneous items into his backpack.

"Gad. Look at this fancy GPS unit." I shook my head at the extravagance of his equipment and handed it to Sarah to tuck into one of the pack's outside pockets. A flash of white caught my attention. "Wait, there's something in there."

Sarah pulled a folded business envelope from the pocket. She arched her brows and handed the envelope to me. No addressee. The paper was the same fine linen quality as the scrap I had found in the well, but this envelope was whole, no torn edges. I ran my fingers over the embossed lettering in the upper left-hand corner and the raised ink of the logo, a ship's anchor.

"Patrick Kinzler," I read. "Ludington, Michigan. He was here. This ties him to the body in the well." The thought depressed me. I had judged him to be a gentle man.

"So, open it," Sarah prompted.

"I shouldn't even be touching it."

"Too late," she said.

True.

Sarah's dark curls bobbed up and down, urging me to lift the unsealed flap. Meagan gave me a single nod. Curiosity guided my fingers. The envelope contained a check, business-size, made of blue safety paper with the same anchor logo in the upper left-hand corner next to the account owners, Patrick and Valerie Kinzler. The signature was a mere scribble.

From over my shoulder Meagan read the firm, square letters on the payee line. "It's made out to Erik Jansson."

Where had I heard that name before? I thought for a moment, and recalled Valerie's strident voice demanding her dog be returned to her. "Erik Jansson is the name of the Kinzlers' boat captain," I said.

"Huh," Sarah said. "His paycheck would have been ruined in the next rain. He'll be thankful we found it."

"It will be good news/bad news when we deliver the check to him," I said.

The words "severance pay" were slashed across the perforated check stub in dark, angry ink. "Patrick intends to fire Captain Jansson."

16

Widow Maker

In the deep woods, dusk disintegrated into night without warning. The moon, if there was one out there beyond the canopy of trees, was no help. Pinpoints of light flitted around like fireflies in the clearing as the scouts prepared for night. Darkness muffled their voices.

"Time to go," Sarah announced.

"Let's leave the backpack here," I suggested. "Patrick—or whoever left it—may come back."

"If it's still here when we leave in the morning, I'll carry it back to Windigo," Sarah said. "If we don't find Patrick or Erik Jansson, it goes into lost-and-found."

After I returned the paycheck to its pocket, Sarah hefted the pack onto a stout branch to keep the expensive gear off the ground and away from curious critters. We said our farewells to Mr. Domkowski and his boys and headed toward our own camp.

Shadows stole our sight, except for the beams from our headlamps lighting the path ahead of our feet. Odd how distances seem longer in the silent dark. Walking required more focus. Still, I would enjoy the quarter-mile hike, the insulation of the night, the knowledge that nocturnal animals were out and about—except for the possibility of a murderer among them.

Sarah led the way. Meagan and I were inches behind her. Suddenly, a sharp crack shattered the silence. We froze in mid-stride. The sound seemed to come from nowhere, and from everywhere.

"What was that?" Meagan grabbed my arm.

"Sounded like a gunshot," I dared to answer, "but far away."

"Shhh," Sarah demanded. "Listen."

We crouched low, waiting.

Another shot rang out.

I knocked Meagan to the ground and protected her with my arm across her back. The three of us huddled in the dirt, breathing the same hot air. I hid my headlamp beneath me. They did the same.

"That one was louder," I whispered. "Closer."

Minutes passed. We heard nothing more.

Sarah moved to stand, and I reached to pull her down.

"We're overreacting," she said, though she was still hunched in a wary stance, ready to bolt. "It was probably a tree popping."

"What?" Meagan and I hissed in unison.

"All this murder stuff has rattled me, but that sounded like a tree popping somewhere." Sarah huffed and stood straighter. "When a branch gets too heavy for the tree, it pulls away from the trunk. Strands of cellulose stretch and snap like rubber bands. Sounds like a gunshot."

"Wouldn't we hear crashing branches?" I tried to reconcile the sound of gunfire with her explanation.

"Maybe the tree is a mile away or maybe the limb will crash tomorrow." Her voice was stronger, more confident. "That's what it was."

I wanted to believe her and got myself off the ground.

Without further incident, our short hike ended when my beam of light fell upon our yellow tent sitting alone in the quiet clearing. I was ready for the security and cozy warmth of my sleeping bag, though I realized that safety was more psychological than real.

Thin nylon walls would not stop bullets or deter rock-throwing murderers, but they allowed me to keep that illusion.

Sarah would spend the night under the stars, and I didn't envy that decision. Without a tent, Sarah's only concession to the elements was a head net to stave off hungry mosquitoes. She spread her borrowed sleeping bag fifteen feet from our tent and bade us good night. Meagan and I were still talking and jostling for position when we heard Sarah's raspy snores.

I switched off the light and punched my pillowcase filled with clothes into a comfortable shape before snuggling down into my bag. Meagan lay on her back, staring at the dome of the tent.

"Mom?"

"What, honey?"

"Thanks for believing I didn't kill that man."

"Don't even think such thoughts, Meagan."

She rolled over in her sleeping bag. The noise of rustling nylon filled the tent. When she settled in, my daughter whispered, "And thanks for not being dead in the bottom of that hole."

"My pleasure." I laughed softly. "Good night, Meagan."

* * *

Hours later something yanked me from a thick sleep. My eyes flew open. I stared at blackness, trying to identify the sound. Meagan lay rigid and quiet beside me.

"What was that?" she whispered.

"I don't know." I held my breath, listening. Waiting for a clue.

In quick succession, two rifle shots tore through the silence, as if a gunman stood next to the tent firing across our camp site. Three more shots exploded.

"Crap!"

"Sarah? What is it?" I yelled in near panic.

"A tree is falling! Right here," she screeched.

In an instant, a series of explosive pops overwhelmed the night. *Run!* my brain told me, but I lay in my bed paralyzed with fear. I thought only to protect my daughter. I flung myself over her and pulled my knees up tight. We clung to each other like twins in the womb, not breathing, not even praying. There was no time.

Deafening sounds obliterated thoughts from my brain. Snapping. Creaking. Crashing. A thunderous thud vibrated through my bones. My air mattress bounced. Meagan cried out.

Then, silence. I held my breath waiting for the next crash, listening.

The earth was still.

Meagan whimpered, her breath hot and moist on my neck.

"Are you okay, honey?" I dare not think otherwise.

"Think so," she whispered.

Her heart pounded against my ear. I pushed myself off Meagan, but an unyielding surface pressed against my back. A knob poked at my spine. A black mitten seemed to be pressed against my eyes. I felt bound, compressed, as if zipped into a body bag. We struggled to untangle ourselves from our sleeping bags, from collapsed tent poles and fabric, from each other.

"I think I can move this way." Meagan grunted. "No, I can't get my legs out."

From the inside, I managed to pull the zipper on my mummy bag down several inches and snake my right arm out. There seemed to be room above our heads and I wiggled in that direction, but the nylon wall held me fast. "The tent zipper is on your side, Meagan. See if you can…"

Smaller twigs and branches cracked amid a confusion of frantic thrashing. I held my breath and felt Meagan stiffen. "Shhh," I whispered next to her ear. An erratic beam of light grazed the blackness, roaming back and forth. The yellow tent fabric glowed.

"Amy! Holy crap," Sarah cried. "Meagan!"

"Sarah," I called. "We're here."

"We're okay!" Meagan kicked in frustration at the tent fabric. "Get us out of here."

"You're not hurt?" Sarah's voice was pitched high in disbelief. "You're okay?"

"I think so." Though I hadn't done a checklist of all my parts. "We're stuck, caught in something."

"Branches. Tree branches flattened your tent." Her breathy words were accompanied by the sound of logs hitting dirt. "I'll dig you out."

Meagan and I struggled in darkness against the bondage and a claustrophobic feeling that brought sweat to the surface of my skin. "Can you get to that zipper?" I asked Meagan.

"I'm trying."

Each yank of the zipper jerked the tent fabric that bound us together. Suddenly, the solid mass at my back shifted, jabbing my shoulder and pushing me further into my daughter. Branches and limbs scraped against each other, shifting, rolling. I cried out in alarm.

"Oh crap," Sarah gasped.

All sound ceased.

"Are you guys okay?"

Meagan tensed next to me. "Yeah," she breathed.

"It's getting tight in here," I called out to Sarah.

"The tree is shifting." Panic was evident in her voice. "I'd better not pull out any more branches. The whole thing may roll." Her light beam bounced erratically as if attached to a spider monkey.

"Don't move," I called out to Sarah. "Do you have your knife with you?"

"Yes, yes, of course."

I heard the soft hiss of the blade sliding from its leather sheath on her belt. "Slit the tent—here." I poked a finger of my free hand into the nylon wall until Sarah's beam of light zeroed in on the area.

"Hold still," Sarah demanded. She grasped the taut fabric and pricked the nylon. I felt an improbable sense of loss as Sarah's four-inch blade sliced through my faithful tent. Cool air rushed into the opened space. Breathing became easier. Meagan and I both sucked in big gulps of relief.

"You'd better cut the rest," Sarah said. "I don't want to nick you."

I shredded what I could reach of the yellow nylon and handed the knife to Meagan. With each slash we were less constrained until, finally, I crawled from my mummy bag and to my knees amid a tangle of tent poles, pine needles, and branches. Under Sarah's spotlight my daughter and I played a dangerous game of Twister as we extricated ourselves from the tree, which shifted with each branch broken in our escape.

Sarah dragged me over the last of the dying limbs and into her embrace. "I can't believe you're alive." She then gathered Meagan in her arms. I heard a small sigh escape my daughter as she accepted our friend's hug.

Belated fear clutched at my heart. "Sarah, you were sleeping right there. How did you not—get…?" I thrust aside the image of her crushed beneath the pine tree.

"I ran." She paused for a moment to clear her throat and seemed to have trouble getting words to come. "The popping started. I grabbed my light. I saw that monster coming at me and jumped out of the way." She lowered her voice to a whisper. "When I couldn't see your tent, I thought…I thought…" She cleared her throat again.

We leaned against each other at the side of the massive pine, wondering at our survival. The beam of Sarah's light wandered back and forth over the crown of the ancient giant. I shuddered and stared. Ordinarily, I would mourn the death of such a venerable living thing, but this one had tried to take us with it.

* * *

My adrenaline dissipated as we waited for dawn. Wool socks and long johns were no longer enough to keep a body warm, so Meagan and I poked amid the tent wreckage for our clothing. Sarah made coffee, and we all huddled with our backs against a log under a salvaged sleeping bag. Sarah, who could sleep anywhere, dozed.

Morning's light came by inches. In silent vigil Meagan and I monitored dawn's progress, side by side, her head upon my shoulder. A heavy mist resisted the new day. Dew formed on every level surface, pooled, and dropped to the ground. From within the fog, the fallen behemoth appeared. We roused ourselves to inspect the massive white pine.

Sarah whistled beneath her breath. "How big do you think that thing is?"

"Fifty feet, maybe more," I whispered.

I gawked at the near-miss. The twenty-four inch trunk had crashed to earth between our tent and where Sarah had lain on the ground. On one side, shredded yellow nylon showed beneath the brush pile protected from the pine's weight by a tripod of limbs. On the other, a thick branch skewered Sarah's borrowed sleeping bag into the dirt.

My bold, courageous friend set her jaw and blanched.

Meagan slipped her hand through the crook of Sarah's elbow. The three of us stood shoulder to shoulder and marveled at the miracle, each with our own thoughts, but sharing the moment, our reprieve.

Clinking metal and marching feet caused us to turn. Yellow helmets bobbed above the bushes along the trail leading from the work crew's summer home. The MCC group stopped and gaped at our devastated campsite. Linda paled and covered her open mouth with her hand as she looked from the ruined tree to Sarah and back again.

"Sorry about your sleeping bag," Sarah said. "I'll get you a new one."

Linda took a few tremulous steps toward the crown of the massive pine. "I'm so sorry." She directed her words to Sarah. "It would have been my fault if you—if you hadn't escaped."

"Your fault?" Sarah tilted her head and draped her arm over the younger woman's shoulders. "Hey, we're okay. Trees fall. It's no one's fault."

Linda looked on the verge of tears. "That pine was scheduled to be cut down at the end of the season." The shocked woman shook her head. "I judged that it wouldn't be a danger until next year. Me!—I reported its condition. I'm so sorry." Her doleful gaze met Sarah's. "You could have been killed."

"But we weren't," Sarah said. "It's crazy to put blame on yourself."

I was struck by the connection between these two strong, independent women. Lean, muscular, nut-brown Linda, with her hard hat and the heavy tools of her trade, being comforted by big, gregarious Sarah. I wished I had my camera.

Meagan and I also assured the distraught Linda that we had not been injured. Yet she would not accept our absolution. She waved away our offers of a seat at the picnic table and a hot cup of tea. Her brusque leadership skills kicked in as she gave instructions to the work crew. Half of them continued on the path toward their trail project. The others turned in the direction of their camp.

Linda walked around the crown of the tree, fingering needles, breaking small twigs. We followed her to the base of the tree.

"Look how healthy this is." A deep furrow between her eyebrows marred her face, still fresh from an early morning scrub.

The fallen trunk had shared its base with a second, equally large tree, still standing. A splintered gash separated the two. The scent of raw lumber emanated from the heart of the dying tree; wet with sap, oozing its life blood.

"Why would it fall?" I wondered aloud and ran my hand over the heartwood.

"The two trunks grew in a tight vee, making a weak union." Linda spoke as if her mind were elsewhere. "The base reached a certain girth, and they pulled apart." She yanked out a heavy branch that had wedged between the severed trunks.

"The crotch between the two limbs is the weak point. There must have been more rot there than I saw." The poor woman put her hand to her forehead and continued her inspection of the pine, surveying the angle of the fall and the earth around the base.

Sarah shook off her look of helplessness. "We still need breakfast." She announced that oatmeal would be ready in fifteen minutes and wandered away. Meagan headed for the creek with our water bottles.

I examined the gash in the tree, amazed at the power needed to rip the base of the tree to shreds. The moist core bristled with curled strands where the cellulose had pulled apart. A row of indentations embedded with bark marred the clean, fresh gash. Bits of bark clung to my fingers. It wasn't pine.

I picked up the stout branch Linda had removed from the base. "Linda, what kind of tree is this from?"

She glanced at it. "Sugar maple."

"I don't see a tree like it near here."

Linda glanced up and around the vicinity of the fallen tree. "Birch. White pine. Huh. The nearest maple is twenty feet away."

"Then how did the branch get wedged into the base?"

Linda shrugged, perplexed. She watched as I held the six-foot limb against the pine's heartwood, pretending it was a crowbar. I wondered... If the maple branch was jammed into the crotch and leverage was used, could a person pry the two weakened trunks apart? Did someone hear the tree popping and wanted to hurry along its demise? Was the killer still in the area and wanted us dead?

"Meagan! Where are you?"

I raced down the hill in the direction of the creek, yelling for my daughter, until I spotted her serenely filtering water from the little stream. Startled at my approach, she jumped up.

"Mom! What's wrong?"

Out of breath and relieved, I heaved a major sigh. "Sorry to scare you, honey. My imagination is running wild." I put my hand on her forearm and shook my head. "I was afraid Brad's killer was still around."

Meagan scanned the ravine and hugged her water bottle to her chest. "I haven't seen anyone."

"Good." I calmed myself. "I'm sure he's gone."

Still, my eyes darted toward every leaf twitch and scrambling squirrel in the thick underbrush. We quickly finished the task of purifying enough water for our day's hike and returned to the campsite.

Roaring chainsaws greeted us as we crested the hill. The MCC crew had arrived armed with gas-powered saws, ropes, and hand saws, prepared to dismember the giant white pine. Linda and Sarah, with the maple limb between them, stood at the base of the tree examining the gash and repeating the crowbar movement I had made earlier.

"I'll bet you're right." Sarah stroked her jaw and squinted at the lethal, spiked trunk. "Some sicko saw this tree ready to fall and tried to rush it along—wanted to crush us as we slept."

Meagan shuddered. "What? Are you saying this wasn't an accident?"

We moved away from the din created by the chainsaws and went through the theory again.

"Eventually, the tree would have come down on its own," I explained, "but someone wanted us dead last night."

"Or really scared," Sarah said.

"Well, my nerves are shot." Meagan closed her eyes. "I don't feel so good."

A sickly blue tinted my daughter's ashen face. She swayed. I grasped her elbow to steady her, but she twisted away from me and ran to the edge of the clearing. She doubled over and vomited into the bushes. I rushed to Meagan's side and did what I could to comfort her, holding her hair out of the way and patting her back. I worried that stress had sickened her—or was this food poisoning or maybe giardiasis in the water?

"I'm sorry, honey," I murmured. "This has all been too much."

She wiped her watery eyes and her mouth with the bandana I had handed her. "Can we just get back to civilization, Mom?"

17

Day Seven - Back to Civilization

While my daughter rested, I hurried to pack the remains of our gear. Sarah collected the abandoned backpack from the group site and related the night's events to the scout leaders. We bade the MCC crew good-bye and offered Patrick's sleeping bag to Linda. The crew leader reluctantly accepted the bag and assured us that she and her young charges would stick together for safety. Sarah gave Linda one of her trademark hugs, and we headed for Windigo. The sun had not yet topped the trees.

Fields of wildflowers and thickets of juicy thimbleberries barely registered in my mind as we hiked steadily toward the relative civilization of the Windigo ranger station. Meagan's illness left her. She hiked strong. My thoughts were free to concentrate on suspects and motives.

"This is a load of crap." Sarah stopped in the trail ahead of Meagan and me. Her fists were balled up, ready to pummel an unseen enemy. "Some scumbag throws rocks on you in the well and then tries to drop a tree on us, and all we can do is run back to Windigo." She had worked herself into a red-faced lather. "We should have found footprints and tracked him down and beat the crap out of him."

Sarah's vehement passion always impressed me, but my smile would not have been appreciated at that moment. I nodded in agreement. "Maybe if we had a bloodhound to follow his scent."

Meagan disagreed. "If a lunatic is out to kill you, the prudent thing to do is to get away."

"I'm worried about Linda and her crew." Sarah raked her fingers through her curls. "And the scouts are in danger."

With her and my daughter so clearly upset, it was time for a break. "Let's sit for a minute and analyze what we know." I stepped down from the puncheon and took a seat on its edge. Meagan and Sarah joined me. Still collecting my thoughts, I reached for my water bottle and took a long drink.

"First," I said, "one or all three of us are targets."

"But why?" Meagan propped her elbows on her knees and leaned toward me. Her color had returned, but her beautiful face appeared haggard.

"Brad is the connection," I said. "Because we know him, or maybe because I'm asking questions, someone wants to silence us."

Sarah and Meagan shook their heads, unable or unwilling to believe such evil exists. "Who?" they asked in unison.

"Our list of suspects has to include everyone that has been near the well and Island Mine." I started to count on my fingers. "Taylor."

Sarah scowled. "I'd never believe that."

"Linda and the work crew."

"Are ya kidding me?" Sarah bristled and drilled a stare into me.

"I'm just naming everyone in the area in the last two days."

"Then what about the scout leaders and the little boys?" Sarah stood with her hands on her hips. "You're being ridiculous."

Meagan came to my aid. "Mom's just giving the facts. She doesn't really suspect them." My daughter turned toward me. "Do you?"

I shook my head. "Let's say I'm giving the kids a very low probability rating."

Sarah plopped down on the wooden planks again. "Who else is on your list?"

"Patrick's gear was in the clearing," I said, "so he's on the list, though maybe his wife carried the pack in."

"Nope." Sarah sniffed. "I still say her royal highness couldn't handle fifty pounds." She jerked her thumb at the pack on her back.

"Erik Jansson's paycheck is in the pack," Meagan reminded us. "Who's he?"

I held up a sixth finger. "Taylor mentioned the French woman who sprained her ankle." Low probability, but she went on my list.

"You have to add anyone who ever met the detestable man." Meagan groaned and leaned on her knees with her head in her hands. "The investigator will put me on *his* list."

I hugged my daughter to me. "We'll figure this out before they ever get to accusing you," I assured her. "I'm going to start by questioning Joannie to see what else she knows about Brad."

Sarah raised her eyebrows at me. "Is she on your list?"

"Low probability. She wasn't in the area." I frowned at the thought. "At least I don't think so." I added another digit and studied my eight fingers. How would I ever pinpoint the right one before the rangers questioned my daughter about her confrontation with Brad at the well?

* * *

Several hours later we marched into Windigo, made a pit stop at the real toilets, and dumped our heavy packs on the outside deck of the ranger station. Joannie flinched when she saw us and busied herself by shuffling paper. We made a beeline for Zak's office.

"Oh, excuse me." Sarah came to an abrupt halt at the office door, causing me to bump into her. She backed up and turned Meagan and me around, but not before I caught a glimpse of an austere man sitting behind Zak's desk. He flashed us a baleful stare. We retreated.

"Where's Zak?" Sarah whispered to Joan.

The woman smirked and pointed toward the lunch room. We found Zak Weckman at the table chewing on a sandwich. My stomach grumbled over our meager breakfast. Zak handed me a loaf of whole wheat bread and waved us into seats.

"Looks like Frankenstein in a suit took over your office," Sarah said. "Who is that?"

Zak held up a finger while he swallowed. "Peanut butter," he said and took a drink of water. "That—is the investigator. He and the park manager flew in this morning. Grilled me first thing."

I slathered crunchy peanut butter on a slice of bread and passed the jar to Meagan. "What did he ask?"

"Everything. About the body in the well. The British girl's injuries. He wanted a list of everyone on the island. Incident reports. He's reviewing Cody's pictures now." Zak laid his sandwich down and looked away. "Sorry. I told him about the stapler and the note from Deborah."

Sarah paused with jelly dripping from her knife. "Forget about it. We have bigger issues."

She filled the ranger in on my escape from death in the well and about the tree crushing our tent. "Someone is out to kill us."

The young ranger paled and headed for the door. "We have to tell the investigator."

"Wait." Sarah grabbed his arm and sat him back down.

I glanced at Meagan. "I'm not ready to see him yet." Ever mindful of Joan's eavesdropping, I peeked down the hall to see her still at the counter. "There are some things we have to figure out."

"You're on the list." Zak looked at me and frowned. "He's interviewing every person on the list before they leave for the mainland."

"I'm on his list?"

Zak nodded. "You were the first one to find the body."

Meagan put her hand over mine. We chewed our peanut butter and jelly in silence. I kept an eye on the door, expecting Frankenstein to come for me at any moment.

"Did Deborah ever return?" I asked.

Zak made a sound of disgust. "She hiked back from Daisy Farm an hour ago and went right to bed. Investigator Morden has her scheduled for an interview tomorrow."

The ranger balled up his napkin. "A murder on Isle Royale," he murmured. "Never happened before." His shoulders hung low. "This ugly business isn't for me. I've requested a transfer to the north end to survey invasive species."

The skinny young man seemed to have shrunk since I first met him—back when he took on the investigation of the attack on Deborah—when he strutted around under the weight of his badge. I felt sorry for him.

Sarah stood and grasped Zak by the shoulder. "Hang in there, buddy. After we figure out this mess, the island will get its magic back." She looked pointedly at me as if I'd solve the mystery. All I wanted to do was steer the investigation away from my daughter—and stay under Frankenstein's radar until the murderer was caught.

Investigator Morden may have had a fearsome demeanor, a gray suit, and access to all the files, but I had my list. A mental tally of everyone who had been near the stone well the day Brad Olson was murdered. I had spotted the Kinzler yacht from the deck of the Windigo visitors' center. The vessel was tied at the main pier, shimmering in the afternoon sun. Sleepy waves lapped against the hull. Though low probabilities, Patrick and Valerie Kinzler were on my list.

"Did any of you catch the name of that boat at the dock?" I wondered if Patrick's yacht was on Deborah's computer spreadsheet. My daughter and friends shook their heads.

"If that's Valerie's boat," Meagan motioned toward the lake with her sandwich, "I want to go down and visit Remington—if she'll let me."

"All those floating palaces look alike." Sarah put her hands on her hips. "That one will have to get out of *Voyageur*'s dock space before tomorrow morning."

"I heard Kinzler had some kind of trouble," Ranger Zak said. "Dented his hull on the way in."

No wonder Patrick wants to fire Captain Erik Jansson, I thought. "Do you mind if we review the permit file, Zak? I'd like to check the owners of *Spending Their Inheritance*."

"Not my domain since Deborah's back." Zak sighed as he put the lid on the peanut butter. "Joannie might help you."

"Fat chance of that." Sarah took the jar from the ranger and put it in the refrigerator.

"Can you lure Joan away from Frankenstein's office?" I asked Zak. "I'd like to talk to her—out of the investigator's earshot."

Zak stood to leave, but his heart wasn't into the intrigue. "I'll relieve her at the counter and tell her there's fresh coffee back here."

Three minutes later Joan slouched into the doorway. She stopped and straightened. Her eyes shifted from Sarah, to Meagan, to me.

"Come join us, Joannie." I put a steaming cup of coffee in front of an empty chair. "They must be working you overtime with all that's going on around here."

"Yep." She sat, but studied the brew as if I might have added strychnine.

The three of us pulled out chairs and leaned in like vultures. Not wanting the woman to bolt, I relaxed and put my feet up on another chair. I positioned myself to see her facial expressions. "I suppose you heard about the death up at Island Mine."

She smirked. "Matt and Cody discussed it. You found the body, so Investigator Morden plans to question you tomorrow."

"Yes, but we want to solve the mystery before that." I ignored the obvious pleasure she got from my uncomfortable situation. "You can help, Joannie. We need the boat permits for the last few days."

She took a sip of coffee and wrinkled her nose. "I could."

"Good." I smiled at the woman in her ill-fitting volunteer uniform and felt guilty for my fake companionship. "I knew you'd be the one to come to."

She wiped her olive-oil skin with a napkin and shot me an imperious look. "Investigator Morden depends on me, you know."

"Of course." I almost reached out to pat the woman's hand, but couldn't bring myself to touch her. "You seem to be handling the death very well."

"Why shouldn't I? People die."

I lowered my voice to a whisper and took a shot in the dark. "I thought you were friends with the victim."

She leaned back in her chair, shaking her head.

Her lack of emotion concerned me. I feared my fishing expedition had come up empty, but I threw in another hook. "Didn't he come to visit you several times here at the station?"

Joan's face went white.

I saw a crack in her hard attitude. "Didn't Brad ask you to write that note and sign Deborah Mitchell's name?"

She jumped to her feet. Her chair clattered to the floor behind her. "Brad? No! Cody didn't say the dead guy was Brad." Joannie grabbed the edge of the table.

"I'm sorry, Joan," Sarah stammered. "We thought you knew."

Joan shook off Sarah's hand, choking on sobs. She slammed against the exit door's crash bar and ran across the deck. Meagan, Sarah, and I were left to stare at each other.

"What was that all about?" Ranger Zak entered the break room to admonish us. "We have visitors waiting."

"Sorry, Zak. We mentioned the body at Island Mine to Joan." Sarah shook her head. "She's upset. I'll go find her."

"But I told her..." Zak frowned and watched Sarah push open the back exit. "Here. I made copies."

I scanned the group of six or seven handwritten permits. "*Spending Their Inheritance*," I read. "Owner: Ken and Nancy Shetino. Captain: Ken Shetino."

Meagan took several sheets from my hand. "Here's the Kinzler yacht. *In the Dog House*. Captain: Erik Jansson."

I suspected Patrick named the boat after his own predicament. Clever. I looked at the date. "Where's today's permits?... And I don't see Brad Olson's anywhere."

Zak shrugged his shoulders. "That's all I found. Maybe the investigator pulled the Olson permit for the investigation." Zak peeked down the hallway. "I'd better get back to work. I can't get any more involved with this."

We thanked the ranger and let him go.

"Let's visit *Spending Their Inheritance* first," I suggested to Meagan. "We'll find out if the yachting crowd knows anything about the death of one of their own."

18

In The Dog House

Meagan and I snuck out the back exit of the visitors' center. I hoped to avoid crossing paths with Investigator Morden before we had enough evidence against the real killer—before Frankenstein dragged either of us in for questioning. The sensation of being watched followed me past the tinted windows and across the deck.

Sarah caught up to us on our way to the marina.

"Joannie rejected my offer of consolation." Sarah rolled her eyes. "She headed back to work."

I regretted that I'd dumped the news of Brad's death on Joan, but marveled at her recovery. A flicker of doubt crossed my mind. Had Joan's eavesdropping turned up a clue we missed?

"Mom, I'll catch up to you." Meagan made a detour into the ladies' room as we passed the shower house.

"We'll wait," I called after her.

"I'll catch up!"

"Joan did say that *Spending Their Inheritance* is leaving today," Sarah said. "Maybe we should get down to the dock."

Spending Their Inheritance was bigger up close than she looked out in the open bay. Tied to cleats by bristling ropes, she took up much of the length of the pier. Smaller boats crowded into spaces on the opposite side of the same pier. A man bent toward *Spending Their Inheritance*'s hull, scrubbing her exterior with a long-handled brush.

He leaned on his brush when our metallic footsteps on the floating dock alerted him. Streaks of damp hair lay across his pink scalp. His Hemingway fisherman's shirt strained against his low-slung belly. Khaki shorts threatened to fall onto his leather boat shoes.

"Good afternoon," he called, looking Sarah up and down in her volunteer uniform.

"Beautiful boat," she said, whistling low and long. "What length is she?"

He beamed and petted the mahogany gunnel like a favorite grandchild's head. "Sixty-three feet. She's a work of art."

"That she is. Must take hours of maintenance." My gaze swept the yacht. A dinghy was parked on the stern near water level. Electronics bristled from the roof of the towering midsection. The bow, narrowed to a spear, pointed to open water.

"Endless maintenance." He chuckled, dipped his brush in the bucket, and swabbed the hull to reveal another swath of gleaming white beneath the dull film of lake residue. "But Nancy and I love the life." He propped himself up on the brush handle again and motioned to the woman in trim-fitting denim who appeared from the cabin's tinted sliding glass doors. She raised her hand in greeting.

"Nancy loves company. Come aboard." He stuck out his meaty hand. "I'm Ken Shetino, captain of this vessel, hailing from Minneapolis, Minnesota."

It was easy to smile at the affable man. Sarah and I introduced ourselves and climbed the stairs to the main deck to meet the mistress of the yacht.

Nancy Shetino waited for us behind a table with her manicured nails tapping the glossy teak finish. I hid my broken nails at my sides, but brightened my smile to assure her of our friendly intentions.

"So nice to meet you, Mrs. Shetino. I'm Amy Warren. Sarah here is a volunteer docent at the visitors' center."

"Oh, a volunteer." A smile transformed her face. She had been an attractive woman in years past. Even now, beautiful bones hid beneath her softening skin. "Can I get you a soda? Water?"

"No thank you. We were just admiring your gorgeous boat," I said. "I can't believe the two of you manage all of this without a captain."

"We hired a few when we first bought the boat," Ken said. "It took several years to get comfortable with sailing her myself."

"Maybe you know Captain Erik Jansson?" I asked. "He sails the boat moored at the big dock."

"He didn't do a very good job of it." Ken scoffed and got a poke from his wife's elbow. "Sorry." He rubbed his ribs. "No, I don't know him. We hired Troy Lundgren six, seven years ago and… Who was the other one, honey?"

Nancy curled her arm around her husband's. "Adam Bontz." Her hand disappeared into Ken's big paw. Cute couple.

"Do you have GPS and depth finders and all that?" Sarah had been eyeing the electronics since we boarded.

Ken perked up and disengaged himself from Nancy. "Come on. I'll give you the tour."

Sarah and Ken stepped through the smoked-glass doors into the interior of the yacht. I took a seat next to Nancy on white cushioned chairs at the high-gloss teak table on the open deck. The sunlight and the breeze coming off the lake were perfect for lounging. Ken's voice drifted from below talking about batteries and engine size, so Nancy and I chatted at length about yacht life, her grandchildren, and her husband before I got around to the questions I really wanted to ask.

"Does the phrase Wolf Pack mean anything to you?"

She looked at me quizzically, but didn't flinch. "Isle Royale is famous for its wolves. Is that what you mean?"

"No," I said. *"Spending Their Inheritance* was on a list in a file by that name."

Nancy shook her head and shrugged.

"Do you know Deborah Mitchell?" When no recognition registered in Nancy's eyes, I cocked my thumb toward the visitors' center. "She works here."

Her eyebrow twitched. "Then I may have seen her when I got the permit. Let me get you a glass of water."

I put my hand on Nancy's forearm to keep her in her seat. "Does the name Brad Olson sound familiar?"

She eased her arm away from me. "No. Why are you asking me these questions?"

"I'm sorry to push, but Brad Olson harassed me and assaulted my daughter."

With a start, I realized Meagan hadn't caught up with us. I jumped to my feet. My heart pounded in my throat while I scanned the shore, the dock, and the tree-lined path. Hidden in shade, Meagan sat on a bench at the end of the dock reading a book. My breathing resumed, and I waved to my daughter.

"That's terrible." Nancy twisted in her seat to follow my stare. "A man attacked her here? Is she okay?"

"Meagan was shaken up, but she's fine now." I sagged back into my seat. Perspiration stung my armpits. "I worry about her like she's still two years old."

"Of course you do, dear." Mrs. Shetino put a motherly hand on my arm. "What else do you want to know?"

Brad's arrogant smirk floated through my mind. "Does the Captain's title make them think they're all hot stuff?" I pondered aloud.

Nancy Shetino's blush alerted me. She had a story to tell. "Did either of the captains Ken hired harass you?"

She turned away and bit her lip.

"Was it Adam Bontz?"

Nancy shook her head.

"Troy Lundgren?"

Her long lashes lay on her reddened cheeks.

"What does this Troy Lundgren look like?"

The woman's lip curled. "He'd be about forty-five now," she whispered and glanced toward the galley stairway. "He had broad shoulders, six feet tall. I don't know—blond."

She leaned toward me. Her expensive perfume scented my breathing space. "Please don't tell my husband." She gripped my wrist. "Ken and I were going through a bad time then, and I was an old fool. Troy was young. I let that bastard seduce me, and he never lets me forget it!"

The dollar signs on the list on Deborah's computer popped in to my mind. "How long have you been paying him?"

Taken aback, Nancy hesitated, but decided to share her secret. "Two payments every summer for five, no, six years. And every time he asks for more."

She shuddered, but whether in anger or repulsion, I couldn't tell. Maybe both. The poor woman seemed relieved to unburden her conscience. "Two years ago he tracked me down in Minneapolis. At my own home. Disgusting. That was the last time I saw him. Thank God."

I had been listening carefully for a telltale word that would incriminate her, or her husband, in Brad's death. She hadn't seen him? "Then how do you make the blackmail payments?" I blurted.

"That's why I insist we sail to Isle Royale each year. I left cash this morning—up in the museum."

The audacity of the man! I stumbled around for my next thought. "But how... Where?"

"In a hidden compartment behind that big light thing."

Nancy caught my dumbfounded expression and lowered her head as if confessing. "You don't understand. Troy threatened to tell my husband of our...our..." She shivered. "Just thinking of him makes my skin crawl."

Her mouth twisted as if tasting curdled milk. I could taste that milk myself. I wondered if we were talking about the same man.

"I met a boat captain," I confided. "Cornflower blue eyes, ruddy complexion, longish blond hair. He sometimes pulls it back in a ponytail."

"That sounds like Troy!" Nancy clutched my hand. "Is he blackmailing you, too?"

"No." I patted her arm, but couldn't tell her, or even admit to myself, that I had had a moment of attraction to Brad, or was it Troy? "Someone matching that description is dead, killed up at Island Mine two days ago." I watched for her reaction.

"Good. If it is Troy, maybe I can keep my day of stupidity a secret, and I don't have to break my husband's heart." She looked with tenderness at Ken Shetino in the galley of *Spending Their Inheritance*. Her lip quivered. "I love my husband and would do anything to protect him."

* * *

Sarah waited until we got on shore before she burst into praise about *Spending Their Inheritance*. She was pumped about the mechanics of the yacht. "Meagan, you should see the immaculate engine and the bank of batteries." She whistled. "That thing holds seven hundred gallons of gas! Three bedrooms, two baths."

Meagan put aside her book and indulged Sarah's enthusiasm. I let her run on, too. When she slowed down, I asked, "Did you find out anything about Brad Olson?"

"Oh." Sarah grimaced. "Sorry, no. I told you, I'm no good at this detective stuff."

I held up my hand to forestall her excuses. "Turns out, Captain Troy Lundgren and Brad Olson are probably the same person."

"Mrs. Shetino told you that?"

"Nope, but he fits the description and has the same detestable personality," I said. "Captain Troy was blackmailing Nancy for an indiscretion she had years ago."

"You're kidding," Sarah exclaimed. "Isn't she a little old for getting caught in a scam like that?"

"Maybe a woman with her youth slipping away is the perfect target."

"I guess. A little flattery. The excitement," Sarah said. "Did you tell her he's dead?"

"Yep, and she thinks the world is better off without him."

"I'm not following any of this," Meagan said. "I assume Mrs. Shetino is the woman on the boat. Who is this Troy?"

We sauntered along the path to the visitors' center and speculated on Nancy Shetino's story. "So, either Troy Lundgren and Brad Olson bear an uncanny resemblance to each other," I said, "or Troy gave an alias when he demanded we leave the shelter at Siskiwit."

"So who is the dead guy?" Meagan asked.

"Joannie didn't know it was Brad," I pointed out.

"I'll ask Zak, if he's still here, which name was on the death certificate," Sarah said. "He must have seen the paperwork when Matt and Cody brought the body back." Sarah looked at her watch. "Gotta run anyway. I'm scheduled to work the visitor counter this afternoon."

"Mom, this is getting crazy," Meagan said. "Who did I shove into the well?"

* * *

The ropes securing *In the Dog House* to the dock were wrapped around the cleats in a cluster of sloppy knots. The yacht appeared deserted. Meagan and I stopped at a courteous distance from the bow to hail the Kinzlers.

"Hello?" Meagan called.

A muffled bark came from below deck. We waited. My daughter held her breath and hid a smile behind her clasped hands. Clear, cold Lake Superior lapped against the hull. The boat that had looked so sleek and streamlined while underway, appeared clumsy tethered to land. My fingers itched to put those knots into neat figure-eights.

Meagan called again, hoping, I suspected, that Remington would scamper out to greet her.

"Must be out," I said. "Let's…"

The door leading below opened and a bedraggled Patrick Kinzler ascended the stairs. "Mrs. Warren?"

Remington darted from between his feet and ran through the galley to the stern. The bundle of white fur danced and bounced, panting with excitement. Meagan reached over the railing to have her fingers licked by the little guy.

"You'd better come aboard before Remington leaps off." Patrick held out his hand to help us up several steps onto the yacht.

Remington jumped into Meagan's arms, licking her face. Meagan cooed to him.

"He likes you." Patrick smiled, though his eyes were dull, his skin pale. He moved tentatively, with effort.

"You don't look well," I said. "Should we come back another time?"

"No, no. You've been so good to Valerie and me." He roused himself and motioned us to the seating area in the shaded galley. "What can I get for you?"

"Nothing, thanks." I waved away his offer, but slid onto the bench seat behind a pedestal table. "We came to return Remington's tags." I pulled the diamond studded collar from my pocket.

Patrick barely glanced at the expensive bauble and handed it to Meagan. "I guess he should wear his tags even if he can't get off the boat. We're stuck here for a few days until a new captain flies in."

"What happened to your captain?"

"We had to fire him."

Remington perched on Meagan's lap while she buckled the collar. Patrick sagged into the captain's chair, but noticed that I scanned the boat. "I'm sorry Valerie isn't here to greet you."

He nodded toward land and made a weak sweep of his arm. "She hiked out to collect more thimbleberries. She knows I love fruit salad."

In spite of his illness, he appeared content, even happy.

"Was Erik Jansson your captain?" My abrupt question brought a frown to Patrick's broad forehead. He gave a small questioning nod, then closed his eyes and rested his head against the back of his chair.

I pushed on. "Where is he now?"

The exhausted man lifted his head and stared at me through dull eyes. "I don't know. I fired him back at Siskiwit."

Meagan and I darted looks between us. I hesitated to interrogate the sick man, but pushed ahead. "This could be important, Patrick. Will you describe Erik to me?"

Fire flashed through his eyes. "Erik Jansson is a liar and a bastard!"

The outburst woke Remington. He jumped to his feet, ready to attack. Meagan soothed him with a touch.

Patrick held his hand up. "I'm sorry, ladies."

He lifted his chin and closed his eyes for a moment before running through a litany of Erik's physical traits. The list was an echo of Mrs. Shetino's description of Troy. I didn't have time to speculate on the probability of a coincidence—Patrick had more to say.

"He can't be trusted. I couldn't stand anymore... The way he treated my wife." A groan came from deep within his barrel chest.

I trod on the beaten man's emotions as lightly as possible. "What do you mean, Patrick?"

"I swear Erik threw Remington overboard and told my wife I did it." Patrick's pale face broke out in sweat. He held his belly. Trading one sort of pain for another, he continued. "I let Jansson flirt with my wife. He made her feel better, but how much can a man take?"

I felt terrible for poking into Patrick's private torment. Meagan and I prepared to leave.

"My wife's a wonderful person." He motioned us back to our seats, his eyes brighter. "Try her fruit salad. She worked so hard on it."

He hoisted his bulk from the seat like a much older man and retrieved a plastic bowl from the refrigerator. He put so much effort into spooning the pink concoction into individual dishes, I felt obliged to sample Valerie's fruit salad. Meagan accepted her bowl and sat next to me on the leather seat with Remington resting his chin on her knee.

"Coffee? Water?" Patrick asked.

Meagan had already dipped her spoon into her bowl when I got a good look at our desserts. I grabbed her wrist.

"Patrick, where did you get this fruit?"

My tone must have startled the poor man.

"Valerie gathered everything fresh here on the island," he stammered. "Raspberries, thimbleberries, blueberries. Tastes great, except the nuts are a little bitter." He held up his spoonful.

"Don't eat that," I demanded.

He stalled with his spoon in midair.

I separated a blue berry from the yogurt sauce and squished it between my fingers. "Look. Blueberries do not have hard seeds. These are the fruit of the bluebead lily."

He cocked his head. "She told me those crunchy things were nuts."

I hesitated to consider how to tell a man that his wife tried to poison him. "Patrick, Valerie and I discussed bluebead lily several days ago. At the visitors' center I showed her the poison plant display."

He pursed his lips and his hand rested on his bloated belly. Without a word he grabbed the dishes from the table and threw the salad, bowls and all, into the garbage bin.

"How much have you eaten, Patrick?"

"A lot." The big man sank into the seat and covered his face with his hands. "She's trying to poison me." Sadness and defeat crushed him. "She's convinced I threw her dog overboard. She claims I don't love her, and that I hate Remington." His chin quivered. "He and I get along quite well, really. I'm just allergic to dogs."

While the forlorn man struggled with his emotions, I wracked my brain trying to remember the antidote to poison plants. "Go back to bed, Patrick. I'll run up to call a doctor."

"Wait." Patrick pulled at my arm. "Say it was an accident. She didn't mean... She won't survive in...in..." He grimaced and gave up. Tears blinded him. He stumbled down the stairs into the yacht's private quarters.

"That woman is sick," Meagan hissed once Patrick was below deck. "I don't want to be here when she gets back."

"No, and we don't want to be between them when he confronts her."

Meagan cuddled the silky white dog in her arms. "But I can't leave Remington in the middle of a fight, either."

"Valerie will be gone for a while," I reasoned, "if she hiked out to collect thimbleberries." I didn't want to risk my daughter's safety on a miscalculation. "I'll hurry. Stay on the dock and don't get lured below. Don't trust either of them."

* * *

The door to the visitors' center slammed behind me, causing several patrons to glance my way. Sarah jumped up from her chair at the counter, waving both her hands in excitement, but spoke in hushed tones.

"Where's Meagan?" Before I could answer, she rushed on. "Guess what I found. It was in the wastebasket in Deborah's office. See, torn on the edge. Maybe it matches that scrap from the well." Sarah shot a look at Joan, who was with a customer in the library, and dragged me behind the counter. Joan's head jerked up at the hint of a good eavesdropping opportunity.

"Whoa, girl." I held up my hands to stop Sarah.

She turned her back on Joan and thrust an envelope into my hand. Sarah stood back with a smug grin. "Look at that."

She was right. The envelope was of fine quality. Its torn end could easily match the scrap stashed in my backpack and was identical to the one containing Erik Jansson's final paycheck.

"Dang. The scrap's back at camp." I examined the linen paper and ran my fingers over the remains of Patrick Kinzler's return address.

The back of my neck prickled. Startled, I realized I had forgotten my mission. "I've got to get back to the yacht." Nightmares rose in my mind. "Meagan's alone with him."

My loyal friend's face went white. "What...?"

"Call an EMT. Patrick Kinzler needs a doctor." My words came quick. "I have to go."

Sarah was already on the radio. "Is it that wife of his again?" She shooed me toward the door. "Matt? It's Sarah. We need first aid at the Windigo marina. Are you nearby?"

I heard only static as I rushed to my daughter.

Sarah's voice followed me. "I'm coming with you."

19

Blackmail and Betrayal

Screams, coming from the marina, reached the deck of the visitors' center as I pushed open the heavy exit door. Seconds passed before I identified bits of my daughter's shouts from amid chaotic shrieks and yips. I ran along the deck railing until the scene below, partially hidden by *In the Dog House,* came into view.

On the concrete dock next to the gleaming white yacht, a crazed Valerie Kinzler wielded a long stick, swinging wildly, trying to hit a home run with my daughter's head. Meagan ducked, screaming at Valerie to stop. My daughter backed away until her heels hung over the edge of the dock, eight feet above the dark water. She ducked again and fended off the woman's weapon with one arm. Her other arm sheltered Remington, who was barking and snarling at the attacker.

"Hey!" Frozen in place, I shouted with absolutely no effect.

Sarah came up behind me. "What the…"

She took the steps three at a time and was down the hill before I came to my senses. I ran, getting to the shore twenty paces behind Sarah—in time to see Patrick Kinzler bound off the yacht. He grabbed his wife from behind, around her waist, and lifted her off her feet.

"I want my dog," she screamed. She thrashed against him.

Patrick removed the aluminum mop handle from Valerie's grasp and talked into her ear. She quieted, nodded miserably, and hung limp over his forearm like a boneless cat.

Meagan, with her arm still outstretched, stepped away from the edge. She glanced once at the icy water and put Remington's feet on the concrete pier. The little dog refused to move away from Meagan's ankles. He stood his ground, growling at his owners.

Valerie began to cry.

"Who called for first aid?" Matt yelled from the shore. His boots pounded down the length of the long dock. The first-aid backpack hung from one shoulder. Unbuckled straps dangled, flying loose behind him. His voice of authority calmed the chaotic scene. Even Remington sat on his haunches to see what would happen next. Patrick put his wife down, but pulled her to his side like an eagle protecting its brood.

I rushed past the couple and made a beeline for my daughter, who submitted to my fussy hugs. I held her at arms' length and turned her around, scanning her face and arms. No bruises showed. Meagan flashed me a nervous smile to say she was okay before kneeling to scratch Remington behind his ears.

Matt's short, stocky bulk filled the space between us and Kinzlers. "What's going on here? Is anyone hurt?"

Sarah nudged me forward.

"Meagan's okay, but this man needs your help." I pointed to Patrick still comforting his wife. "He may have eaten bluebead lily seeds and doesn't feel well."

Matt's eyebrows arched only slightly before he spoke in low tones to the Kinzlers. The rest of us stepped away to a discreet distance.

"He ate bluebeads?" Sarah tilted her head down at me and spoke from the side of her mouth.

"In a fruit salad," I said.

"Don't tell me…" Sarah aimed a glance at the tiny Mrs. Kinzler still under her husband's wing. "Does he know?"

"He does now."

Matt ushered Patrick onto the yacht and below deck, but Valerie hung back. Like a finger-sucking waif, she held a red acrylic nail between her bleached teeth. She bristled when Meagan stooped to pick up Remington.

My daughter stroked the dog's silky fur and whispered to him as she walked toward Mrs. Kinzler. The little pup cocked his head, but allowed himself to be placed in the woman's arms. He endured her hugs and kisses with the poise of a prize-winning Havanese show dog.

"Oh, Remmy, *mon cher*," Valerie murmured. "*Mon petit*. Mama *vous donnera un* cookie." She scurried aboard the yacht with Remington pressed to her chest.

We watched the pathetic woman disappear behind the tinted sliding doors. Sarah rolled her eyes. Meagan and I shook our heads in wonder, then linked arms and followed Sarah. At a picnic table on the beach, we sat to await Matt's prognosis. The small crowd that had gathered at the end of the dock to watch the mini-drama dissipated.

"Okay, someone tell me what the ruckus was all about," Sarah said. "What set the little princess off?"

"Nothing." Meagan threw up her hands. "She came up behind me like a maniac. Claimed I was trying to kidnap Remington. She wouldn't listen."

"I was afraid she'd whack you with that mop and shove you—and her dog—into the lake." The image of my daughter floundering in the icy water made me shudder. "Valerie just moved herself higher on my list of suspects in Brad's death. I wish we had the chance to ask her and Patrick about the envelopes."

We lowered our voices and considered the possibility of Mrs. Kinzler being a murderer until a sound above us caught my attention. Behind the top of a row of leafy birch trees Joan hung over the visitor center's deck railing. Once spotted, she jumped back and made a show of organizing flyers and announcements on the bulletin board.

"I guess I'd better get back to work, before Joannie breaks her neck trying to hear what we're saying." Sarah swung her legs out from the picnic table. "Let me know what Matt says about Patrick."

Meagan stood up, too. "I've had enough of the crazy Kinzlers. I'm going to grab a snack and take a nap. Do you want your granola bars, Mom?"

She looked peaked. "No thanks, honey. The PB&J was enough for me. I'll wake you in a couple hours." I worried as my daughter and Sarah walked away. Meagan seemed drained. Her run-in with Valerie must have been more frightening than I thought. Or did something else weigh on her mind?

I leaned back against the picnic table and closed my eyes, trying to let the magic of Isle Royale ease my thoughts. Lake Superior lapped at the pebbled beach. The cool air smelled autumn fresh. Paper birch rustled in the breeze. And images of Brad's body in the well ruined my peace of mind. Until the murder was found and Meagan cleared, I couldn't relax. Instead, I paced to the pavilion and back.

Finally, Matt called a good-bye and exited the Kinzler yacht. He shrugged into the straps of the medical supply backpack. I met him at the end of the dock and peppered him with questions.

"Thank you for your concern," Matt said, "but I can't comment on a patient."

"Did the bluebead make him sick?" I persisted.

"Ingesting bluebead fruit will cause mild symptoms— intestinal distress, fatigue."

"Could they kill a person?"

"Not likely." Matt's patience wore thin. "Mr. Kinzler is a big man. It would take a lot to bring him down."

To stop my questioning, I suspect, Matt turned the tables on me. "Mrs. Warren, I haven't yet interviewed your daughter about the body found at Island Mine. Where is she?"

I stepped back. A hairball of fear stuck in my chest. With effort, I arranged a kindly smile on my face. "She's scheduled with the investigator tomorrow. Surely, he'll ask the same questions."

Matt quick dark eyes hadn't missed my reaction. "Investigator Morden needs our complete report."

"Meagan's taking a nap," I insisted. "She doesn't feel well."

"Sorry. I didn't realize." He nodded his head and kept his eyes on me. "Maybe I should check on her."

"No."

Dang him. He knew I was hiding something. I paused to calm my voice. "She just needs to rest after the incident with Mrs. Kinzler. She'll be fine."

Matt let it go. I watched the muscular EMT take the hill in an easy stride. Had I drawn suspicion onto Meagan or myself with my faltering excuses? Determined to get more evidence against the real murderer, I marched up to the visitors' center to find Sarah.

* * *

Sarah squatted amid boxes in the book display. "Hey." She waved and put the last of the new field guides on the rack. "What did Matt have to say?"

Her loud voice echoed through the visitors' center. Three female hikers near the wolf display looked our way. I cringed and darted a look toward the offices.

"Heck. They're all out somewhere. The investigator hitched a ride with Cody in the patrol boat." Sarah shifted to her knees, stood up, and dusted the seat of her pants. "Joan left by the back door when I came in the front."

Sarah rolled her eyes, but it was clear that the hostile situation was painful to her. "So, what did you find out?" she asked.

"Matt says Patrick will have stomach pain for a day or two. He'll be okay." While my mind struggled with the implications of the day's events, my fingers straightened a row of books. "I'm afraid Matt will track Meagan down and question her. We've got to figure out who killed Brad—or whatever his name was."

Sarah took the books from my hands and plunked them on the shelf. "Did the envelope help at all?"

"Not yet. I'll confront the Kinzlers when I can." I glanced out the windows to see their yacht innocently bobbing in the lake. "Obviously, the envelope came from Patrick or Valerie, but who was it given to?"

"Deborah. Right?" Sarah scrunched up her face. "It was in her trash."

"Maybe. *When* was it thrown in the wastebasket? She was out in the field for days. Who else could have been in her office since the cleaning crew was last in?"

Considering my question, Sarah covered her mouth with her hand. Her cherub cheeks became more pronounced. "Lots of people, I guess. Several volunteers, Zak, the investigator. Maybe the park manager. My money's on Joan as our suspect."

"Doubt that," I said. "Joannie isn't smart enough to hatch a plot."

"She's up to something, though—way too sneaky."

"True." As we talked, I eyed the beautifully varnished display stand supporting the lighthouse lens and glanced around to make sure no one, especially Joan, was listening. The women across the room had moved on to the moose exhibit.

"Mrs. Shetino mentioned that she left her blackmail payment behind the display. Will you help while I search for the hidden compartment?"

"What do you want me to do?"

"Stand between me and the camera," I said. "Don't turn around."

201

Too late. She looked over her shoulder directly at the camera lens.

I breathed out slowly. "Act naturally. Pretend we're discussing lighthouses." I made a circuit around the large display, trailing my fingers over the smooth pine boards. No hinges or irregularities. No knotholes.

"Nothing." I stood back for an overview of the hexagonal alcove and waited for inspiration to hit me.

Sarah repositioned herself to keep me out of the camera view. "Try tapping, like you're locating a stud. Listen for a hollow sound."

Carpentry was one of Sarah's many useful strong suits. I shot her a quick grin. "You're so smart." I began another circuit, rapping my knuckle at two or three-inch intervals. Halfway around the display, I hit a clunker.

"Eureka."

The uppermost section of board, a foot long, jiggled. Hidden under the lip of the display was a gap, about the width of a mail slot. The tongue and groove slat shifted from side to side beneath my hand, but didn't come loose. I knelt to peer more closely. "Sarah, lend me your glasses."

"What about the camera?" She stood stock still, making herself the biggest shield possible. Bless her heart.

"I'll pretend to read the placards. Just hand them to me."

Even with her reading glasses, I couldn't see how the board could be removed, but noticed dents in the soft wood across the lower edge of the slat. Tool marks, I guessed. "Sarah, I need something to shimmy this loose."

I heard the soft hiss of her knife being drawn from its leather sheath. "Be careful. I just sharpened it." She handed the blade to me, hilt first, and went back to being my shield.

I wiggled the knife edge under the board.

"The payment Nancy Shetino left this morning will be here."

I pried up the bottom of the board, but excitement made me clumsy. The tip of the blade glanced off a nail, nicking my left hand. Slow to react, I watched a pearl of blood form on my knuckle.

"Ouch. Dang it." I put my finger into my mouth, but not before a red streak ran down the blond wood.

The knife, still stuck between the boards, clattered to the floor and the wooden slat fell beside it. The sounds were at odds with the visitor center's quiet atmosphere. The hikers across the room frowned in Sarah's direction. She gave them a reassuring wave while I stayed crouched behind the display.

Sarah stooped down to retrieve her knife. "Are you okay?"

Annoyed with myself, I nodded. The metallic-tasting blood stained my tongue, but I ignored my wound and examined the hidden opening. Empty. Dang. How could my theory have gone wrong? Confounded and disappointed, I felt the bottom, sides, and back of the small cubby hole. No envelope.

"We have visitors." Sarah's harsh whisper was accompanied by the sound of feet on the outside deck. "Hurry. What's in there?"

"Nothing. I was so sure."

"It's Deborah. Quick. Put it back together." Sarah leaned against the display case in a casual pose that would fool no one.

The bloodied board fell into its groove and clicked into place. I swiped at the drip of blood with the palm of my hand and successfully smeared red across the light pine. There was no time to pull out my bandana to give the stain a proper wipe, so I stood up in front of the hidey-hole and grabbed a Park Service brochure from the rack. I jammed my wounded hand in my pocket.

Two seconds later, Deborah stalked into the visitors' center as if on a mission. She slowed her march to glare at the two of us.

"This here fresnel lens had a range of thirty miles," Sarah announced in her visitor orientation voice. "The most powerful light on the Great Lakes in its time."

Deborah wasn't fooled for a minute, but the arrival of Investigator Morden saved us from her wrath.

Investigator Morden looked almost human. He wore standard hiking clothes, a ball cap, and dusty scuffed boots, but his casual outfit did not enliven his mortician's face. What had he been doing in the back room? From behind wire-framed glasses, his shark eyes took in every detail of the room and swept over Sarah and me. I felt as though I'd been through an airport screening machine; x-rayed, analyzed, and exposed.

"Come into my office," he demanded.

His harsh voice beat me down. I was a mouse again. I heard echoes of deans, priests in the confessional, my ex-husband. His command pulled me toward him, shamefaced. But Sarah hooked my arm, stopped me, brought me to my senses. I forced myself to raise my eyes to Investigator Morden and saw that his stare drilled into, not me, but Deborah. I leaned into Sarah for support.

Deborah had stopped in her tracks. She shot us an SOS glance as if we could or would save her. Emboldened by my reprieve, I dared to smile at the obnoxious woman as Investigator Morden disappeared into the office he had commandeered. Deborah sneered back at me, puffed out her ample chest, and straightened her shoulders, but her steps toward his office faltered. She didn't fool me. He scared her, too.

Sarah and I retreated behind the lens display. Sarah screened me again while I scrubbed the bloodstained wooden slat with my bandana and a little spittle.

"That guy should be kept on a leash," I said. "Where'd he come from?"

"Joan told me he went to the crime scene at Island Mine early this morning. I didn't hear Cody's patrol boat come back." Perplexed, Sarah shook her head at me. "Done? I have to help them." She nodded toward two visitors headed for the information desk.

"I'll come back later with a wet cloth." I crawled further behind the display, tapping my knuckle along the top row of slats. No other hollow spot presented itself.

Sarah watched my progress. "You found the drop box, so where's the blackmail money?"

I got off my knees and walked with her to the counter. "Obviously, the blackmailer picked up the payment within the last few hours. Who have you seen here?" I kept my voice low and my eye on the investigator's door.

"The new volunteers were here earlier and went off with Deborah." Sarah squinted her eyes and thought. "Joan, of course. She said Zak reported to the park manager and then got a lift to Rock Harbor from Cody."

"Zak must have been on the patrol boat with the investigator." It was my turn to scrunch my forehead, trying to squeeze out ideas. "Mrs. Shetino probably put her cash in an envelope, too. Wouldn't you think? Were there other envelopes in the wastebasket when you found the Kinzlers'?"

"Don't remember. Sorry. I was so excited to see that one with their logo." Sarah shrugged and held up a finger. "Excuse me." She put on her trademark grin and rounded the visitors' desk. The two hikers paid me no mind. I wandered behind the official counter and tipped the first wastebasket toward me with my foot. Empty. The second bristled with papers and crumbled forms. I picked through the basket and kept my ears perked up. Deborah's strident whine reached through the investigator's door, though I couldn't make out her words. Sarah shot me a warning glance.

My rummaging yielded nothing. I eyed the door to Deborah's empty office. Should I check out her wastebasket or escape before the shark-eyed investigator called me on the carpet? Another opportunity to snoop might not present itself.

"Don't even think about it," Sarah hissed. "They'll be out any minute."

"Okay, okay." I glanced at my watch. *Voyageur* would soon dock. The place would be swarming with new visitors, volunteers, and rangers. "Will you at least stand guard while I sneak into the storage room to get a look at the security video?"

"Are ya kidding me?" Sarah looked at the ceiling and shook her head. "No. I'd like to keep this job. Besides, I already checked. That door's locked."

Sarah's face darkened and her eyes narrowed. I followed her stare out the window to the water sparkling in the afternoon sun. *In the Dog House* had angled itself away from the dock. The water behind its rumbling engines roiled and sloshed. The Kinzlers were leaving.

I ran out the door and down the steps of the deck. My flying feet took me halfway down the hill before I realized there was no way I could stop the yacht. Any answers I'd expected to pry out of Valerie and Patrick were history.

I muttered a few choice words.

As if responding to my anger and disgust, the big boat churned through a wide starboard turn and glided into the inlet to my right. I hustled three hundred yards down the path to the secondary piers in time to see *In the Dog House* nudge the small metal dock. Ken Shetino was at the wheel.

Patrick Kinzler climbed from the stern of the boat with mooring ropes in hand. He wound the ropes around the cleat and fumbled with several knots. Ken secured the bow in a fast figure eight and went to Patrick's aid. The two big men, one tall and muscular, the other short and rotund, talked amiably while Ken showed Patrick the art of securing a boat. Patrick clapped the shorter man on the shoulder in thanks. *He must be feeling better,* I thought.

Nancy Shetino stood on the shore end of the pier watching her husband. The contrast between her crisp, white outfit in a nautical motif and my scruffy hiking clothes made me self-conscious and

206

reluctant to approach her. I reminded myself that this elegant woman once allowed herself to be lured by the smarmy Troy Lundgren/Brad Olson.

She broke into a smile when she spotted me. "Hi, Amy." The seriousness of our last conversation was apparently forgotten.

"What's going on here?" I asked.

"Mr. Kinzler doesn't know how to pilot the yacht and asked Ken for help." She lowered her voice to gossip level. "They fired their captain, you know, and Patrick's sick." A frown wrinkled her skin-glow cosmetics. "A ranger insisted they move to this pier. Couldn't wait for the new captain to fly in. That bossy redhead really ticked off my husband."

My eyebrows jumped up. Redhead? Deborah?

Mrs. Shetino put her hands on her hips and bobbed her head up and down. "Really," she said. "That ranger boarded their yacht and threatened to ticket the Kinzlers for mooring at *Voyageur's* dock."

"If it's Deborah Mitchell you're talking about, she's not a real…"

"She's a real bitch."

That described Deborah.

Nancy Shetino covered her mouth with delicate fingers. "Excuse my French. She was so rude."

French? An idea dawned on me. Valerie was speaking French to Remington. I stopped listening to Nancy's complaints against Deborah and itched to get on board *In the Dog House* to question Valerie Kinzler. Maybe she was the "French" woman near Island Mine—the one whose ankle Taylor Lorenz had wrapped on the trail.

The narrow metal pier shook under Ken Shetino's bulk. He waddled toward us with a huge grin for his wife. "Come on, honey, let's get underway."

"Sweetie, you remember Amy," Mrs. Shetino said. "She and Sarah visited with us this morning."

"Of course, I remember." He engulfed my hand in his. "Your friend has a sharp mechanic's eye." He nodded back over his shoulder toward the lake.

Only then did I notice that their yacht was missing from the pier. *Spending Their Inheritance* sat at anchor a hundred yards off shore. Instead, an inflatable rubber dinghy bobbed in the water, tethered to a cleat by a thick cotton rope. They must have vacated the pier to make room for the Kinzler yacht.

"I was just complaining to Amy about that nasty ranger."

"Don't waste your breath on her, my darling." Ken threw his hand in the direction of the visitors' center. "The investigator said he'd mention her behavior in his report."

Mr. Shetino waded into the clear water up to his knees to steady the dinghy. The gallant gentleman offered a hand to his lady and settled her into the bow. He then hauled his big belly over the gunnel while Nancy held on for dear life. I stifled a giggle and tossed Ken the rope. The engine, which appeared too big for the toy boat, roared to life.

We yelled our good-byes. Concerned that Ken asked too much of the dinghy, I watched them buzz over the water. The plucky little craft stayed afloat, so I set my sights on the Kinzler yacht.

20

Water Rescue

Patrick lay shirtless on a chaise lounge, sunning his bloated belly on the deck of *In the Doghouse*. His stomach appeared less distended than earlier, yet I was loath to disturb the man's restful recuperation. Peace and relaxation, I suspected, were a rarity when living with Valerie in the confines of a boat, even a yacht as luxurious as *In the Doghouse*. Still, I needed answers now, before Investigator Morden questioned my daughter.

"Hello on board!" I called.

Patrick started up, shading his eyes from the glare of the sun. "Oh, Mrs. Warren. I'm sorry..." He grabbed for his shirt and fumbled with the buttons before welcoming me aboard.

I accepted his hand to help me onto the yacht and smiled up at him. "You look better, Patrick. Less pale."

"The worst is over, I think." His gaze avoided mine. He shuffled his feet and picked at his unevenly buttoned shirt.

Was his bare chest the source of his embarrassment, or did he anticipate the reason for my visit? Maybe he'd been questioned about his wife's behavior before. To cover my suspicions, I stroked the teak tabletop with my fingertips and chatted about wood grain and varnish.

"This is a gorgeous boat," I said. "The craftsmanship is wonderful."

Pride showed through my host's discomfort. I laughed lightly to encourage him to relax. *"In the Doghouse* is so clever. Did you name it in honor of Remington?"

"Valerie thinks so." He lowered his voice and glanced toward the interior of the yacht. "I'm afraid *In the Doghouse* was my little joke. It describes my usual situation." A small smile came and disappeared in an instant.

"Sorry I have no lunch to offer you, Mrs. Warren. Erik Jansson was our captain and cook, too."

With the fruit salad episode fresh in my mind, there was no way I'd accept food.

"Water or lemonade?"

"Don't worry about me." I softened my voice to broach a dangerous subject. "Patrick, you said you fired Erik because he flirted with your wife. Do you think he was guilty of something more than that?"

The man's chin fell to his chest. His cheeks flushed with shame. "I think.... No. I'm sure. Yes...he was." Patrick Kinzler leaned forward with his elbows on his knees, his face hidden in his hands. "You've seen how she is." He pleaded with me to understand. "I'm not enough for her."

His need to talk surprised me. His humiliation silenced me. I averted my eyes while the man, who adored his wife, tortured himself with self-doubt. The multimillion dollar yacht's opulence disguised a marriage in chaos.

Patrick moaned. "Erik calmed her, but the thought of him touching my... He was smug, so arrogant. He had to be stopped."

I held my breath and leaned forward. Did Patrick Kinzler just confess to killing his wife's lover? He glared at a distant island, but said nothing more.

"Patrick?" I waited for his thoughts to return to the present. "Did you follow Erik to Island Mine?"

"No, of course not. Island Mine? Erik went to Rock Harbor." Patrick sniffed and snapped his fingers. "He claimed he'd be hired on another boat just like that." He narrowed his eyes at me. "Why do you ask?"

An ugly thought popped into my head. If Patrick had murdered the man in the well, I could find myself at the bottom of Lake Superior. My mouth went dry. I glanced at people buying gas at the marina. Others were just yards away. I forged ahead. "A man I knew as Brad Olson was found dead near Island Mine."

Patrick's spine stiffened. He shook his head, perplexed. "You think Erik killed this Brad Olson?"

"No, he…"

"Erik could be a murderer?" Patrick thumped his hand on the table, fingers splayed, as if reaching toward me for help. "Valerie might have been killed!"

The big man sat on the edge of his seat ready to dash below to save his wife yet again. I laid my hand on his arm to settle him. "She's in no danger now, but a murderer is certainly loose on the island."

Either Patrick Kinzler was truly shocked or he gave an Oscar-worthy performance. He stayed in his seat, ready to listen.

"Your description of Erik Jansson matches Brad Olson," I said. "I think they're the same person."

Patrick put the pieces together, much as he'd assembled the tent back at Feldtmann Lake. "And he's dead?"

"I know Brad Olson is dead, and we know Erik hiked as far as Island Mine. Your backpack was abandoned at the group campsite there," I said. "Inside was a paycheck made out to Erik Jansson."

I pulled out the torn envelope Sarah had retrieved from Deb's wastebasket. "This appears to be your stationery."

Patrick shifted uncomfortably in his seat. I suspected he wanted to deny ownership. "Yes, that's mine. I gave Erik his severance pay in that envelope."

"Would anyone else have access to your envelopes?"

"I keep extras in the desk in the spare bedroom." His gaze wandered to the door leading below deck. "My wife, of course, uses our office supplies." His husky voice faltered. "Anyone on board could have taken an envelope. Erik could have, too."

"A federal investigator is on the island…"

Before I could inform Patrick of his pending interview, Valerie emerged from below with Remington in her arms. The little fluff of white squirmed from her grasp and ran to me, wagging his entire body. Ignoring Valerie's pout, I bent over to scratch behind his ears. Remington took that as an invitation to leap into my lap and make himself cozy.

Patrick jumped from his seat to escort his wife into the sunshine. "How are you feeling, sweetie?"

Valerie's slight limp became more pronounced. Above her gold lamé sandals, she sported an Ace bandage. "Not too well, Patrick." She sighed and leaned into her husband.

"Hello, Mrs. Kinzler."

Valerie pursed her lips. She frowned at the torn envelope in my hand, but pretended not to see me. She scooped Remington from my lap and plopped herself onto a seat cushion on the other side of the deck. *"Mon cher,"* Valerie purred, rubbing her cheek against the little dog. He whimpered beneath her tight show of affection. She glared at me from above his silky coat. "What are you doing here? Haven't you caused enough trouble?"

"I'm sorry to bother you." I forced a smile. "Patrick was so ill earlier, I came to check on him."

She threw the evil eye at her husband as if his illness had betrayed her. The self-absorbed woman shot back up to the top of my list of suspects. "Do you speak French, Valerie?"

She raised her chin and sniffed. "Of course. I spend several months a year in Paris."

"How did you sprain your ankle, Mrs Kinzler?"

Taken aback by my abrupt questions, she stammered. "I didn't… I mean, I don't remember."

Oblivious to the intent of my verbal attack on his wife's innocence, Patrick tried to maintain the peace. "Wasn't it a couple days ago when you went for a walk? Remember, sweetie? You said a hiker bandaged your ankle for you. A biologist, you said."

"What does it matter who wrapped it?" The shrillness of her voice caused Remington to writhe in her arms. "Why are you here asking all these questions? Why can't you leave us alone?"

The little dog freed himself from Valerie's grip and jumped to the floor. He backed away, barking at her as if she was an intruder.

Patrick reached out to his wife. "Now don't be upset, honey."

She flung his hand away.

"Mrs. Warren brought news about Erik." Patrick ignored his wife's rebuff and softened his voice. "They found the backpack I gave him." He moved to console her.

"What's that to me? He was an employee!" Valerie spat out the words as if they tasted vile. "I don't know anything about what happened."

She ignored the barking dog and her husband's attempt at détente. Her gaze darted into the galley to a butcher block with knives sprouting from it. Probably my imagination, but I swore she studied the array of cutlery as if she wanted a weapon in her hand. I backed off, afraid she'd grab a cleaver and bury it in my chest.

"Get off my boat!" Valerie shouted and took a step toward me waving an empty fist. Remington dashed in front of me, yipping. He danced around, feigning charges and snarling at the woman.

Mrs. Kinzler dropped her fists and reached for her pet. "It's okay, Remmy, come to mommy." He nipped at her fingers and scurried under the table.

Valerie's face contorted. She screeched at me. "See what you've done!" She kicked at the little dog and lost her sandal. He darted under her foot and sunk his teeth into her bound ankle. The dressing unravelled. Remington shook and worried the bandage until it trailed across the deck. Valerie danced about, howling.

Patrick caught his wife to soothe her and control her wild arms. She whipped herself away from him and shrieked in his face. "You! You're taking her side." She stabbed a red acrylic nail at his nose. "You threw Remmy in the lake, and now he's scared of me. You hate him, and you never loved me!"

The more Valerie screamed, the louder Remington barked. I retreated to the far side of the deck and the little dog scampered to hide behind my legs. He coughed and gasped. His pink tongue lolled from the side of his mouth. I picked him up to comfort him.

That was the wrong thing to do.

"See? Even Remmy despises me. You're all against me." With the fury of a wild cat, Valerie slipped from Patrick's grasp. Driven by anger, she ran blindly toward the bow of the yacht. Patrick hustled after her, but the big man stumbled along the narrow walkway and grabbed for the railing.

Valerie ran out of room at the tip of the bow. In her perfect coif, sparkling jewels and white capris, she plunged overboard. I rushed to the side railing expecting to see Valerie floundering in the water, thrashing and gasping for help. Instead, I spotted her several yards away from the boat. She was in perfect control. Her strong Australian crawl pointed her toward the open bay.

"It's too cold. She'll drown out there," I cried.

Patrick already knew the danger. He dove into the water like an Olympian weightlifter. When he surfaced, he scanned the lake in a panic. He spotted his wife's steady arm strokes and plowed after her.

I clutched Remington to my chest and scrambled off the yacht onto the pier. A boat owner paused with a red gas can above his tank to gape at the drama taking place in the bay.

"Help them," I pleaded, as I grabbed his sleeve and gestured to where the Kinzlers splashed out toward Beaver Island.

"Frank, jump on board," a young woman shouted. She was at the steering wheel of the ski boat and had already started the engine. Frank obeyed her command, and Remington and I leaped into her boat without invitation. The craft roared away from the dock and covered a hundred yards in a matter of seconds.

Patrick had caught up to Valerie. He tried to turn her around, but she fought against him. The water roiled and splashed around them as they grappled. "Valerie, stop. Calm down." His pleas could be heard above the engine noise and her angry protests.

The swimmers ignored our shouts and Remington's barking. Frank and I hung over the railing, reaching toward the couple, waiting for a chance to intercede. The Kinzlers' heads bobbed above and below the surface. Arms thrashed. She grazed his temple with a fist, but his big hand closed around her wrist.

"Leave me alone. I hate you!" She pushed off his chest with her feet, pulling against him and holding him under until he released her arm. Patrick flailed beneath the water. Valerie swam off, headed for Lake Superior while her husband floundered and gasped for air.

"Swing her around, Nikki," Frank yelled as he threw several seat cushions to Patrick.

The captain of our agile craft expertly maneuvered the boat into Valerie's path. Valerie pulled her head up from the water to glare at our boat. She changed course only to find the hull again.

Nikki herded Valerie back toward where Patrick bobbed in the waves.

Valerie tried to swim past her husband, but he caught her foot and yanked her in. She sputtered in protest, but her thrashing had become more a performance than a real attempt to get away. Patrick overpowered his wife with one arm, while clinging to a seat cushion with the other. His strength made escape impossible.

Nikki and Frank hauled Valerie out of the water like a hostile dolphin and wrapped the petite woman in beach towels. Her face had paled to a thin blue. Red blood had already rushed to her body's core to protect vital organs, leaving her arms and legs to tremble and fend for themselves.

Remington and I sat in the bow of the twenty-foot boat. I didn't want the sight of us to throw Valerie into another fit. She loved the theatrics too well. I hid behind the captain's windshield and relaxed. A ranger's patrol boat headed toward us, probably Cody and Matt doing their jobs.

"Woof."

I hushed the little dog. He slipped from my arms and scampered along the vinyl seats to crane his neck over the railing. Like a sentry, Remington barked at seat cushions floating past. "Shhh, Rem, we'll get them later." I scooped up the little pup, but he squirmed away and continued barking. I glanced at Valerie huddled under the beach towels with our new friends ministering to her. Something was missing. I counted heads. Patrick? I twisted in my seat next to Remington.

"Patrick!" I screamed.

The big man floated off the port side, just beneath the surface. Remington's barks filled my ears. Panicked, I bent my body in half over the railing, reaching with outstretched arms. My fingers hooked Patrick's collar. My arm twisted, but I refused to let go, trying to lift his face to the air. I grunted and clung to the railing. Patrick moved his hands weakly, unable to right himself, or

216

perhaps not caring to. His weight and the motion of the waves threatened to yank me overboard, but other hands grabbed my waistband.

Frank splashed into the lake. He released my fingers from the knotted collar and held Patrick's head above water. Frank pushed away from the slapping of the hull and cupped his hand beneath Patrick's chin. Patrick choked on water and allowed himself to be towed. Within seconds Cody's boat was alongside.

Amid the chaos, Valerie Kinzler made herself comfortable. She hugged her knees up to her chest and pulled the towels tighter. She must have seen them haul Patrick into the patrol boat, seen him gasp and cough up water. She must have heard the concern in the EMT's voice. Did she not care that her husband had nearly floated into the afterlife?

Neither did she offer one of the towels to Frank when he climbed back on board his ski boat. Nikki tended to the shivering man, while I held the steering wheel. I glanced at Valerie huddled in the corner. Impassive, staring. I imagined that blank face above the stone well, hurling rocks. Yes, I decided, she could have split open Brad Olson's head.

* * *

The patrol boat and the smaller craft zipped back to the marina where the Kinzlers were reunited. From under a National Park Service blanket Patrick thanked his boating neighbors and signed Cody's paperwork. Valerie, veiled like a nun in a Florida beach towel, clung to his side. After shaking hands all around, Patrick shepherded his wife aboard their yacht in search of dry clothes. They disappeared below to their private quarters, away from the gossip and speculation buzzing on the pier.

"What happened here?" Cody seemed tired of asking me that question. I suspected that his suspicions of me had grown since Matt took my first statement at Island Mine.

I related the facts of today's story from my perspective, leaving out any reference to Island Mine and the Kinzlers' ex-captain, Erik Jansson. My speculations about Brad Olson's death weren't developed enough to present to the authorities.

Frank and Nikki supported my version of events and added that the couple on the yacht had feuded before I arrived. After scribbling his notes, Cody put his pen behind his ear and leveled his gaze at me.

"When do you and your daughter leave the island, Mrs. Warren?"

"Wednesday." I had lost track of time and counted on my fingers. "Three days."

"Please tell Meagan that tomorrow either Matt or I will take her report about the incident at Island Mine." Cody could have been the poster boy for the National Park Service: efficient, helpful, intelligent. He didn't deserve a snide remark from me.

"Yes, of course." I smiled pleasantly as if it was an everyday event to have my daughter asked to incriminate herself in a murder.

The ranger tucked his clipboard under his arm and frowned at *In the Doghouse*'s empty deck. He may have drawn conclusions of his own, but didn't voice them. "Thank you for your help today, Mrs. Warren." He hopped onto the waiting patrol boat, and Matt kicked the motor into gear.

Frank and Nikki were joined by other boaters and hikers eager for gossip. They congregated on two boats moored side by side and shared beverages and their versions of the events. No one had new details, so I disengaged myself from what was turning into a party. I headed for shore and wished there was time for a nap.

"Mrs. Warren!"

I hadn't yet reached the end of the pier and turned at the sound of Patrick's voice. His color had returned. Combed and dressed in a blue fishing shirt, he waved me back to *In the Dog*

House. Behind him, Remington nudged open the door from below deck and trotted to Patrick's side.

"May I speak to you?" Patrick beckoned me onto the yacht and offered me a seat in the stern. Remington curled up in my lap.

"How's your wife?"

"That young ranger says she's physically fine. I've given her medication so she can sleep." He layered his big paw over my hands on the table. "Before we leave, I wanted to thank you for all that you've done for us."

"You're leaving?" My mind panicked. Valerie was my prime suspect. I pulled my hands away from his gesture of friendship.

"Yes. I called this morning for a seaplane to pick us up tomorrow. Valerie must see her doctor." He cleared his throat. "This last episode..." His eyes dimmed and wandered to the floor. "Now, I'm not so sure we can go."

His football-player fingers drummed on the table. I stilled them with the touch of my hand.

He heaved a heavy sigh. "I know my wife is a troubled woman. She just told me..."

I let him talk. In halting speech he relayed Valerie's story. She had confessed her indiscretion and said that she had followed Erik Jansson to pay him and to beg to be left alone.

The big man shook his head. "None of that matters to me. I love her and will protect her—no matter what."

I murmured my condolences, but listened for scraps of hard evidence of her guilt in the murder. My conscience bothered me only a little.

"I must tell you—" He lowered his deep voice to a whisper. "Valerie saw your daughter shove Erik into some sort of well."

"What?" I yanked my hand back and lurched to my feet. Remington tumbled to the deck.

"I'm sorry, Mrs. Warren." His big, open face was level with mine. "We have to tell the investigator that your daughter may have killed Erik."

"No way, Patrick. Meagan did *not* kill anyone." He flinched as my voice took on the tone his wife used on him.

I clenched my teeth, filled my lungs with air, and sat back down.

"Patrick," I said in my patient, mom tone. "In the past two days the murderer has targeted me *and* my daughter. Meagan certainly is not the killer." I bit back a sarcastic remark concerning his wife's innocence. "Someone wants me dead because I'm asking questions."

When had his boyish demeanor blackened? Hawk eyes now glowered beneath heavy brows. A shadow of a beard darkened his jaws. How far would he go to protect his wife? Adrenalin surged to my muscles. I scooted to the edge of the seat and judged the running distance to the exit steps.

"What can I do to help, Mrs. Warren?"

Seconds passed before I took in his meaning. I needed several moments more to refocus my energy. I exhaled with more force than intended—relieved that he'd cooperate, that he knew Valerie needed help.

I concocted a plan on the spot. "Brad—Erik as you knew him—must have had an accomplice in his blackmail scheme. I want to draw him out."

* * *

Ten minutes later, Patrick held an envelope to be delivered to the blackmailer's drop slot. Rather than money, the envelope contained a note informing the blackmailer that the jig was up. The message also suggested a last payment if the blackmailer disappeared without a fuss.

Patrick had insisted on the last payment to keep his wife's indiscretion out of the public record. I hoped that the promise of cash would give us a second chance to catch the blackmailer.

"If you're seen dropping off the envelope and cornered by the investigator, tell him what you're doing and suggest he monitor the video system," I said. "Please leave me out of it, if you can."

Patrick nodded and looked with apprehension toward the door leading below. "She's medicated, but… I'll hurry."

"Don't worry. I'll be here to watch her." I didn't let on that I'd agreed to the vigil so I could keep an eye on my prime suspect. By her own admission, she was at the old well—close enough to see Meagan shuck Brad into the hole.

Remington stood on my lap, cocked his head, and watched Patrick disappear down the pier and beyond a hedge of wild roses. The two of us settled in to babysit the sleeping Valerie. The gossip party had dispersed, but the marina was busy. Small pleasure boats docked to buy gas and motored off again. Others tied up for the night. Frank and Nikki unloaded the last of their camping gear from their ski boat and stopped to ask after Valerie and Patrick before hiking to Washington Campground.

"My daughter's at shelter twelve," I called after them. "If she's not napping, will you tell her I'm here?"

Quiet returned. The warm sun must have pulled me into slumber. I was startled when Patrick rushed down the pier and clambered onto *In the Doghouse*. "Is Valerie all right?"

"She's fine. I haven't heard a sound from her."

"Good. Good." The big man snuck to the galley door and peeked down below. "She's still sleeping," he whispered when he tip-toed back to the stern.

"How did it go up at the visitors' center? Did you find the drop slot?"

"I found it." Patrick nodded. His gaze skimmed past me, scanning the tabletop, the seat back, the floor.

"Oh, no. What happened?"

Patrick rubbed his football player-sized hands over his jaw. "Investigator Morden asked me into his office."

My heart sank. "What did you tell him?"

"I'm sorry, Mrs. Warren. I'm not a good liar. The investigator asked if my wife had seen a young runner at the well."

I stared at the big oaf. "The investigator knows my daughter was there?" I slapped my hand on the expensive teak table. "How could you?" I knew how he could. He swore he'd do anything to protect his wife.

Remington tumbled off my lap, scrambled to his feet, and stood on alert. Patrick shrank into his Hemingway fishing shirt.

"I'm leaving," I said. Anything I might have added would have turned ugly, so I scooped up Remington, gave him a last scratch under his forelegs, and tucked him into a beach towel on a seat in the open stern. I ignored Patrick and climbed off the yacht. A whimper made me look back. The prize-winning show dog propped his front paws on the back of the leather seat. He gave one small woof. I couldn't tell whether it was a friendly good-bye or a reproach for leaving him in that luxurious doghouse.

"It'll be all right, little buddy." I wasn't certain whether I reassured myself or Remington. Meagan and I would tell her side of the story to Investigator Morden. I headed for our campsite to wake her. We'd face Frankenstein together.

21

Medical Emergency

One of my least favorite people dawdled near the marina's gas pumps. Hidden under a floppy hat, Joannie craned her neck to look past me. "What happened on that yacht?"

"That's none of your business, Joan." I wouldn't trust the woman with my shoe size. "You shouldn't be snooping around."

She smirked like a seventh-grade girl about to ravage an ex-friend's reputation. "You're the snoop, *Amy*. Everyone knows you're causing trouble."

I stepped back, stung by the nugget of truth in her contemptuous remark. For a moment I compared myself to the odious woman in front of me.

No. I didn't snoop for pleasure. My motivation was to protect my daughter from a murder charge. Joannie could not pull me into her muck. She had been a perfect ally for Brad and his accusations against Sarah. Had she also been an informant in his blackmail scheme? I wondered if she'd seen Patrick drop off the fake payment.

"You did Brad's dirty work for him, didn't you?"

The smirk fell from her face. Her eyes narrowed as she collected herself. "You don't know anything." She waved a small paper between her two cigarette fingers. "Maybe I won't give you this note from your big, bossy friend."

I restrained myself from snatching the paper. "I'll go see her instead."

"It's about your daughter."

"Give me the note," I demanded.

I itched to slap the oily smile off her face, but she held out her hand and let me snap the paper from her fingers.

"You don't have to thank me," she purred. She stepped back to watch my reaction to Sarah's message.

Meagan is sick. Matt and Cody went to your camp. —Sarah

Joan enjoyed my panic, but I didn't care. I ran to my daughter.

* * *

The lane to the campground was less than a mile, but seemed like ten. I raced a quarter of the way down the gravel lane through a tunnel of flowering shrubs until my labored breathing forced me to slow to a fast walk. I blasted myself for ignoring Meagan's symptoms, the vomiting, her pale skin.

The view opened near the utility sheds. I strained my neck trying to spot the EMTs transporting my daughter back to the ranger station. Would she be on a gurney? Or strapped into that one-wheeled contraption? I wished fervently for civilization—for the blare of ambulance sirens signaling that Meagan was on her way to safety.

The island's isolation suddenly seemed a detriment.

I stopped for a moment at the signpost indicating the turn to Washington Campground. I listened. Nothing. Everyone must be camping elsewhere—or out for a late afternoon hike. Was quiet a good omen? Thundering heartbeats in my ears said no.

I plunged into the shadows under a leafy canopy where sunlight never reached the boggy ground. Cool air wetted my eyes. My boots on the wooden path echoed like stilettos in a hospital wing. My blurred vision and the puncheon slick with dew challenged every foot placement. Still, I jogged toward shelter twelve until the clink of metal off to my right stole my attention away from my balance. I stumbled off the edge, crushing the life out of bluebead lilies.

The boaters from this afternoon were seated at their picnic table with their cooking pots. They raised their hands in greeting. Their names escaped me. I regained my footing and sped past them.

Our familiar shelter came into view.

"Meagan?"

I hopped from the end of the puncheon and ran into the empty campsite. The shelter was deserted. They had already taken her. How did I miss them? I ran to the water's edge to see if Cody's patrol boat had beached there. Only moose footprints marked the soft mud.

My breath came in rough gasps. My mind struggled to clear. I tried to bring logic around to my side by reexamining Sarah's sticky note. The small square paper held the secret. I stared at it to see beyond the meaning of the words, turned it upside down and back.

The handwriting was wrong. The cramped, careful printing could not be Sarah's. Her bold script would have run off the sheet.

Who had written the note? Somebody who knew I'd come after Meagan, who wanted to lure me to the camp—or away from Windigo. But why?

I searched the campsite for a clue to my daughter's whereabouts. Footprints around the picnic table obscured each other. A walking stick Meagan had begun to whittle leaned against the rough exterior of the shelter. The site presented a perfect picture of camping tranquility. Maybe she was simply out for a hike. There were no signs of a struggle inside the shelter. Our gear and sleeping bags were neat and in order. Her backpack hung on a peg. I rushed out again and slammed the screen door behind me.

"Is something wrong, Amy?"

I whirled around. If I'd had a baseball bat, I would have swung. The two people at the corner of the shelter jumped back.

"Take it easy. It's just us." The man held out his hands in a peaceful gesture as if trying to reason with a madwoman. "Remember? Frank and Nikki from the ski boat. We helped pull that woman from the water."

"Oh. I'm sorry." I rubbed my fingertips between my eyebrows. The pressure eased my panic. "Of course, Frank and Nikki." I dropped my arms to my sides. "Sorry. I'm not thinking straight. I got this note saying my daughter is sick, but can't find her."

"We may have seen her. Tall? Honey-blond ponytail?"

I grabbed the woman's arm. "Yes. When did you see her?"

"I think we saw her headed for the Minong Trail fifteen minutes ago." Nikki pointed to the north and glanced at Frank for confirmation. "She looked well. Hiked fast."

"Did she say anything? Was she with anyone?"

Frank still had his hands out, trying to calm me. "We just waved. She was with a ranger, a volunteer, I think. The one with red hair and big…" He glanced at his wife. "…and a tight shirt."

"Deborah." My feet started running. "Thank you. Thank you. If you're going back to Windigo, tell Sarah about this. I gotta go. I have to find Meagan."

My boots pounded along the maze of puncheons, retracing my route. I burst from the shade into bright sunlight and turned away from Windigo toward the interior of the island. I ran until I couldn't breathe. At an intersecting trail, I bent over with my hands on my knees gasping for breath.

Which way?

The answer came from ten feet up the smaller trail to the west. I trotted toward a pink cloth laying on the ground. I knew the bandana was Meagan's before I reached it. We had purchased a three-pack of them in Duluth as our girlie addition to our serious camping gear.

Had she dropped the bandana by accident or did she intend to leave me a sign? Either way, I knew I was on the right path. If Sarah got the message to follow me, would she recognize the bandana? Would she realize Meagan was in trouble? I wanted Sarah as my back-up. I fished around in my fanny pack for trail markers and came up with Kinzler's envelope. I tore off the logo and left it next to Meagan's bandana. Unless another Leave No Trace enthusiast picked up my litter, Sarah would find bits of fine stationery every two hundred yards or so along the trail.

I chugged up every hill with the confidence that I could catch up to Meagan; that I followed in her footsteps, but each steep incline seemed more difficult than the last. My breathing grew more labored. Time dragged on and worry crept in. I rested at the midpoint of a bridge over a deep ravine. A person could slip so easily on the mossy boards or lose their footing on loose rocks at the edge, especially if someone shoved them from behind. Horrible images entered my mind. To disarm their power, I forced myself to scan below amid the tumbled rocks, flood debris, and trees fallen helter-skelter.

Nothing unnatural littered the rocky gully. I sent a thank you skyward. Hope drove me forward, up from the ravine and around the curve of a hill. I ran out of stationery. Bits of paper would have been lost among the foliage anyway. Wild rose bushes obscured the trail and snagged my nylon pants. Few hikers used that minor trail. After another half mile, I began to wonder if I had missed a side path.

Just when I needed reassurance, a hint of color showed through the leafy green. A purple water bottle stood upright in the middle of the narrow trail. That was not an accident. Meagan had placed her bottle there. I surveyed the woods for my daughter and then searched for a turn. A thicket of wild rose had been pushed down and broken. Maybe a moose had plowed through, or maybe

Deborah and Meagan. I fought my way through the thorny bushes and came out with a network of bloody scratches on my arms and face. Animal musk in the air reminded me that I was in the West Pack's territory. A faint trail marked with canine paw prints—and human boots—led over a rise. I felt eyes on me.

Wolves, no doubt, prowled the deep woods hidden by thick stands of pine and birch. Civilization lay miles behind me. The forest was alive with every sort of northwoods creature. Humans were out of place. Deborah had lured Meagan—and me—off the tourist map. I flipped open my jackknife and followed their footprints into whatever trap she'd planned.

* * *

Prickling at the base of my neck heightened my awareness. I perked up my ears. Woodpeckers had stopped drilling for bugs. Juncos no longer flitted in the bushes. The whir of insects had gone silent. They were on alert, too. I tiptoed forward.

"Over here!"

Deborah's voice came from a distance. I straightened up and scanned the foliage until I spotted her dyed-red hair. She stood in waist-high bushes, halfway up a hill.

"This way, Mrs. Warren. Meagan's hurt over here."

"Where is she?"

Deborah waved her arm and disappeared.

Compelled to find my daughter, I thrashed through the bushes. Deborah's manufactured concern and urgency didn't fool me. I tried to out-think the woman. I climbed upward to approach her position from above. I wouldn't give her the chance to hurl rocks down the hill at me.

"Deborah! Where's my daughter?"

No answer came. I inched forward to where she'd last stood, digging my boots into the loose dirt to arrest my slide. A vine grabbed my toe and I crashed to a knee. I stifled my cry, but my knife fell from my hand. Dang. I scrambled around, searching for my weapon in the thick foliage until I heard a muffled voice.

"Meagan!" I slid down the rest of the way and landed in a flat area in front of an opening in the hillside. I righted myself. "Meagan?"

Vines and wild roses grew in abundance, obscuring a wooden frame around the four-foot hole. One would have to know where to look before seeing the entrance. Was it a cave or an adit into an abandoned copper mine? Deborah must have had access to historical maps. I ducked my head into the dusty gloom. "Meagan?"

Echoes bounced back to me, but came with a welcome sound. "Mom."

"Where are you?"

Logic battled with instinct. I wanted to run into the dark cave to retrieve my daughter, but was leery of Deborah's intentions. I stopped near the entrance until my pupils adjusted to the dark and listened for my daughter's response. No answer came. Further in, a glow of light played against the earth and stone walls. Hairy roots hung from the low ceiling. Bits of dirt fell. One-hundred-year-old walls couldn't be stable.

"Meagan, come out here."

"Your daughter broke her ankle while we were exploring the cave. She can't move."

"Meagan, is that true?"

"It's true."

"Deborah, I don't want to hear from you. I want..."

The sound of scuffling came from within the mine. "Mom! Don't..." Meagan's words were cut short. I bent low and rushed toward my daughter's voice, toward the light.

Twenty steps into the cave, I ran into a wall of pitch blackness. The light was gone. Shards of rock and mine debris crunched beneath my boots and gave Deborah my location. I felt for the side walls, ran my fingers along, and crept forward.

I heard her harsh breathing and an angry grunt just before her shoulder drove into my ribs. Air left my lungs and I crumpled, falling flat on my face. The ground beneath my cheek vibrated with her footsteps. I dragged air into my chest and turned my face toward the faint glow at the cave entrance as Deborah dashed out into the daylight. I hauled myself onto hands and knees and crawled forward to find my daughter.

Meagan's breathing sounded muffled, ragged, but drew me to her. I felt along the stony ground until I bumped into a warm, soft body lying prone. Like a blind man, I saw the scene through my fingers. They trailed over her arm, her shoulder, her cheek. I cupped her face in my hands and kissed her forehead.

"I've got you, honey."

She moaned and struggled to sit up. Her arms were bound, elbow to elbow, behind her back. She gagged on the cotton cloth tied across her mouth, too tight to pry loose. I found the knot that had snarled with her hair and worked my fingers at the tangled mess. She whimpered with the worst of my fumbling. "I'm so sorry, Meagan." I wanted to cry.

Finally, the knot loosened and came away with a wad of Meagan's hair. I pulled the gag from her mouth.

She coughed and sucked in air. "She…" Meagan forced words out of her parched mouth. "She'll bury us."

I shot a look at the entrance. Like the moon moving across the sun, a dark object eclipsed the faint light. I jumped to my feet, crouched low, and ran toward the last bit of halo. Darkness become complete. A sheet of plywood sealed the entrance. I backed up and rammed the barricade with my shoulder and hip, but bounced off, falling into a carpet of mine debris. New pain merged with the ache in my ribs. I rolled on the ground for a moment to suck in a breath, then kicked at the wood with both feet. It flexed, but would not break.

Laughter came from the other side, from the daylight world.

"Deborah, you can't do this!" Metal scraped against the outside of the barricade.

"I think I can."

Late afternoon sunlight leaked into the mine from a seam at the edge of the plywood. I put my eye to the line of daylight. Deborah appeared carrying a small boulder. She dropped the rock at the entrance. The plywood shook.

"Deborah, what do you have against me and Meagan? We've done nothing to you."

"Someone has to pay for Brad's death. And I need the money."

"We didn't kill Brad!" She had moved out of my vision. "Deborah?"

I found a loose stone and scraped a tiny hole in the edge of the mine wall. The beam of light gave me hope—until Deborah returned. Another rock crashed against the others in the pile.

"What money? Are you blackmailing the Kinzlers? Mrs. Shetino? Don't make it worse for yourself by killing my daughter and me. Do you hear me, Deborah?"

"If they don't find you, it won't matter." She chuckled and went for another boulder.

Deborah hauled rocks back and forth, but ignored my pleas. Between her visits, I scraped a peephole large enough to see several feet to either side of the mine entrance and down the hill. I dared not make it too big. She'd plug up my light. Time ran short. Her pile of wall building materials grew.

"What's going on, Mom?" Meagan's disembodied voice travelled to me on a thin ribbon of old dust.

Should I crawl back to untie Meagan or stay to persuade Deborah to come to her senses? Meagan needed me, needed hope, needed light. I unzipped my fanny pack and fumbled for emergency supplies, including a mini-flashlight. The LED emitted a pinpoint of light.

Meagan winced when I pulled the cruel bindings away. Rope burns marked her biceps. She rubbed her swollen wrists. Even with my jacket and my arms wrapped around her, she shivered. We leaned against the rough walls to rest and regroup. Though there was no way we'd be overheard by our captor, we whispered.

"Why are you here, Meagan? How could you follow that woman?"

"I'm so sorry, Mom." In the darkness her misery was as plain as day. "She told me you were here exploring old mine shafts—that a hiker found you injured, and she'd help me find you."

How could I fault Meagan? I had fallen for the same type of story.

"Why is she doing this?" My daughter sounded small and close to tears. "I heard you yell about Brad and money."

"She wants us to disappear, I think." I heaved a sigh. "If we've run away, they'll blame you for Brad's death instead of Valerie. Deborah is blackmailing the Kinzlers."

"Valerie killed Brad?"

"That's my guess." I nodded without conviction. My entire theory needed a reshuffle.

"Deborah's capable of killing."

Another rock crashed onto the pile, punctuating the truth in Meagan's statement. With as much speed as the low ceiling and our pinpoint of light permitted, we rushed to the entrance of our prison.

"Deborah!"

I pounded on the wood barrier. She ignored my shouts and began to build her wall. I watched her unnatural hair bob up and down with her movements and heard the thud of rocks against the plywood.

"At least tell me why!"

"Because you're a hard person to kill," she shouted through the barrier.

Hard to kill?

The despicable woman grinned.

Meagan's arms slipped around my waist. I patted her hand and leaned my forehead against our prison door. How could I argue with an insane person? Rocks continued to bang against the wood. I put my eye back to the peephole. Deborah bent over her work, concentrating on the placement of each layer.

A slight movement at the bottom of the hill caught my eye. I covered my mouth before a gasp escaped. I prayed Sarah had found my trail of litter and could overpower our captor.

"Someone's out there," I whispered.

Meagan gripped my arm and took a turn at the peephole, but shook her head. I looked again, straining my peripheral vision and studying the thick shrubbery. My heart sank when I recognized Joan's floppy hat amid the bushes. Deborah's flunky crept forward, but ducked out of sight. Why was she hiding? Eavesdropping, of course.

I raised my voice and aimed it at the blackmailer disguised as a ranger, at her pride. "So, Deborah, I figured out Joan's blackmail scheme and that *you* do her dirty work."

That hit a nerve.

"I work alone." She jumped to her feet and slammed a rock against her wall. "Joan's nothing but a useful idiot."

The plywood shuddered. Dirt rained on our heads. I wondered how much more of my goading the cave entrance would take before it collapsed. Deborah walked out of my narrow view. I yelled for all to hear. "I thought Joan and her lover, Brad, blackmailed the yacht owners."

"His lover!" Deborah blurted from off to the side. "Brad called Joan a pathetic grunt—a weasel."

"Was he your lover?"

No answer. She knew I was fishing.

"You killed him, didn't you?" I shouted. "Deborah?"

Rocks thudded onto the wall. The floppy hat disappeared.

* * *

The prison wall thickened. Deborah placed each rock just so—as systematic and precise as the office supplies on her desk. The obsessive compulsive tendency slowed her work, but built a stronger wall. Our peephole would be blocked soon. Meagan and I joined forces to kick at the plywood. We succeeded only in bringing more of the cave's ceiling down on our heads. The solid weight on the other side held fast.

"Now stop that." Deborah reprimanded us like a Sunday school teacher corralling unruly students.

Changing tactics, I tried a conversation, woman to woman. While Meagan took a turn at the eye hole, I spoke through the barrier near where I judged the faux-ranger knelt. "What did you ever have against me, Deborah?"

"You're a snoop," she said reasonably. "I've got a good business going here and need those payments."

"Preying on vulnerable women? Blackmail?"

"They can afford it."

"Brad is dead. Now you have nothing to sell."

"Your daughter set that up." Hatred filled her voice, but she caught herself. "My clients don't know he's dead. I can still get my payments."

I went back to the peephole. "The Kinzlers know. They're done with your blackmail."

She smirked. "You're wrong. He'll keep paying—even more now." She sat back on her heels and pulled an envelope from her shirt pocket. I recognized it as the one Patrick dropped off at the visitors' center that morning.

"That won't help you," I said. "I wrote that note."

Her face fell. "You lie."

I quoted the wording, feeling smug, enjoying my little victory. My coup backfired. I realized too late that her gaze followed my voice to the peephole. I had pushed her too far. The next rock slammed into place, blocking our only source daylight. Deborah ignored our shouts and pleas.

The blackness deadened my spirit. Meagan's LED provided a little glow, but no hope. Rocks continued to crash on top of each other. The sound built toward the ceiling and then stopped. Our captor, our link to the world, was gone. I missed the sound of the rocks, her shouting, her insanity. Silence was a killer.

22

Buried Alive

Amid fallen rock, rotting timbers, and bits of metal left behind when copper miners abandoned the cave, Meagan and I huddled together with our backs to the plywood wall—as close to the outside world as possible. "Don't worry, sweetheart. Sarah will come for us." I patted my daughter's forearm and tucked my hand in the crook of her arm. "She'll follow your trail markers just like I did."

"What trail markers?" Meagan asked, putting her hand over mine.

"Your water bottle and bandana. You left them at the turns."

Meagan groaned. "Deborah took them from me to lure you here. I'm so sorry, Mom."

How had I missed that? I'd been so sure. I sagged in defeat. Deborah would pick up the water bottle and bandana on her way out. "I also left bits of paper for Sarah to follow," I said, mustering as much optimism as possible.

"You, Mrs. Leave-No-Trace, littered?"

My daughter's humor and spunk buoyed me. I didn't have the heart to tell her the paper trail ran out a half-mile back.

The LED light bounced around the cave as Meagan nudged me with her elbow. "If anyone can find us, Sarah will." She laid her head on my shoulder. "Other than the dead body and being trapped in an abandoned mine, this has been a wonderful trip."

I had to laugh. Then we talked. Funny how darkness brings intimacy and allows you to speak from your heart—as if she was six and we again read a story from a Golden Book and laid curled up beneath her eyelet lace bedspread. Whatever had gotten between us this week was gone. She trusted me again…trusted me to get us out of the mess we were in.

Meagan yawned. "What if Sarah didn't get your message or misses the trail?"

"She'll find us," I answered with my eyes half closed. I had gotten comfortable in spite of my sore butt and stiffening joints. I rested my aching head back against the plywood and wished for a brisk northwoods wind to sweep through the cave to freshen the stale air.

My body demanded sleep, but my foggy brain nagged me with warnings. Suddenly, the message got through. If I did sleep, it would be for eternity.

"Meagan, get up." I staggered to my feet. "We're running out of air, honey. We have to dig ourselves out."

"Oh," she said in a dull voice and let me drag her upright, leaning heavily into me.

I felt the ground for a scraping stone and pressed it into Meagan's hand. "Dig." I coaxed and prodded until she understood. Together we attacked the dirt walls at the edges of the plywood.

Desperate for fresh air and fighting lethargy, I scraped at the peephole in the glow of my wristwatch's backlight until my fingers grew raw and my headache tightened my skull. After a time, my lower back stiffened from crouching beneath the low ceiling. I sank to my knees to straighten my spine.

"Meaghan, we need a stick, something to shove through." My words were slow and slurred. We followed her LED beam and shuffled around the cave floor kicking at debris, raising more dust.

"Here. This…" A cough choked off her sentence, but she handed me a metal spike.

"Perfect," I wheezed. My teeth felt coated with dirt. I jammed the spike into a niche between the rocks, heard it clink and scrape. Again and again I worked the metal into the hole. Dirt fell from above with each blow. Dust swirled. I coughed until my eyes teared.

"I'll take a turn, Mom." Meagan's voice was low and husky, her breathing shallow. She took the spike and handed me the mini-light. With the metal levered between outside rocks, she applied force downward, grunting with the effort. She got under the spike and pushed up. Suddenly, Meagan fell back and the spike clattered to the ground as rocks on the outside crashed and tumbled. We held our breath until silence came and dust settled. A laser beam of light pierced the cave.

We whooped for joy and gagged on more dust.

Sweet air rushed through the narrow slit. Cheek to cheek, we drank in the oxygen. For several minutes we indulged in the pleasure of breathing, but pulled ourselves away to return to our work, taking turns chipping at the plywood. The air hole grew to several inches.

But Deborah had built her wall well. Though we continued to attack the plywood, the remaining boulders against the wooden barrier held fast. Our elation and hope dimmed along with the evening light. At least we could breathe.

I illuminated my watch. 8:43. Felt like midnight. The long day had beaten my fifty-year-old body. My ribs ached and my stomach rumbled. My energy flagged, and faith in our rescue dwindled.

"Take a break, Meagan." I tugged her down to a seated position. "Eat something." I held out a baggie half-full with raisins and nuts. She waved the snacks away, but accepted my water bottle and took a small sip.

She rummaged in her own fanny pack and came up with two granola bars. "What do you think, Mom? Will we spend the night here?"

238

"This place is impossible to find even in daylight." My own negativity enervated me, coaxed me to surrender to my weariness. My eyes demanded sleep. What could be more natural than sleeping in your grave?

Meagan shone the light into my face. "We're going to dig out of here tonight, Mom." She brandished the metal spike like a weapon. "We'll spell each other." She pressed her granola bar into my hand and commanded me to eat.

My fierce, businesswoman daughter was right. Action was the antidote. While she attacked the barrier, I inventoried our supplies and worked out a rationing plan. After fifteen minutes, I took my turn chipping at the wall. We would dismantle our cairn, one rock at a time.

Hammering at the wall became rote, leaving my mind free to castigate myself for endangering my daughter's life. *I had been selfish,* I told myself. *It had been folly to bring her to Isle Royale—all because I tried to carve out a new life for myself.*

The spike jammed between two rocks. I grunted and pushed until one of them tumbled away. I beat and pummeled the plywood as I remembered feeling like John's doormat. Splinters flew. Like a dog shocked by a security fence, I had stopped challenging boundaries he put on me.

Sparks jumped from the rock with each strike of the iron spike.

I stayed to give the kids a stable home, right? My children drifted from me anyway.

My arms ached and my blows became weak and ineffective. In blind frustration, I hacked and thrashed at the prison wall.

"Take it easy, Mom." Meagan's gentle voice startled me. She stilled my shaky hands and slipped the spike from my grip. "It's my turn."

Maybe it isn't too late for us.

* * *

239

Only the opaque night could be seen from our peephole. The moon had yet to rise and the forest had disappeared into the blackness. Before taking my next turn with the iron spike, I positioned the LED outside the gap in the plywood. Afraid to lose the precious light source, I secured its lanyard to a nail in the frame of the cave entrance.

The Fresnel light on top of Rock of Ages lighthouse had saved countless lives on Lake Superior. I hoped the mini version would save just two. I put the light into blinking mode and aimed the beam at the deep, black woods.

"Good thinking, Mom. If Sarah's out there, she'll find us." Meagan tested the knot and the strength of the nail securing our mini light before turning the iron spike over to me.

I worked by the glow of the luminescent face of my watch. 9:38 P.M. Meagan sagged to the ground. Without adequate light, sleep snuck upon her. Her heavy breathing became the yin to my yang of iron against rock, the rhythm of our imprisonment. Another boulder gave up to the pry bar and crashed to the ground. She didn't stir.

Dust settled. Guilt crept back in.

My daughter is in this hole because of me. I practically killed her myself...falling for Deborah's trap, snooping like I was Miss Marple. Stupid.

I swiped at tears that had cut a trail through a layer of grit. *What if Sarah didn't find us? Four ounces of water would last less than a day.* I paused in my work and looked toward Meagan's gentle snores. *She'll drink my share. I'll insist.*

Weariness prevented me from lifting the iron spike again, yet I didn't have the heart to rouse Meagan. I sank to the ground beside her, leaned against the wooden barrier, and felt her warmth. I closed my eyes for just a minute.

* * *

In my dreams a redwing blackbird trilled from a bluestem prairie grass bent under its weight in the fresh breezes on an open plain. The creek was dry. The bird startled and flew to a higher perch. Its shrill whistle demanded I awaken. I zoned in on the sound, and my eyes flew open to sharpen my hearing. Another whistle pierced the night.

Sarah.

I jostled Meagan and jumped to my feet. The two of us put our mouths to the holes in the plywood and screamed. "Sarah!"

Beams of light bounced around in the woods.

"Amy!"

Sarah's voice came from a distance, but was soon accompanied by the sounds of thrashing through shrubbery. Boots thudded on the ground outside. Light beams blinded me. I stuck my arm through a gap in the rocks, reaching toward our rescuers. Sarah grasped my hand in both of hers.

"That bitch," Sarah said in a broken voice. "I'll have you out of there in five minutes." She released my hand and began tearing at Deborah's wall. Amid grunts and expletives, rocks crashed and rolled, some thrown with force. Meagan and I stood back.

Finally, the wall was dismantled, and we heard the scraping of metal as Sarah lifted the bar holding the plywood in place. The sheet of wood, now ragged around the edges, fell away and fresh air streamed into our prison. Meagan and I burst into freedom.

Two headlamps stared at us. The taller light rushed at me, and I was caught up in Sarah's bear hug.

"Oh, my god! I'm so glad to find you," she said and turned toward Meagan, who returned her hug with gusto.

We jabbered in thanks and welcome, but the second headlight was still, off to the side, illuminating our reunion. I shaded my eyes from its blinding light. "Who?"

"Joan." Sarah's announcement struck me dumb.

"Joan?" I looked in disbelief at the dark shape. The headlamp pointed away.

"She led me here," Sarah said. "I thought I had it right, following the paper scraps, but Deborah, that creature, had me going in circles. When I get back to Windigo, I'm going to beat the crap out of her!"

"Whoa, girl." I loved hearing Sarah prattle and rage, but laid my hand on her arm to get the story straight. "You saw Deborah?"

"No, but I fell for her tricks. She tied Meagan's pink bandana at a turn onto the Huginnin Cove loop. I ended up back where I started. Joan tracked me down and told me about the mine. I never would have found this place without her. Right, Joannie?"

The headlamp ten feet away bobbed, and Joan muttered something. Meagan and I both thanked the woman hidden in the dark.

Sarah leaned down to whisper in my ear. "I didn't trust her, but I had nothing else." She hugged my shoulders. "Joan told me how crazy Deborah got. All the way here I pictured you dead."

Meagan piped in. "I told Mom you'd find us."

Sarah gave a satisfied sigh.

After discussing the pros and cons, we opted to build a camp at the mine entrance rather than hike to Windigo in the dark. I was bone tired. We chanced a ticket from the rangers by building an illegal fire on a bed of rocks. Burning the plywood would have given me a great deal of pleasure, but the board served us better as a lean-to and wind break.

A storyteller's tongue is loosened by lemon-blue flames dancing amid twigs and branches. Each of us told our version of events. Even Joan told of hiding in the bushes and watching Deborah march past toward Windigo.

"Brad said he loved me," she said.

The fire crackled. A white ash twig bent and disintegrated in the heat. Night creatures skittered in the underbrush. Joan wrapped her arms around her legs and put her forehead on her knees. I sat near enough to reach out to comfort the grieving woman, but could not.

From the other side Sarah draped her arm over Joan's shoulders. "They fooled us all. He isn't worth your tears."

Joan shrugged off the gesture of friendship. Sarah drew back and put her hands up as if burned. She rolled her eyes to the stars. "Okay, then."

"Deborah did us a favor." I threw that into the mix to break the tension. "Tomorrow we tell the investigator what Deborah did here and that Valerie Kinzler killed Brad."

Joan sniffed from within her self-inflicted isolation. "You think you know everything."

Try as we might, Joan would not be persuaded to elaborate. I was too tired to play mind games with her.

"I need to get some sleep," I said.

The campfire brightened the area outside the mine entrance, but the yawning black hole set the mood. None of us thought to reenter the mine for shelter. Sarah's daypack proved to be a boon for emergency camping. I unfolded a tarp for Meagan and me while Sarah and Joan each wrapped themselves in foil space blankets.

Meagan seemed reluctant to settle in. "Do you think Deborah will double back here?" she asked. "Maybe she wonders where Joan and Sarah are."

Sarah threw another log on the fire. "I'll stand guard. You guys get some sleep."

A gibbous moon rose and cast shadows through the trees. I tried to relax under the clear, crisp sky, but Deborah loomed in my imagination.

23

To Confront a Killer

We hiked toward civilization in morning's half-light to find Windigo unchanged after our ordeal. Loons called from the bay. Mist wetted the shrubbery and muted our approach. Our destination was the darkened visitors' center, perched on its hill like a remote outpost guarded by slumbering sentries. Sleepy boats bobbed in the marina. Only *In the Doghouse,* with a soft light shining from behind the smoked-glass sliding doors, showed signs of life.

Though daylight warmed the front of the ranger station, shadows still clung to a thick stand of trees in the back where a faint glow emanated. No doubt Investigator Morden was first to arrive and already on duty. I quickened my steps, eager to tell him of Deborah's treachery and demand that he begin the manhunt, but Joan shushed us and motioned for our troop to tiptoe across the deck toward the rear windows. She had perfected the art of sidling and eavesdropping, so we followed the woman who sought revenge for her own reasons.

With noiseless steps, we passed the first window behind which the desk commandeered by Investigator Morden sat in gray shadow, empty. Fluorescent brightness poured from the second window. Joannie stood to the side, peered into the office, and waved us forward. I crouched low and peeked over the sill. The shock caused me to stumble into Meagan, but Sarah caught my elbow. I righted myself and gawked at the scene framed by the window.

Inside the visitors' center in her office, Deborah sat straight-spined at her organized desk pecking at her laptop—as if she had not entombed two women the night before. My fury boiled to the screaming point.

"Watch the back door," I demanded of Joan. Stealth and silence forgotten, I pushed past her and my daughter and ran toward the building's front entrance. Sarah ran ahead of me, key in hand. Meagan was close behind. We charged into the visitors' center and darted across the display room, ready to tackle Deborah if she tried to escape.

When we burst into the brightly lit office, Deborah looked up from her work. She raised her eyebrows, cocked her head, and closed her laptop. "Good morning, ladies. What can I do for you?"

I sputtered in anger and stared at the woman, who seemed unconcerned that Meagan, Sarah, and I faced her like a firing squad. My daughter was first to regain her speech.

"You left us to die!" Meagan pounded her fist on the desk, leaving a smudge of dirt on a sheaf of white forms.

Deborah frowned, slipped the dirtied papers into the recycle bin, and tidied the pile. "Please sit. Fresh coffee's in the break room." She rose as if to play hostess and fetch cappuccino.

"Sit down." Sarah grabbed Deborah by the shoulder of her neatly pressed uniform and backed the woman into her chair, pointing a finger into her face. "Before we call the rangers, tell us why you trapped them in the mine."

"I did no such thing." Deborah straightened her blouse and brushed Sarah's fingerprints from her shoulder.

"How can you deny it?" Sarah roared.

Afraid that the volunteer coordinator was about to be throttled, I stepped between them.

"Deborah, back at the mine you said that you had a good business going here, collecting payments from yacht owners, blackmailing them."

She ran a protective hand over the sleek lid of her laptop. "I don't talk about business while I'm on duty."

I persisted. "If Patrick Kinzler thinks his wife killed Brad, he'd pay big bucks to keep you quiet, wouldn't he?"

Deborah closed her eyes and lifted her chin as if dreaming of the riches to come her way.

Suddenly sure that Valerie Kinzler was innocent—at least of Brad's death—I lowered my voice. "You killed Brad, didn't you, Deborah?"

Her eyes flew open and darted at me. "Mrs. Warren, your daughter murdered Brad Olson." Her voice was devoid of emotion, eerie and flat. "I have submitted my report, and Mrs. Kinzler will swear to it."

Meagan gasped and sagged at my side. I hugged her to me.

"No, Deborah," I said. "Remember that I wrote that last note? Valerie Kinzler confessed her affair and the blackmail to her husband. You have no hold on her. She'll tell the truth." I didn't add that Valerie's last truth incriminated Meagan.

The ice woman gazed out the window at goldfinches flitting at the bird feeder. A knot of worry gathered between her brows.

I silently beseeched Sarah and Meagan for a suggestion for my next move. Both grimaced. Sarah gripped the edge of the file cabinet as if trying to restrain herself, but shrugged.

Why would Deborah kill the source of her revenue, her golden goose?

"Were you jealous," I asked, "of the attention Brad gave me and my daughter?"

Deborah sighed and shook her head. "I tried to keep you out of the investigation, but..." She shrugged.

"By throwing rocks on me in the well? And the falling tree..."

"Accidents happen."

"You're crazy," Meagan shouted. "You buried us alive in the cave."

"I captured you and held you for the rangers," Deborah corrected. Her eyes skittered toward the file cabinet. The same file cabinet she had trashed looking for her canvas bag—the money bag. A puzzle piece fell into place.

"Brad cut you out of the money, didn't he?" I watched for telltale body language. "He didn't need you. The blackmail money would be all his."

Deborah's lips disappeared in a tight, pinched line. She sniffed and looked toward the doorway. "Joan, summon the rangers to arrest these people for stealing my money, for attacking me—and for murder," she hissed.

I glanced over my shoulder and saw Joan leaning against the wall with her trademark smirk. "Yes, Boss."

That weasel saluted Deborah. I shot the traitor a venomous look that would paralyze most humans. She didn't flinch.

"Thank you, partner." Deborah stood, smoothed her pant legs and patted her hair into place. "Now if you'll excuse me, I have a yacht to catch."

Her casual dismissal of us infuriated me. "You're delusional," I shouted. "You're not walking out of here." Sarah's and Meagan's body heat at my side fueled my resolve to bar her way. We formed a battle line.

As if preparing for her daily commute, Deborah slipped her laptop into a padded case and pulled the fob of the nylon zipper, but she stepped from behind her desk without the case. Instead, in a smooth practiced motion, she produced a hunting knife from a side compartment and whirled around, pointing its lethal blade at Meagan's midsection.

Mesmerized by the serrated edge and the horrid possibilities, I froze and watched events as if in slow motion. Meagan's foot shot out. She bent, fists clenched, into a Tae Bo position and kicked the knife from Deborah's hand. Metal clattered against the window pane and fell to the floor. Sarah threw chairs out of her way. Deborah scrabbled after the blade.

An image of the woman slicing Megan in revenge thawed my muscles. Before Deborah got control of the knife, I grabbed for her, finding a hold in her thin, red hair. She yowled. I swung her around like a roller-derby champ, away from the knife, away from my daughter. As roots gave way, Deborah stumbled into Sarah, who shoved her against the wall like a punk in a drug bust.

"That's enough!"

The command filled the office and brought all movement to a halt. Sarah stopped with her elbow jammed into the nape of her captive's neck. Deborah's cheek stuck to the wall, her lips squeezed into a grimace, but she strained her eye to look toward the door. Meagan caught her breath, still in a fighting stance, her fists held high to guard her chin. Tufts of red hair fell from my fingers as I turned and saw Investigator Morden filling the doorway with his craggy visage and mortician's suit.

"Thank you, Ms. Bernudi. You may go."

The smirk left Joan's face. She looked as if she might protest her dismissal, but slid out the door behind the man.

"Release Deborah."

Sarah sputtered, but stepped back from the woman on the wall.

Deborah tugged her shirt into place, snickered at us, and smugly turned toward the investigator. "There's your murderer." She extended her arm and pointed at Meagan.

"No," I cried. "She…"

Meagan and Sarah objected in chorus with me, but Investigator Morden cut us short.

"Sit down, all of you." His tone brooked no argument. He motioned us to fallen chairs and dragged another from across the room for himself. "We will talk."

Sarah found chairs for herself and Meagan. I righted a chair as far from his glowering eyes as possible and tried to read his intentions. My knees gave way, and I fell into the chair. Deborah folded her arms and remained on her feet.

"You too, Ms. Mitchell."

Deborah huffed and took the seat behind her desk. "Thank goodness you're here, Bill. These women assaulted me. I have proof that Meagan, there, shoved Brad Olson into the well at Island Mine. She killed him by smashing his head with a rock." Deborah rolled her shoulders back and pointed her breasts at the investigator.

We're cooked, I thought. *Bill? How well do these two know each other?*

Bill ignored her and turned his Mount Rushmore face on me. "Mrs. Warren, I am Investigator William Morden, National Park Service." He rose and extended his hand to me.

I hesitated to touch the stone-cold man's flesh, but felt compelled by his piercing eyes. The warmth of his hand surprised me.

"You and I are on the same team, Mrs. Warren." Morden's barren face tried to smile. "Yacht owners from ports in three states filed complaints about blackmail and extortion. Isle Royale proved to be the common denominator. Your investigation has been one step ahead of me all the way. Thank you."

I slid back from the edge of my seat. From across the circle of chairs, Meagan hid a half smile and Sarah flashed a thumbs-up. Deborah fidgeted behind the desk, eyeing the door. Sweat pasted strands of red across her forehead.

"From what I overheard just now, you've drawn the correct conclusions," the investigator said, but frowned even more deeply. "But how did you make the original connection?"

I stumbled over my tongue, but found my voice. "Boat names. I found a list on Deborah's computer but couldn't get back in."

Deborah's fingers tightened on the laptop.

"I have the passwords," Joannie piped in. Somehow her declaration sounded like a whine.

"No need for that, Ms. Bernudi," Investigator Morden said without turning to acknowledge that she had snuck back into the office. "Thank you for your assistance these past few days. You may go."

Joan clucked her tongue and slumped out of sight. Only a slight flare of the investigator's nostrils testified to the restraint he must have needed to endure Joannie Bernudi's assistance.

"This morning Patrick Kinzler invited me aboard their yacht," he said. "Mrs. Kinzler recanted her statement accusing Meagan of Brad Olson's murder."

His heavy, monotone words jolted me. I sought my daughter's eyes and watched them tear up as the vindication became real to her.

"She confirmed that you were at the well, Deborah," Morden said, oblivious to emotions in the room, "and that you took her last blackmail payment while at Island Mine. Mrs. Kinzler ran off after meeting you, but she didn't trust you. She sneaked back in time to see you lift a rock over your head and heave it into the well."

I frowned at the image in my mind and looked to see Deborah's reaction.

The woman brushed her strands of hair from her forehead and cocked her head to the side. "We'll work this out," she said. "I've been a loyal volunteer on Isle Royale for ten years."

"Cody," Investigator Morden called out. The young ranger stepped inside the office. "Please escort Ms. Mitchell to the sea plane. I'll be along in five minutes."

Cody took Deborah's elbow and helped her to her feet. He wrestled the laptop from her grip, placed the padded case on the desk, and led her from the room.

Sarah whistled under her breath.

"I must apologize, Mrs. Warren, for not giving you the protection you deserved while I followed false leads." Investigator Morden's steely eyes softened to dove gray. "Your friendship with the Kinzlers and the information you pulled out of Deborah just now made her arrest possible. What other evidence did you uncover?"

I appreciated his respect for my investigative attempts as Sarah, Meagan, and I recounted our experiences with Brad and Deborah, the envelopes in the well and Patrick's backpack, the blackmail hidey-hole, and our terrorizing hours in the cave. He listened avidly. How had I ever thought of him as Frankenstein? He took his job seriously, that was all. I smiled into his strong, authoritative face and admired his cleft chin, but stopped myself from inventorying his other attributes when I caught Sarah's knowing look and raised eyebrows.

"The National Park Service owes you its gratitude, and I personally thank you for your involvement," he said as he stood and took my hand. He bent from his height to place a tiny kiss on the back of my hand. I sat there, stunned, and watched his straight back leave the room.

Sarah whistled. "You've got another one."

Meagan nodded. "She's right, Mom. He's really attracted to you."

"Don't be silly," I protested. "He was being polite."

"He didn't go all Sir Galahad on me," Sarah pointed out.

I couldn't argue. Still in shock, I touched my fingers to the warm spot on the back of my hand. Roller coaster emotions drained the last of my energy, and last night's fitful sleep caught up with me. "I need a nap."

"Hey, I'll fix you up in the dorm," Sarah said. "You'll be more comfortable than at the campground, and Deborah's cot is available." She threw her arm around me as we crossed through the display room and onto the deck overlooking the marina. We heard the drone of the sea plane at the dock and waited for the craft to taxi across the water and lift above the treetops. Too far away to see faces, we waved to the sky. The plane tipped its wings and flew out of sight.

"Good riddance," I said.

"Which one?" Sarah asked, her eyebrows arched high on her forehead.

"Deborah, of course."

"Mom," Meagan interrupted. "I'm going to hike down to the shelter and get some sleep."

She looked peaked, and I was concerned for her.

"Not the dorm? We'll be warmer indoors tonight."

My daughter gave me a wan smile. "You know I sleep best under the stars and love waking up in the wild."

I grinned ear to ear.

"What?" she said. "I've always loved camping."

"I know, Meagan."

24

Isle Royale Magic

The next morning at our lakeside camp with dawn lacing through aspens and strewing prisms around a heron's silhouette, Meagan and I squabbled over breakfast. But the barbs and hurt were gone. We laughed at ourselves.

"Good God. We're acting hormonal," I said. "I think menopause makes me goofy."

Meagan laughed. "Not you, Mom, you've been great, and I just need another cup of coffee." She put her cup to her lips and looked at me over the brim. "What would you think of leaving a day or two early and spending time in Duluth or Grand Marne?"

The idea of seeing the sights with my daughter suddenly sounded like a perfect ending to our week of craziness. "I'd like that."

We packed our gear and headed for Windigo to inform Sarah of our early departure. Patrick Kinzler met us near the path leading to the marina. The big man looked rushed and harried.

"Oh, Mrs. Warren, I was on my way to see you."

"What's wrong, Patrick? Is Valerie okay?"

"Yes. Yes. We've balanced her medications, and she's doing well now that her stress level is down." He wrung his hands as if his wife's stress had transferred to him. "You've already been so good to us, and for that I'm grateful. I need another favor."

"What can I do for you, Patrick?" I couldn't help but like the man, in spite of his choice of women.

"Remington." Patrick threw up his hands and then let them drop against his thighs. "Valerie can't stand the sight of him anymore. We're flying out this morning. Will you look in on him on the yacht until you leave or until a captain gets here to pilot the boat back to Ludington?"

"Oh," I stammered. "We're leaving, too, when *Voyageur* sails this afternoon."

His shoulders slumped. "I don't know what to do. She won't have him in the plane, and I have to get him back home and then find a place for him, maybe someone with kids..."

"Wait a minute, Patrick." I held up my hand to get his attention. "You're giving Remington away?"

My daughter's eyes widened, and she nudged my arm. "We'll take him. Right, Mom?" Her eagerness was contagious. I opened my hands and let it happen.

"You will?" Patrick broke into a grin and pumped Meagan's hand. "He loves you. I'll get his traveling case ready, so he can sail with you."

Patrick hurried toward his yacht, but turned back. "Here. I almost forgot. We can't use our reservations at Nanaboujou Lodge. It's all paid for. Maybe you can stay there on your way home." He pushed a brochure into my hand. The cover pictured an old-world lodge on the shore of Lake Superior, a lovely place. I looked up into the man's earnest face.

"Please accept my gift. Dinner, too...or I can arrange different dates," Patrick said. "You saved my life—more than once." He blushed and waited for my answer.

"We'll take it, if they allow dogs." Meagan bobbed up and down in happiness.

"Thank you, Patrick. This looks like the perfect place to wash off a week's worth of Isle Royale dust."

We watched Patrick rush off to deal with his wife. I hoped we had eased his worries.

Meagan jumped up and down like a little kid. "Thank you, Mom, for not talking me out of taking Remington. Ed will love him, and I'll make it work."

I enjoyed my daughter's excitement but also wished I'd grabbed the chance to bring the prize-winning Havanese pup home with me.

* * *

Joannie sat at her desk in the visitors' center and smirked as we entered. "She's up at the store."

How did she know? "Good morning, Joan. Nice to see you." I tried to view the odd creature in a new, positive light, but shrugged and backed out the door. "What's with that woman?"

I asked no one in particular, but Meagan answered, "Yeah, like she's permanently menstrual."

"Harsh," I said, "but true." I laughed until Meagan's face went white. "What's wrong?"

"I'm late."

"Late for what?"

"I'll be right back."

Meagan raced up the steep hill to the store—one of those places packed with at least one of everything a person might want, but with no variety. I shook my head at my daughter's behavior and took my time trudging up the hill to find Sarah. I replayed my daughter's last words. *Late. Late?*

"Oh, my God." My hand flew to my mouth, and I came to an abrupt stop as Meagan flew past me toward the shower house. I ran after her. "Meagan?"

"I'll be right out."

I paced outside the pebble-brown building, counting the sidewalk squares. I couldn't take it any longer. "Meagan? What is it?" I pounded on the stall door.

"Hold on, hold on," she called.

"Two lines!" She threw open the door, waving a test strip. Her wide eyes beaming from her glowing face told me two lines was good. "I *am* hormonal, Mom. I'm pregnant!"

I think I screamed before I hugged her to me. We danced a jig in the shower house, laughing like hyenas, before I realized what we were doing.

"Meagan, stop. You need to sit down. You need to take care of the baby." I was so excited I could barely talk.

* * *

"Don't you touch that pack," Sarah commanded Meagan, snatching the heavy pack from a picnic bench under the pavilion and hoisting its weight to her own back. "You have a baby to take care of."

Meagan allowed herself to be pampered and toted only the canvas dog carrier down the long cement dock.

Since hearing the news, Sarah hovered over my daughter, ready fetch water or to catch her if she tripped. For his part, Remington stood guard from inside his mesh travel case, waiting patiently to set sail. I had little to do but stand back and enjoy my growing family.

On *Voyageur*'s starboard side we handed the backpacks over the lapping water to a crew member and extracted his promise to treat Remington's case with care. He recognized Sarah and gave her a friendly salute.

"I hate to see you go," Sarah told us. Guilt played around her face as she tried to explain why she'd stay longer. "Deborah left us in a mess and the investigator took her laptop—including the schedule for incoming volunteers. Zak's back in charge and has asked me to stay for the rest of the season to get it sorted out." She waggled her eyebrows, impersonating Groucho Marx. "Linda's going to help me with that."

"Really?"

"She draws, too," Sarah said. "Pen and ink."

"Did you impress her with your watercolors?" I asked.

"Yeah! I mean, she said she liked them. We're going to do matching scenes of Isle Royale."

"Like Van Gogh's and Gauguin's sunflower paintings?" I asked, amused with her enthusiasm.

"Exactly. Cool, huh? She promised to teach me sign language, too." Sarah's animation reddened her cheeks. "Her older brother is deaf and taught her to sign before she could talk. She has a cabin in Ely, Minnesota. Not too far."

I was happy for Sarah and let her prattle on about Linda until most of the passengers crowded aboard.

Sarah gave me a final bear hug. "Good bye, Grandma," she teased. "Take care of them both."

Meagan got in line for her hug. "Thanks for everything, Sarah. You've been a great friend to my Mom—and me."

We stepped aboard *Voyageur* and leaned over the railing, saying good-bye.

"You know, Sarah," Meagan called out. "This baby needs a godmother. Would you consider..."

I'd never before seen tears in my friend's eyes. Sarah put her hand over her mouth and nodded. She turned quickly, waving over her head, and hurried away from *Voyageur*.

"Thank you," I whispered to my daughter.

Meagan glowed with nature's blessings—as ripe as an Isle Royale thimbleberry.

END

Isle Royale Wolves in Danger

When research for this book was done several years ago, the Isle Royale population of wolves had dwindled to dangerous levels. The delicate balance between moose and wolves was destabilized.

As of 2014 only eight wolves remain on the island and they are not expected to survive much longer. Due to in-breeding, the wolves are in poor health, with spine deformities and trouble giving birth.

The National Park Service has three controversial options:
1) Do nothing and let nature take its course, which has been their policy.
2) Bring in healthy wolves from the mainland to add to the gene pool.
3) Let the wolves die out and then repopulate the island with healthy wolves.

The bitter cold winter of 2014 may be good news for the wolves. Lake Superior's frozen surface has created bridges from the Isle Royale to the mainland. Wolves may have naturally wandered onto the island and will mate with the native packs.

For updates about the animals on the island, take a look at reports from the long-term Wolf-Moose Project conducted by the Michigan Technological University. There are great pictures and facts on their website www.isleroyalewolf.org

For other information about Isle Royale National Park visit: www.nps.gov/isro/

ABOUT THE AUTHOR

In the 1990s Jeanne Meeks was committed to poetry, belonged to Poets and Other Writers, and gave poetry performances as part of that group. Her work appeared in several anthologies. She also self-published a book of poetry, *My Sister's Quilt*. She regularly writes human-interest articles for *Schoolhouse Life* news magazine.

After twenty-eight years of self-employment, Ms. Meeks and her husband recently sold their security surveillance company. During her business career, Jeanne was recognized by the Illinois governor as the Small-Business Person of the Year. She was the Tax Collector for New Lenox Township, the President of the New Lenox Chamber of Commerce, on the board of a local bank, and on Silver Cross Hospital's Community Trustee Board.

Ms. Meeks now writes full-time and belongs to Mystery Writers of America, Sisters in Crime, and writers groups in Illinois and Florida. In July of 2013 she won a first place cash prize for a slice-of-life story from Midlife Collage. Her novel, *Rim To Rim*, was nominated for a Lovey Award - Best First Novel-at the 2014 Love is Murder convention in Chicago. When not writing, she backpacks, kayaks, volunteers with the local historical society, and plays tennis or golf. Married in 1969, she lives with her husband on Florida's gulf coast and in a suburb of Chicago.

Also by Jeanne Meeks

RIM To RIM - Death in the Grand Canyon
(First in the Backcountry Mystery series)

The awesome Grand Canyon scenery is marred when Amy and Sarah find a mangled body in a ravine. The women, who each hike for their own reasons, must face the physical hardships of the five-day trek— plus stay alive as an eerie danger stalks them.

"A Dandy Chick Lit Work: Empowering Women, Dispensing Adventure. Ladies take note: Jeanne Meeks has created a first novel that puts her up in the company of fine adventure/mystery writers..."   - Grady Harp, Los Angeles reviewer

"Couldn't put it down. You owe me a night's sleep."
                    --Kathy Eversman, Rhinelander, WI

Rim To Rim was nominated for a Lovey Award - Best First Novel at the 2014 Love Is Murder writers convention in Chicago. It is available in e-book and print from Amazon, at Barnes and Noble, from the author, and from other retail outlets.

To sing along with *Rim to Rim* as performed by Eve&Me (lyrics by Jeanne Meeks, vocals by Mary Beth Hafner, and keyboard, guitar, and bass by Mike Evon) visit my website, www.jeannemeeks.com.

Dear Reader,

I hope you've enjoyed Amy's adventures on Isle Royale as much as I enjoyed writing about them. May I ask a favor? Will you help spread the word about these stories? Your opinions will help another reader decide to open the cover and begin the journey. I'd appreciate your feedback in any of these ways:

* Leave a comment on *Wolf Pack*'s page on Amazon or Barnes & Noble,
* Write a review for Goodreads.com,
* Pin a picture of yourself with the book on Pinterest,
* Post your opinion on Facebook and Twitter,
* Ask your library to carry my books,
* Or simply mention my novels to your friends.

I am available to discuss my novels with your book discussion group or will speak about my publishing experiences or hiking adventures to your women's group. Contact me and let's talk.

e-mail   - ChartHousePress@aol.com
Website - www.jeannemeeks.com
Facebook - www.facebook.com/JeanneMeeksAuthor
Pinterest - http://pinterest.com/jeannemeeks

Thanks so much for reading. I'd love to hear from you.
Jeanne

48278215R00148

Made in the USA
Charleston, SC
30 October 2015